To my Rebecca
Hope ...
adventure ...
Love y...
A.J.
x+oo

The Sands are Changing

A Novel

There is a fate that makes us brothers,
None goes his way alone.
All that we send into the lives of
others
Comes back into our own
Author unknown

JEANNE ARLETTE

A world of love
makes a world of peace.
J.

The Sands Are Changing

Published by Wheatmark*
1760 East River Road, Suite 145
Tucson, Arizona 85718 USA
www.wheatmark.com

ISBN: 978-1-62787-356-7 (paperback)
ISBN: 978-1-62787-357-4 (ebook)
LCCN: 2015954129

The Sands Are Changing is pure fiction, however the location of cities is real as is most of the history. For several years, the author lived with her husband in a country she fell in love with . . . Saudi Arabia. She learned Arabic and lived through many of the experiences she writes about; however this novel is a work of fiction, sometimes inspired by true events and locations. The characters, names, incidents, dialogues, events, situations, and plots are coincidental, fictionalized and used fictitiously. Any resemblance to actual persons, living or dead, is pure coincidence and is the product of the author's imagination.

Contents

—1—
Justice Served

The experience infinite: A surrender of man's will to Allah.
Life and the worthlessness of the transient earthly existence of man
permeates all Muslim thought and actions. The Koran is the way
of life for the Muslim . . . a surrender of man's will to Allah.
The Koran

A green fire engine is parked on the edge of a large open area, now filled with bystanders. Two Americans wait among the Muslim crowd. A dusty red and white police GMC van drives up, its door opens wide. A youthful dark-skinned man emerges, his shackled feet are without shoes. He wears a soiled dirty-white long sleeved shirt to his knees with pantaloons of the same color. His eyes are tightly closed, covered with a thick black cloth. Tranquilized and confused, he does not know which direction to go without help. His hands are cuffed behind his back.

Jet black curls cover this man's downcast head, partially hiding his facial features. He visualizes nothing, but his senses of touch, taste, smell and hearing are still functioning. The sixth sense of perception also remains, for he perceives what is about to happen. He has witnessed this punishment many times before . . . always on Friday after religious services at this ancient Grand Mosque. But now, at this moment, it is *his* hands tied behind *his* back. He detects that which is about to happen to him is only moments away.

He, the prisoner, is prodded along with a big stick firmly driven into his rib cage by a soldier. He is roughly pushed into the wide clearing in front of the Mosque where a large piece of plastic covers a cement walkway. Roughly shoved, he falls on his knees, landing on a small square of carpet that was just quickly placed there by someone in the crowd . . . a family member perhaps? His tightly tied blindfold blocks out all peripheral light.

The young man is aware of the usual anticipation filtering and spreading throughout the silent crowd. But the only noise he hears is the heavy excited breathing and an occasional cough or sneeze by some who wait and watch. His whole being feels the beams of many eyes coming from everywhere among the huge crowd— like lasers honing in on the kill—anticipating the awful, ancient surgery that is about to be performed on him.

A familiar guttural Arabic voice from the direction of the nearby Mosque describes the awful sin he has committed. "This man raped a young girl as she lay sleeping in her bed. There were witnesses. We, the Palace of Justice and the King, decree this punishment, an Islamic law for over a thousand years. *Allah* demands it." His voice, now in a high-pitched yell, stimulates the crowd into a frenzy. "Allah's will be done. *Allahu Akbar, God is the greatest.*"

Someone yells out, *"Aiwa, Allahu Akbar. Hut . . . Hut . . . Hut!"* *Yes, God is the greatest.* Added is the emphatic and ominous "hut, hut, hut" by the crowd. The Americans standing close by, shiver to think about the inexplicably grotesque thing that is about to happen.

An executioner waiting, tall and stately in manner, has wooly chocolate brown hair and medium-dark skin. He is gowned in pure snowy-white, in stark contrast to the prisoner's dirty, spotted clothing and dark Ethiopian skin and hair. The executioner appears dignified. Straightening his chest bandoleer and waist band adds a speck of perfection to his person. Slowly and meticulously, he rolls up the right long sleeve of his gown. The solemnity of the occasion is nervously contemplated by all standing and watching.

Suddenly he pulls a long, shiny curved sword from its scabbard. For one brief instant, the heavy, gleaming blade dazzles in the bright sunshine like a solitary lightning strike appearing out of nowhere. The crowd is startled.

The soldier, standing beside the executioner, roughly pokes his large stick again into the kneeling blindfolded man's side, harder this time causing a sudden exaggerated reflexive rising of the prisoner's head—producing an automatic upward neck extension, ready for the swords action.

The prisoner's response was instantaneous—and so was the blade. The flash of the shiny metal gracefully swirls in a high horizontal circle, the skillful descent of the lethal stroke takes priority over everyone's senses . . . the aplomb and rhythm of executioner, stick and blade are akin to a graceful Bedouin dance minus the drum rolls. The teamwork is faultless. The bleeding severed head, like Rodin's 1887 sculpture of John the Baptist's decapitated head, hits the plastic cloth rotating. The thick black eye-covering flies off.

Simultaneously, a voice emanates from the nearby Mosque, "*Allahu Akbar, Muhammadun Rasulu'llah-lah.*" God is great and Muhammad is the messenger of God diffuses into a hum throughout the square. Now headless, the convulsing body crumples among spurting blood while the hemorrhaging head, bulging eyes now seen, continues its rotation. Smashing into the front of the crowd it causes a catastrophic disruption of the silence, substituting quiet for noise, "*Shuff, qariib.* Look, it's coming near!" Jumping and pushing follows the murmuring of many voices.

Without warning, a resounding "whoooop" of a satisfied crowd is followed with the pouring forth of a concert of voices. Singing of praises *"Allahu Akbar"* swirl throughout the square . . . God is great!

The retrieved head's fountain of blood pouring forth is finally controlled by the pressure of a doctor's gloved hand. Attached to a tall post, the bleeding body part is raised for full viewing—a reminder of a very effective, if not archaic, capital punishment.

The doctor checks the body before it is placed in a waiting ambulance. Shortly after, the head is retrieved and sewn back on. The whole body is then wrapped in the plastic sheet, driven off to an unmarked desert grave.

"Allahu Akbar," like a muted final song, is sighed and repeated by the Muslims in the slowly dispersing crowd who are satisfied that justice has once again been served.

Expatriates, Lilli and Frank Martinez walk among the droning hum to their parked car.

"No wonder westerners call this Chop-Chop Square. I can't believe this has been going on for centuries. I am shocked with this horrible experience. I will never forget that head rolling toward us with blood spraying everywhere. Really scary and unreal."

Frank replies, "Never seen anything like it! At least this penalty is decided upon rapidly. They tell me the death penalty is definitely performed for murder and rape."

"Guess that's the reason there is very little crime here, Frank and why I always feel safe walking with you around this city at night."

— 2 —

Lilli

Lilli's mother, born in New England into a wealthy French-Canadian family, who purchased thousands of acres of orange groves and cattle in Central Florida where they eventually settled.

Her mother met Lilli's Dad, a good 'ole Southern boy, while he was stationed in Britain after WW II. A handsome Naval Pilot, he was on a rest and recuperation leave, Mother on a vacation. Mom told Lilli they practically ran over each other while viewing a Rodin sculpture inside Westminster Abby . . . a serendipitous meeting and love at first sight, she admitted to her daughter. They had a passionate two weeks together, the result of which Lilli was conceived. One week after their ecstasy the young pilot was killed in action. Lilli's mother returns to New England where her fatherless baby is born.

Her mother married a Florida gentleman after living in Boston till Lilli was twelve years old. They settled in south Florida. Now, visiting her mother and step-dad's home in Miami, this graceful five foot six bubbly Southern belle, is spiced with a delicate mixture of proper French aloofness and southern friendliness.

Lilli's occasional tempestuous and passionate nature is revealed only in fleeting glimpses. A paradoxical but interesting combination—an adventuresome woman of cool French elegance and Southern manners with a hidden warmth and passion that seems to come from deep within.

In the process of searching for her real father's Florida family, she discovers that her dad's family lives in middle Florida. They own a Phosphate Company that now helps Saudi Arabia develop its new found massive phosphate deposits. She hopes to meet them one day.

Days later, she meets Cuban Frank Martinez while shopping in downtown Miami. Frank, is mesmerized when he sees this beautiful woman passing by. He purposely bumps into her. They converse, discovering they both work in Chicago and have southern parents. He invites her to lunch at his father's nearby restaurant, the "El Camino." *(The Road)* She is impressed.

Frank begs Lilli to come work for him at Boxwood International of America. After socializing with each other's families and feeling their positive input, she agrees. They fly back to Chicago together. Frank interviews Lilli for a secretarial position. He is immediately struck by her unusual regal good looks, her calm coolness, her self-assurance, but her fantastic smile melts his heart. He had sworn off women; but this one intrigued him. Lilli was modest about her Cum Laude degree from University of Mass. where she majored in languages. She went on to get a Master's in Archaeology from University of Chicago. After graduation, she held a university secretarial position with the hope a teaching job in languages or archeology would soon become available. But, the meeting of this handsome Cuban, Frank, will change her life forever.

Lilli gives up her present job and Frank hires her as his secretary. Subsequent to a devastating affair, Frank swore off women.

That was before Lilli burst forth into his life. After three whirlwind dates, he proposes.

A beautiful bride, Lilli has the illusion of a 'till death do us part type of wedded bliss with her soul mate, Frank Martinez. The vows were exchanged in a small New England chapel in her birth city where her Mom had grown up. Her mother and step-father, with Frank's parents, flew in from Florida on a snowy day. They were wonderful about the speedy marriage, providing a lovely reception in a quaint French restaurant with only their closest friends and family. "The perfect man for Lilli," the parents had remarked when meeting charming Frank. Impressed with his new partner and family, Frank writes a poem after the wedding.

Dearest Lilli,
Aware that my love appears on the surface as quiet
and calm brilliant stars on a clear wintery night,
glistening throughout a forest of snow laden pines.
When conversely, within the depths and recesses of mi alma
*   (soul),*
love loudly blossoms and bursts—exploding for all eternity.
I will love you forever, mi amour, always you will be mine.

A virginal twenty five, three years younger than Frank, she was in total awe of him. He became not only her husband, but her mentor, lover, companion . . . her everything . . . perhaps the father she never had. She worked as Frank's private secretary until he got promoted. Frank got a new secretary. Lilli, assigned another boss, was not happy. Slowly they saw less of each other during the daytime, lunches together dwindled, special projects took him out of town for longer periods of time and gradually they drove separate autos to work and almost became strangers in the same house. Frank evolved into an egotistical, chauvinistic executive, absorbed with little else than his own advancement . . . and he was advancing rapidly.

Gradually Lilli viewed the man she married through different eyes. She saw right through the gregarious superficial exterior. What she was seeing, she didn't like or agree with—a man whose prime ambition in life was to become "a millionaire by the time I am forty." Lilli sensed his aggression and ambition was embedded in a constant search for more power.

"With position comes power and ultimately wealth," he admonished her when she questioned his seemingly non-stop thirst for position.

"Why do you always invite only people who can help your advancement? Can't we have any friends just for friend's sake?" she had questioned. No answer from Frank.

After two years, Lilli finally realizes they are complete opposites, as different as sweet chocolate and raw chicken. She rationalizes staying in the marriage by using the old cliché, 'opposites attract and enhance each other.' She didn't want an old horse(man leads) and carriage(woman follows) type marriage anyway. She wanted independent relationships, sort of like two roads running parallel, heading in one direction, but passing different towns and landscapes until further on, they merge and end up in the same distinct and beautiful place. She knew that she had been dreaming . . . couples have to have more togetherness than that, or they have nothing in common to build on. She and Frank were on parallel roads all right . . . running miles apart sometimes in the opposite direction, and recently, opposite goals became apparent.

Frank, ambitious and power-happy, Lilli career-minded to a point. She believed a family came first . . . a warm, loving home, eventually children, sharing it all with that one important, special person that you loved. She had missed out on having a real family for eight years, then she had a father . . . sort of. She treasured thinking of having a real family.

"Frank, you know the basis for society's preservation is a solid home foundation with a family. Why don't you want children?"

"I'm too busy to be raising kids and we'd have to settle down. I'm not ready for that. If you like our standard of living, then you know I must travel to get the big contracts. That's my job."

To her, Frank was being mysterious. "Dearest, why do you always wear blue underwear, ties with mostly red colors, navy pants and jacket, and white shirts? And why the conglomerate of red, white and blue socks? You never told me the reason for wearing these three different colors and no others."

"Well, Lilli, after you my dear, America is second in my life. Coming from Cuba and communism, my way of showing dedication to my new free homeland has always been to wear red, white and blue socks . . . not a flag," he chuckles. "I've worn these socks since college days. They are my good luck coverings. To me, white socks mean all is well and calm. Blue indicates I have control of the situation and red socks represent danger, circumstances are unstable. I haven't worn red very often, thank God."

"You are so creative, Frank. I have to admit, life with you is different and exciting . . . frequent employee business parties, interesting people to meet, the few times I am invited to travel with you, and the incredible stash of money we are accumulating to invest and buy whatever we want."

That is the upside. He will change, as he matures, think positively she tells herself. I'll help him. He really does need me, but he also uses me. The downside, is the continuous absences. She tells him so.

"You want me to be charming and entertain your friends, to be ready in a moment's notice for your sexual needs or whatever you want to do," she accuses him. "Having been your secretary, I know you must leave for a week at a time, but your token phone calls are brief and cool. I never know what you're doing or who you're with. You say you're still on business. All I know is that I am left in the evenings waiting . . . very boring for me. "

"Darling, I love having my woman to come home to; but I am sorry, my job must come first if we are to survive."

She muses, *He doesn't have the inclination nor does he make the time to cherish and support our marriage even with such a work situation.*

"The fact of the matter is this conjugal contract is in severe disarray and slowly dissolving. You use me," Lilli raised her voice to him one day. "Your smugness and complete introversion with me is very discouraging. I don't think you give me a second thought beyond your own needs."

"I love you, Lilli and I know I do need you. Your beauty and brains help further my career in my boss's eyes. You are a blessing to me. I am sorry if you think I use you."

One day after a board meeting, his boss told him, enviously, "Your wife is a real looker and bright. Where did you ever meet her? She is definitely an asset to you m' boy with her friendly easy-going nature. We feel fortunate having her here in the office." Frank knew all that was true.

That night he told her, "Lilli, I am so proud of you, your friendliness and phenomenal linguistic ability to speak French, Spanish, and now Arabic. Your talent in history and archeology are impressive, if not brilliant. I love you, girl."

~3~
Frank

F rank Martinez, a Cuban whose family fled from Castro's Cuba in 1957, leaving all their possessions behind. They felt lucky to be away from the Communist regime that confiscated the family restaurant that Frank's grandfather had established years earlier. Cuban free-enterprise suddenly disappeared in Cuba. Arriving in Miami penniless, his family had no money for Frank to complete his last year of college so he washed dishes in a local side walk café on S.W. 8th street. With the Cuban influx, this area became known as Little Havana. He would never forget the psychological trauma of going from riches to rags. What he didn't know was that his smart *Padre (father)* had smuggled some of their savings out of Cuba. Temporarily living with Frank's uncle, his father opened a Miami restaurant which slowly became very successful. The first year of adjustment, with no friends for young Frank, was rough. Finally, he was able to return to college, graduating with a Master Degree in Business Administration from the University of Miami.

This handsome six foot plus Cuban charmer explained to his Lilli, "I watched my parents rise from the hardship of starting all over with very little money, to having the best Spanish restaurant in Miami. Though I will always remember those days of struggle,

I am Cuban-proud, the good-life days or the bad ones in Cuba, I will never forget. Here, in America, the impact of being treated as a foreigner, a minority and one in poverty, has also left an indelible lifelong mark on me. In school, I was on the defensive all the time, feeling like an inferior American."

Lilli thought, *this is the probable reason for his becoming aggressive and power-happy.*

Before his marriage to Lilli, and at Boxwood International of America, he learned the lessons of struggling to win with persistence, slight aggression, leading and most importantly, being politically astute. He pleased and showed respect to his bosses in order to fulfill his goals. He applied this knowledge quickly on his first job. His public relations aptitude is unquestionable.

Frank's dark wavy hair, broad smile, coffee brown eyes, gentle but forceful personality and demeanor is reassuring to female counterparts at work. He was worthy of their admiration. The single ladies there tried to restrain themselves from falling head over heels in love with this tall, handsome Spaniard married to a beautiful woman, but found him an emotionally difficult man to get close to.

Finally Frank feels like he belongs . . . a real American. He is ready for new challenges. That new challenge might come from many directions . . . and places. The thought of Boxwood trusting and perhaps sending him international one day, pleased his psyche.

It happened sooner than he ever expected.

— 4 —
Where???

"My dear Lilli, we may have a contract in Saudi Arabia. The Board of Directors might give me a new position as Assistant Vice-President of International Affairs for Boxwood," he bragged. "This will bring me in contact with powerful people. Mostly wealthy Arabs, men in high government positions harboring enormous oil wealth." *The ideal climate for my desired goals: the three P's . . . Power, Position and Possessions.*

"Pray we get the contract, Lilli. Even though we will have a Saudi partner who owns 51% of our business profits, we will own the 49%. This is how Saudi does business with foreign companies. Smart, aren't they to take more profit than the owner? Some Saudis take an active part in managing, too and some do not. But, you know, I'll get a big pay raise also."

"Lilli, B.I.A. will provide Saudi Arabia with construction supplies for their awesome five-year development plans . . . goals the Saudi's have imposed on themselves enabling growth into the twenty-first century, to eventually become self-sufficient. After a few five-year plans, they will be free of foreign manpower. Now, they must rely on Western technology and expertise. They need

13

training from the Western world for professional leadership and their country's development."

Arriving home early for the first time in a week, Frank's face is glowing as he nonchalantly announces to Lilli, "B. I. A. is close to having a contract! If we win, it will be over ten other international companies. Perkins wants me to fly to Riyadh, the capital, to do some Public Relations and marketing and possibly get a deal signed for selling supplies. This is another chance of my lifetime that I can't miss. You were my first, sweetheart. I hope you're with me, mi amour. I can take my time in becoming a millionaire, my dear. This is our opportunity."

His smugness belies his emotions, he is clearly pleased with himself and very excited. He awaits his highly emotional wife's reaction as he pops open a Mexican beer. Frank is still her handsome cross between a Macho Spaniard and good 'ole southern boy.

"I'm with you, my Frank! Such a coincidence. My Master's degree thesis was on the Middle East and the archeology inherent in those countries. You know, it wasn't too many years ago slavery of women was finally abolished in Saudi. Girls were then free to attend school. The need for manpower is so great now that a Royal Edict proclaimed 'birth-control is forbidden.'"

"People are now Saudi Arabia's biggest necessary asset. More youth are needed for the country's survival into the future," Frank adds.

"Yes, and all youth must be educated. But that is undesirable to some of the strict religious Wahabis and their beliefs, because it includes girls being educated, especially as teachers. The religious sect does not want female independence. This country must and will slowly change."

"Well, Lilli, the Saudis are only too aware that their oil production revenues, by most estimates will last another eighty years at the present volume of barrels per day. The smart leaders of this oil rich, but technology-poor country, do not want to depend on outside brains and supplies forever because when the day arrives that they can't pay for services, that country will become a myriad of desert ghost cities again." Concentrating intensely, he justifies his plan of patience.

"Like a civilization lost in time, a destiny not unlike some other ancient and Middle-East civilizations," Lilli adds. *Frank's only vices now appear to be his quest for riches and his overt ambitious drive for power and position. I'll be by his side forever.*

— 5 —

First Flight 1974

Frank makes the long trip to Riyadh after obtaining an interview appointment with Boxwood's business partner in Arabia, the government Saudi Deputy Minister, Salah abu Bayatri. Luckily, not many people were on the plane. He was able to get through a customs turmoil expediently carrying only his valise. He was told hotel reservations were at one of three decent hotels, the Palace, directly across from the airport. When he arrived, he found out it was an old, two story edifice that appeared rather ancient.

Inside this nondescript room, he sits on a double bed's sagging mattress . . . a dusty chandelier hangs over his head. French doors lead to a back veranda. Two tubes of cloth filled with sand lay on the floor blocking a two inch space between floor and door bottom. But the tubes were too short for the door's width so a small space existed inviting outside light and air to enter.

In the bathroom, Frank notices water dribbling from the faucet. A bidet sat next to a toilet that had a three quarter inch wide crack in its seat.

Washing his hands, he glances at his watch. "Dinner time," he mumbles.

Entering the lobby, many small people, maybe Yemeni he thought, were sweeping and brushing off the sand-covered carpet. "No vacuum cleaners here?" Frank said aloud.

A little penguin of a man welcomed him into the dining room, escorting him to a table for two. Drapery hanging by his table is a heavy blue brocade, soiled, dusty, and faded. He thought, *probably very pretty at one time.*

Ignoring the flies on everything, he enjoyed his first meal served with silver utensils. It was delicious. As he sipped his Nescafe Instant coffee, the mai-tre'd began to rid the dining room of flies by spraying Raid all around the tables and curtains. Inhaling that, Frank decides it is time to leave.

Returning to his room, he waits for the shower-less tub to fill with enough water to bathe, anticipating his meeting tomorrow. Falling asleep after a hot bath, he is awoken by a shining light filling the room, entering from the space under the French doors. Suddenly the light becomes an eery mustard color turning the bright room into a sullen, mysterious space. "What on earth is this?" Breathing becomes difficult. He jumps out of bed.

Gazing out the French doors, nothing is visible except for clouds of sand from the ground to the eye's zenith. Flashes of lightening illuminate sand particles being blown in the room by the powerful winds.

Taking bed pillows, he covers the ends of the short tubes on the floor which stops the dust shower. *This fine orange dust is every-where. My valise and suit bag are covered. Thank God, I'll be out of here and on the plane home tonight.*

Looking at his watch, *Seven a.m. here. My appointment is at 10. Better get ready.*

Riding a taxi to Salah abu Bayatri's villa, he notices the sky

is now clear, the sun shines, sand is everywhere, covering everything . . . but it is a beautiful day in the desert.

Arriving at a mini palace gate, he is shown into a front waiting
room by a young Saudi boy. It is just 10 o'clock. He sits and waits.
One hour, two hours. Hearing the call to prayer, *"salaat, salaat"* by
the muezzin, *(the caller),* he knows the wait will be a little longer.
This is noon-time "salaat," (prayer time) he says to himself. *Hopefully
Mr. Salah abu Bayatri will not take the customary siesta after salaat
and wait until after our meeting.*

At 12:30, he is beckoned to follow the boy into a large living
room, the perimeter is surrounded by cushions with arm rests, the
floor covered with overlapping Persian carpets of varying colors and
designs. Off to the side, a "desert cooler" pumps ice water through
large yellow straws that keep the room a comfortable, cool temperature. "I know about these coolers," he mentions to the young
fellow. "No air-conditioners here yet?"

"Aiwa," (Yes.) he replied and left.

Frank sat his tall frame down just as a slight brownish amber-
colored man enters the room. He scrambles his long legs and stands
up.

"*Ahlan,* (Welcome). I am Salah abu Baytri, but please call me
Salah. I am sorry for the long wait. You wanted to see me about
providing materials for our various construction projects?"

Salah's English is a perfect London variety, "Yes, Salah. My
company appreciates you giving me the opportunity to talk to you
face to face."

They talk at length about personal matters after which Frank
gives his sales pitch. Luckily, Salah takes an immediate liking to
charming Frank's undeniably gregarious personality and seemingly genuine caring nature. His Public Relations presentation is
perfect . . . a contract will be coming, he hopes.

Salah likes the warmth and apparent sincerity of this American and is feeling a camaraderie with him through Frank's Spanish heritage.

"You know, the Spanish and Arabs have had close familial ties throughout history because of the Muslim occupation of Spain for 800 years," Salah says.

Salah trusts this man immediately. "I feel like I've known you for a long time, Frank. I have traveled in the U.S.A. and graduated from Cambridge University in England. I am familiar with Americans and I like them."

After an hour of business talk, Salah closes the meeting with the signing of a multi-million dollar contract that Frank had brought with him. "Will you join me for dinner at seven at my villa?"

"I will love that, Salah, as long as I am at the airport for my eleven p.m. flight. I will be packed and ready to go after dinner."

"You will be on time. My driver will take you there from my villa. And he will pick you up at the hotel at seven and bring you here."

In the lobby, suitcase packed, contract in his pocket, Frank waits for Salah's driver. The ride is short on the somewhat bumpy dirt road. They arrive at the villa. Frank is invited to a table with other family males. No women are present and he doesn't see any all evening. The conversation, in perfect English, is all about how Saudi Arabia is growing out of a third world country by leaps and bounds into the modern twentieth century.

Frank is a little taken aback that a movie is being shown after the meal. *Boxwood told me movies were taboo here. I guess privilege will be privilege. Never mind, he tells himself, I have a multi-million contract to take home. The potential riches are unfathomable.*

His flight home is smooth and he is elated. He was so very successful. At work the next day, he feels the company's esteem for him has hit the sky and mushroomed into adulation overnight.

His boss, President Ralph Perkins announces in a meeting, "Frank, you did a magnificent job with Salah abu Bayatri in Riyadh. The Board and I decided on a raise for you and a promotion to Vice President of Boxwood—International Division in Saudi Arabia. Congratulations."

~6~
All Life Is Based on Decisions, Some for the Better, Some Not

That evening, Frank, wearing his all-is-going-great white socks, takes Lilli to her favorite restaurant. He announces, "Well, my dear we leave for Saudi Arabia in thirty days. My trip to Riyadh had a reward to it. I am now Vice President of Boxwood International Division. The first step to becoming president. All I have to do is unseat my immediate boss and current president . . . Ralph Perkins." *Have patience, he thinks to himself.* The two hug and kiss intimately.

"You deserve this promotion, Frank. That is no small achievement—obtaining a multi-million dollar contract. I am so proud of you, my darling." Another romantic hug and kiss follows.

"Now is the west's time. It will be a while before all Saudi five year plans are completed, take effect, they become independent and Westerners are no longer needed. Their people will then be trained to take over . . . Saudi-ization will become a reality. I must make hay while the right set of circumstances presents themselves. Again, I perceive this move to Arabia will definitely be the once-in-a-lifetime opportunity for us. And honey, we will have a paid week off every four months to travel out of the desert when we want, plus thirty days paid vacation every year to go home."

"How wonderful. We can travel the world. I can hardly contain my excitement, Frank." *Finally an escape from my present humdrum existence.*

Frank notices Lilli's huge eyes are delirious with happiness, reflecting her anticipation. "Honey, I always knew, those eyes of yours were truly the mirror of a good, sweet soul."

In spite of her rich looks, she has one paradoxical prejudice which she admits to Frank this day.

"Frank, I surely dislike your snobby, affluent friends. They are all alike—snooty, know-it-all, arrogant and self-centered, especially the women. Hopefully it will be different in Arabia."

He retorted, "The rich help the rich. Saudis are super wealthy, so you had better just ignore these feelings. I need the well-to-do. You're prosperous now, so why the put down? I know, you're jealous of the ladies, Lillita and you needn't be. You are always my forever sweetheart."

"I know I will like this mysterious future, Frank." Her composure and aplomb restrain her overwhelming anticipation for this adventure. The more she thinks about it, the more excited she is. Maybe things will improve over there, the two of them alone in a foreign country, depending on each other, traveling the world together. She is looking forward to this move like no other. *Our marriage will be salvaged, amen.*

"Do you think I can work there? Maybe they need an Assistant to the Archeologist or teaching a language or geography? I can always do secretarial work, too," she mused.

"From what they tell me, there is sometimes a need for secretaries, teachers and hospital personnel. I hope you will find friends and things to keep you busy. Maybe some jobs with other companies, but as a woman, there isn't much available. I did hear that women go nuts over there, though, mostly from boredom, so we'll find you something. Women don't drive and it's pretty primitive living. Eventually, we will have a modern villa, so you won't be uncomfortable. I'll get you a driver and there will be a few other employees there who have wives, too. They say shopping the ancient markets is great."

"I am prepared for anything. Maybe I can study some of the many antiquity sites. Frank, bring on this fortuitous venture. I am overwhelmed with heart-stirring emotion."

"Christ, I wonder how I'm going to exist without beer. Have to brew my own or become friends with someone with a diplomatic passport. They say liquor from a Corps of Engineers employee is available. At exorbitant prices I bet. No liquor, guns or churches are legally allowed."

"Maybe I can be your secretary again?"

"Not a chance. No nepotism for Westerners there, plenty of that for male Arabs though, so I hear."

So that was it . . . just something to be kept busy, she mused.

Her heart's desire had secretly been to become an actress, but she found the road too long and uncertain. Her unique beauty and charisma could have taken her to the top; but, there came Frank sweeping her right off her feet with gifts, Spanish ardor, and good looks – for her it was head-over-heels love at first sight. A serendipitous meeting to abide by her still first and only love.

Before the wedding Frank bragged to one of his colleagues, "Lilli is an interesting woman to know with incredibly good looks and not lacking in brains, either."

"Her smile is like no other," his friend replied.

"Yes, I know." *Frank thought, Lilli's smile will be her passport wherever she goes.* Lilli had not been the happiest of women for the past married years. So when Frank announced his decision to accept this Saudi job, she felt her unresolved marital feelings had a reprieve. *Maybe a new beginning will be forthcoming?*

— 7 —

An Adventure Begins

APRIL 1974

Cruising above the European/Middle East continent at 37,000 feet, Lilli and Frank Martinez are comfortable at last on a Saudia 737 jet; destination Riyadh, Saudi Arabia. Lilli, slightly more relaxed now, forgot her initial apprehension on boarding. "Frank, the interior of this plane is shoddy, unkempt and very old-looking. I hope the engines are in good condition."

If Lilli had any doubts about this adventure into a third world country, they were surfacing now . . . but too late. Besides, she had been ultra-busy with excitement from packing, selling their home and bidding farewell to family and friends. Most people had never heard of Saudi Arabia, except for them now. Still, she had no idea what to expect. *Does this city have electric lights?*

"This sure can't compare to yesterday's British Airways flight over the Atlantic to London. Somehow I get the feeling they are trying to economize, but in reality, they are known for their lack of maintenance and technical knowledge. Anything purchased must be maintained by whatever country they bought it from. That's why they are hiring two million foreigners right now. They need us," Frank glanced at Lilli's worried expression. "We have nothing to worry about, my darling, I am sure they have ex-pats now maintaining planes."

"Well, I hope this is a safe trip." She nervously eyes the torn fabric on her seat and continues twisting her wedding ring. Her prayers are continuous and silent.

"Lilli, plane crashes come in threes, haven't you heard? We recently had a third in the series, so we are safe for the time being," he jokingly comments with a vocal arrogance and smug expression, "So don't worry so much."

"You need not patronize me, Frank." Normally cool-tempered and easy-going . . . this nervous Lilli was furious. *Here it is, his usual super confidence that comes from thinking he is always right. So pompous, couldn't he have any doubts at all?*

Three years of his egotistical nature would have been her demise, except she couldn't deny, he was a handsome and loving husband, away on business most of the time anyway. Even his love-making was on his own terms; when, where, how . . . so planned, so structured, so business like . . . so opposite her Aquarius nature for creativity and surprise.

Frank softened his tone, "Lilli, the mechanics are Brits or Americans and so are most of the pilots. Those that aren't, have been trained in England or the USA. You're worrying for nothing."

—8—
History

Suddenly, an announcement over the plane's intercom, "Ladies and gentlemen this is your captain. Northern Iraq is now below us. We will be over historic Babylon soon. Later, look to the starboard side and you will see the closest meeting point of the Tigris and Euphrates Rivers as we pass over Baghdad. You can follow along on this historical area in the pamphlet given to you by the stewardess. Please leave them on the seat before leaving." The deep, heavily accented voice continues, "Snacks will be served later."

Lilli, gazing out the window, sighs with anticipation for a new life, *perhaps new excitement for me and Frank.* "Did you hear the pilot, Frank?"

"Ah huh, sweetheart," Frank comments as he drifts in and out of sleep. She removes a camera from her purse, ready for photos. She brushes her thick luxuriously long sable-brown hair, highlights so bright, as if they had been touched by an artist's brush dipped in gold. Then touches up her makeup a few shades darker than her natural skin tone. Not a sun-lover, her flawless skin was never tanned. High cheekbones give the ageless face a glamorous aura.

Poking Frank, "Wake up, dear. The view is fabulous. There isn't a cloud in the sky."

Arriving over Baghdad, Lilli reads aloud from the booklet. "The city, destroyed by floods many times, so the people just moved their city from one bank to the other. In 1955 Iraq built the Samara Dam to solve that problem. But, Iran was unhappy because Iraq then had control of the Tigris and Euphrates rivers all the way south to where the rivers merge and empty into the Arabian Gulf at the port of Basra. I already know all of this from school."

Franks sits up, kissing his beautiful wife, bending over her to see out the window. "I wonder if Iraq is as rich in oil as Saudi Arabia. Saudi probably has more oil reserves?"

"I don't know. I hope there is more history and archeological findings to discover on the Arabian Peninsula. See here on this page it says, 'One of the beginnings of man's civilization is here. Iraq, at that time was known as Mesopotamia. The first kneaded bread, potter's wheel and cuneiform writing was invented here.' I know Egypt had an early civilization, too," she adds.

Frank wonders aloud, "Maybe we can visit this area while we are here. Is there any connection between the Iraqis and Saudis because of their geographic proximity to one another?"

"It says here, 'After the death of the Muslim prophet Muhammad, Muslim Arabs conquered Iraq. This began a Muslim era under two Caliphs. Struggles between them ensued causing two new sects to evolve, Shiites (Iraq) and Sunnis (Saudi).' These are the primary groups of Islamic Muslims today. The Shiites do not accept the Sunnis interpretation of Islam and vice versa. A centuries old problem still existing today, Frank. Am I boring you?"

"Hell, no, sweetheart. This is very interesting. I know that because oil was discovered by the Americans in 1934, Aramco has been pumping oil for them to sell ever since and the Saudis are getting richer and richer. Their lives are changing . . . they can afford help now."

He pulled her over to him again to kiss her sweetly, "I love you dear girl." *Hhhmmmm, she thought. This excitement is good. Maybe things are going to work between us after all.*

A woman's voice from the intercom drifts about the inside space, "Ladies and gentlemen, we will now be serving a light snack before our landing in Riyadh."

After the snack was served, Frank comments, "These gals are not very friendly; in fact, they are downright brusque and not well dressed. They are also most unattractive with their eyes all encircled in thick black."

"That's called *khol*. Around the eyes it is considered beautiful. Most Middle Eastern ladies use it, but especially the Bedouin women. These ladies are most likely Egyptian or Syrian. Maybe someday Saudi will have its own beautiful hostesses."

By darn, Lilli has done her homework, thought Frank. She will be a definite asset to me . . . and with her Arabic, the skies the limit. Little does she know, she is right on and a perfect partner.

Relaxed now, Lilli ponders their situation. Her first European, Middle East flight will be etched in her memory as the beginning of one of the most exciting adventures of her life. Other experiences she thought exciting were mild in comparison; her undergraduate and master degrees, her wedding day, her first home . . . all high pleasure, emotional moments, albeit fleeting. Her high school's Palm Reader's prophesy, "You will travel extensively" is coming true. She feels this adventure will surpass all past experiences and change her life radically and forever. How many have the opportunity to visit a third world country, watch it change, grow and develop as other countries already have? She knows this will happen. *To live and work in Saudi is a privilege, given to us by God.*

Suddenly, over the intercom, the woman's voice in perfect English, "The pilot thought we should give you a short history of Riyadh, the city you westerners are about to work in. Riyadh lies in the central Najid region of Saudi Arabia on a sedimentary rock plateau, six hundred meters above sea level, at the confluence of a dry river bed, Wadi Hanifa and its tributaries, Wadi Aysan and Wadi Batha. Its mountains, sand dunes and desert conditions prevail almost everywhere except the uplands of the south west. We hope you will visit these interesting places when they are dry as well as when they are filled with scant rainfall."

An excited Lilli, "Look down there. We must be over the port of Basr. There is the emptying of the two rivers into the Arabian Gulf or Persian Gulf, whichever you'd like to call it."

"It's a good size city. I see it on the water's edge," Frank, peering out the window.

Lilli says, "For centuries this was the busiest port in the Orient and I know it was known as the city of Sinbad the Sailor."

Frank, now reading, "Yes, the pamphlet says 'the ancient city is no longer there. Since the 16th century a new city stands. Local people call Basra the Venice of the East.' Wow, Lilli, look at the canals down there."

—9—

Pilot Tariq Rashudi

"I think I have time before landing to wash my hands." Lilli slips by Frank.

He grabs her waist as she brushes past, brings her down for a kiss. "My only love!"

"My, you're quite amorous, Frank."

He gives her his usual wink, which she knows is his way of conveying to her he wanted sex at the earliest possible future time.

Standing tall in the aisle, her slim figure becomes a symmetry of grace and manner, accented by her navy wool blazer and camel-colored cashmere skirt, the Harvard crimson silk blouse gives an eclectically chic look and unaffected elegance – a contradiction to the sensual mouth, the top lip a perfect cupids bow, the lower, full, rosy and ripe; lips, flawlessly perfect and made for osculation. Does Frank really know how lucky he is?

All eyes turn her way as she glides up the aisle toward the WC. Suddenly, as if out of nowhere, she is looking up into hot, black piercing eyes. A tall, handsomely dark Arab man stands before her. She gazes at his wide shoulders that fill his ultra-tight, blue gold-braided pilot's shirt; arm muscles rippling through for all to see.

A gorgeous man. The thought penetrates her innermost being. She continues past him. He stops her, gently moving his hand to her shoulder. Entranced, his ebony mustached mouth attempts to speak, but his brain is momentarily speechless. His black velvety eyes are burning and hotly desiring. She feels her clothes melt away as the penetrating orbs scan her very soul. She is now in total breathless confusion, her smile gloriously attracting him even more.

She finds it impossible to sever the magnetic mesmerism of this instant attraction. Their intense gazes locked in the electricity of the moment until a huge, obese man exiting the lavatory wants to get by.

"Ahem, *ana aasif. Yani,* I mean, I beg your parhdon," he says in heavily accented English as his eyes stare at this beautiful lady. "Your smile is Allah's treasure," he hurries to his seat.

Although it seemed forever, only a moment or two passes before she feels a confused, angry blush warm her face when she notices the fullness of this mustached man's trousers, his arousal up, firm, ready for action. He continues standing next to her, studying her face. As if coming to his senses, he says quietly in a deep voice and perfect, flawless English, "I am sorry, you are so beautiful." He walks back to the cockpit door.

She makes it into the minuscule lavatory in a state of total giddiness. Never has she experienced such emotion . . . an enigma of delight, fear and confusion . . . she likes what she saw and felt, but the more she thinks about it, the angrier she becomes. The proper Bostonian inherent in her, surfaces. She becomes more furious and indignant with each passing second. What cheek! However, the romantic Lilli is flattered by the sexiest man she has ever laid eyes on. The encounter brought to mind an incident that happened to her when she was a pretty youngster of only 10 years. Her parent's friends had an elderly father living with them when she, with her mother and step father, paid them a visit. The old man invited Lilli into his garden to see his tomatoes and carrots. Being an inquisitive country girl with a keen interest in gardening, she went along only to find that the carrot he wanted to show her was not growing in his garden . . . but, by leaps and bounds it grew out of his pants as he unzipped and pulled with one hand while offering her a dime with the other hand to "please touch it". She quickly ran back into the house frightened and embarrassed, not saying a word to anybody. The old geezer! She had never seen anything quite like that and actually suppressed the whole incident.

Suddenly the same deep familiar masculine voice resonates throughout the plane, first in Arabic, then French and now in perfect English. "This is your pilot. Kindly return to your seats and fasten your seat belts. We are expecting a short period of turbulence."

So you are the Captain, she thought. "Fine time for turbulence" she says disgustedly out loud, as she sat with her panty hose down around her ankles. Hurriedly, she reaches back with one hand and flushes the WC, pausing momentarily to watch the blue disinfecting water wind its way down the toilet's throat, wondering where it ends up.

She bends over to retrieve her panty hose. There is barely enough elbow room. She wonders how that obese man before her ever maneuvered in here.

At that very moment, her body jack knifes as the plane drops suddenly, like a speedy elevator uncontrolled and non-stop for what seems too long – leaving her air-bound about a foot, until the plane seems to catch up with itself and stop. Lilli drops back down, squarely on the toilet, "Ouch! Good Lord, if someone had shot me, they wouldn't have killed me . . . My heart was in my throat," she muttered as she stood and rubbed her beautiful buttocks . . . a blessing for firm buns. *I'd better get out of this claustrophobic hole,* she thinks as she becomes increasingly alarmed with each quiver of the plane. She does the best she can with the panty hose and pushes the WC door.

Dear God, it won't open . . . (panic) . . . push again. Banging on the door, she notices the letters PULL. She pulls and the door swings open. Relieved, she says aloud "Thank God." She hastens down the narrow isle to her seat. Her snack is in place, but hunger has left.

"That was some altitude drop—a down draft, wind-shear," comments Frank. "Happens every now and then. Are you okay? You look a little pale, Lilli." He reaches for her cold and clammy hands. He massages them, she leans closer resting her head on his shoulder.

"I'm okay now, just a bit of a fright." *But to herself she moans, I have never been so scared in my life.*

Frank, noticing that Lilli is not eating, "You're not missing anything, my dear. Not very good. Tastes peculiar, like nothing I've ever tasted before."

The now familiar voice returns, "Ladies and gentlemen, we are sorry for the sudden loss of altitude. Everything is under control. However, we have one malfunctioning engine. With only one operating engine, we must remain at this altitude until landing in Riyadh in fifteen minutes. Please fasten your seatbelts." Static and a click of the microphone.

"Hold on, Lilli!" She squeezes Frank's hand ever so tightly.

— 10 —
Abdulla

Abdulla, the heavy-set Arab that Lilli had passed in the aisle, was sitting on the opposite side of the aisle. He noticed Lilli, pale and anxious. "Tell your wife not to worry. *Allah* eees watching over us. We will ahhrrrrive safely in Riyadh, *Insha'allah*," he told Frank in a thickly accented voice with rolling rrrrr's.

"What is *Insha'allah*?" Frank asked the pleasant Arab man, as Lilli sat forward, listening.

"Eeet means God willing," his jovial face beaming. Such a nice friendly man, Lilli thought.

He continued, "We Muslims—and all Saudi Arabians are Muslims—believe that God wills everything in our lives. He guides our destiny. We do not control our own lives. Allah wills what will or won't happen to us; we accept His will and submit to Him. He is the most prevalent being in our lives. Before we do anything, we ask his blessing – *Bisma'allah*. We praise Him—*Al Hamdu'lillah*, we do what He wills or permits – *Insha'allah*, we say goodbye using His name—*Ma'asalama or Fi Amen'allah*—go with God. You see, Arabic is the language of our sacred book, the Koran, therefore, it is a divine language. But never mind all that, I am probably boring you. Good, the seat belt signs are off. *Allah* weeel see us safe to

Riyadh, never you mind." He looked directly at Lilli, "My name is Abdulla. It means servant of God in Arabic and I try to be that. *Kaif halik, how do you do? As-Salaam Aleikum, peace be upon you.*"

"*Tayyib, well. Wa-Alaykum As-Salaam, peace be upon you.*" Lilli found herself saying. She glanced over at Abdulla and smiled. She felt relaxed again.

Clearly delighted, Abdulla asks, "You speeky Arabi?" His face glowed with a broad smile.

"Just a little. I studied many languages in college, Arabic included. It is a nice language and I hope to learn more while I am in your country."

"My wife, Fatima would like to learn better English. Maybe you can meet her," he said as he clearly enjoyed looking at the prettiest Engleesi, or so he thought, woman he had ever seen. "Are you Engleesi or Americanee?"

"I am American and I would love to meet your wife."

"Here is my card," handing it to Frank, who passed it to Lilli.

ORIENTAL CARPETS
Importer of exceptional Persian, Pakistani and Afghani carpets.
Abdulla El Bagawi, Riyadh, Saudi Arabia.
Phone number 32116.

"Your phone number is Talata, itnayn, wahed, wahed, sita?" Little did Lilli know at this time, she will be dialing that number frequently. "Were you born in Saudi Arabia?" Lilli asks as she turns to look at Frank who had begun reading a business magazine.

Abdulla looked at her, "Your accent is perfect. No, we settled in Dir'iya, a small oasis town not far from Riyadh, in 1967. Actually, Dir'iya was the capital and birthplace of our first king and founder of the Kingdom of Saudi Arabia, King Ibn Saud Abdul-Aziz. But

I live in Riyadh now. If you and your husband should like to visit one day, I will come to your house and drive you to mine."

"We should love that," she said nudging Frank.

"Yes, indeed, we'd be honored to visit you, ahhh," he looks down at the card, "Abdulla."

Lilli thinks, Arab hospitality already . . . she had heard about their friendliness, especially toward Americans and even enemies. It's their culture.

Abdulla continues, "When I was very young, we moved from Lebanon to Palestine, opened a carpet business, and became famous carpet merchants. We lived there happily; Arabs, Jews and Christians together. Even today my dear friends are of all three faiths. In 1967, we lost everything. I remember the screaming and crying in my village, the Israeli bullets replying to the stones thrown by our youth, killing some and injuring others. Why small Palestinian radical groups kept attacking and bombing Israel, I do not know. The Israeli reply was prodigious. Ordinary Israelis and Palestinians suffered . . . everyone did. In the end it was a disaster for Palestine." People running everywhere, confused, trying to get away. Many ran for fear of death, never to return to their homes that were no longer there. Some did and their houses were occupied by Israelis. We left with only the clothes on our back, my father's store was ruined. We came to Saudi Arabia to find peace, where my father could begin again. It was slow. He died last year so the business is mine now."

"Such a sad situation. I hope peace will come soon. Abdulla, where do you buy your carpets?" Lilli asks.

"Mostly Iran, Afghanistan and Pakistan; but also Lebanon because, like New York, it is a store house of quality carpets. However, I recently went to Lebanon and I think I shall not return again."

Lilli asks, "Why not? I hear beautiful cedar trees grow along the edge of the Mediterranean Sea with a backdrop of picturesque mountains rising skyward. It's one place I must see."

"Beautiful it is . . . the most beautiful in the Middle East; but, politically there is much strife. The minority Christians control the government and the majority Muslims have no voice in the government. This inequality cannot last forever. The street rumors are that a rebellion is not far off. No, I think I have made my last trip to Lebanon. I shall concentrate on the beautiful Iranian and Pakistan markets. And, I doubt you will get to visit there, either." Abdulla did not know how prophetical his statements would turn out to be.

⸻

Lilli felt the plane's engines slow for its descent into the capital city. She noticed a group of western-dressed women lined up by the W.C. (toilet). Each had a black bundle under her arm. A few minutes later, each one emerged completely dressed in black. A black cloth covering the face with only eyes peering out into the universe. A transformation from western dress to middle-eastern. *This surprising phenomena is very interesting. I will definitely find out more about it. I wonder if Abdulla's wife covers up like that. I know women cover up, but not that much.*

She nudges Frank as the black tents pass by leaving a strong perfumed scent in their wake. "I don't think I could ever support that custom. Those girls were all very pretty and now they are hidden underneath ugly black robes. "

"Well, Miss Lilli . . . May I call you that?"

"Surely."

"Well, Miss Lilli, we have a long history and many customs. Saudi archeological history is just now, in this year, being uncovered by our new archeologist, in conjunction with the University of Chicago in America. I overheard your wonderful history of this region. Our customs are a part of that history. Fatima will help you with the woman's part."

"One of my big interests in college was Archeology and I am very interested in customs, history and artifacts," Lilli told their new friend.

"I will introduce you to Omar, a good friend of mine. He is working hard to open the first museum here."

"Abdulla, I should really like to see the museum, *shukran,* (thank you)."

The conversation was interrupted by the intercom. "This is Captain Rashudi. We are preparing for our landing in Riyadh. Please have seatbelts on."

Abdulla explains, "Tariq Rashudi is a dear friend of ours. His family arrived in Arabia from Pakistan many years ago. He studied in America and England, I believe. It is not often I ride in the plane he is piloting."

Lilli didn't utter a sound. Pilot Rashudi's deep, base voice sent chills throughout her body.

Frank put the business magazine he had been reading into his Halburton valise when Abdulla asked, "What company do you work for?"

"Boxwood International of America. I am Vice President of the International Division."

"Aiwa, *(yes)* I know of it. You provide the kingdom with war materials, vehicles, and construction supplies. There is so much construction going on these days. A few years from now, we will have a big city instead of a small town."

Frank asked, "Are you afraid that growth will bring unsatisfactory cultural changes?"

"For me I am only a little upset. I know this country must progress; but our religious leaders, the Ulema, are upset. We have strict Wahabi Islam practiced here, Wahabism. The Ulema's say we might end up like your country with high crime rates, dying family units, loss of religion, greedy people only wanting money and power, working mothers neglecting their children and disrespect for the old by placing them in nursing homes. In Saudi Arabia, we have extended families. Everyone has a home, especially the old."

"If your country's growth situation is of such importance and magnitude to you and you anticipate your country may ultimately become westernized, why have westerners here?"

"*Aiwa, (yes),* these are very real potential problems for my country and yet we need western technology and instruction if we are to advance and become self-sufficient. That is our ultimate goal, although we do not want to fall into the trap of losing our moral values to a technological, anti-religious society. Therefore, our government is extremely cautious and the Ulema keep a check on us to assure we abide by the Koran, our holy book in all things. We are a religious, Islamic state under *Allah*. Only persons who are church members can enter our country. We do not welcome atheists, Jews or our enemies."

They feel the plane circling around for its landing approach. Abdulla continues, "I hope you will visit me one day and we can talk more of our two countries. Your wife will like my wife. By the way, we will be having an after Ramadan celebration called the "Eid", in late October. I shall phone you at work if you would like to come to our villa."

"We look forward to visiting your home for that holiday, Abdulla. By the way, I am Frank Martinez. You can reach me at this number," handing the Arab his card.

"*Taib, good,*" he begins to collect his belongings.

Lilli whispers to Frank, "I've heard about Arab hospitality. This must be it, inviting total strangers into your home. It certainly would never happen in America."

Whispering, "You're right, Lilli and he's probably a good contact."

"Frank, stop it," Lilli says disgustedly. *That's my husband. A genuine gesture of friendship from the heart and he has to think of contacts.* Looking out the window as the plane tilts, she is amazed by hundreds of twinkling city lights turned on while a sun sets, adding shadows to define the perimeter of an unpretentious small town surrounded by mounds of desert sand dunes.

"Frank, a desert surrounds this city! Very few roads lead away from the main center down there. They end at nothing but sand dunes. At least the city has electric lights," *she thought aloud.* She realized she really didn't know what to expect, in spite of the history she had read and studied. They were are at the other end of the world in a culture they knew little about. *I expected things foreign, different; but do I really know?* Certainly Abdulla seemed normal – not unusual.

"Lilli, I realize all cultures are different. I think this country will take time to adjust to its oddity. But, future adventures fill me with anticipation. I can't wait to begin work."

Filled with excitement and curiosity, "How exciting for us to be here, Frank."

─11─
Ahlan wa Sahlan— Welcome

As they hit the tarmac, a thickly accented woman's voice replaces Captain Rashudi's, first in Arabic, then French and lastly English. "The time is eight p.m, Riyadh time. The temperature is thirty-five degrees centigrade or ninety-five degrees Fahrenheit. Thank you for flying Saudia and we hope to see you again soon. Please wait for the plane to come to a full stop before removing your seat belt." Intercom clicks. Lilli thinks, *in these clothes, I will swelter.*

Lilli glanced at her watch, 11 a.m., Eastern time. Riyadh is nine hours ahead. *I must set my watch ahead.* "Frank, she thanked us for flying Saudia. We had no choice. No other airline flies into Riyadh. She surely will see us again, when we go home. But, what if the 'powers that be' don't want us to leave?"

Before the plane comes to that full stop, most Arabs jump up and begin pulling their possessions from the overhead compartments. Abdulla was already halfway to the exit.

"Please remain seated until the captain turns off the seat belt sign," from the thickly accented voice. No one paid attention. The plane jolted as the brakes were applied. People swayed, holding on to the closest seat back.

"Let's wait a minute," suggests Frank. "A month ago, the plane was almost empty."

They collect their overhead luggage, make their way to the front door where Captain Rashudi stands in front of the cabin. His eyes are on Lilli, only Lilly, and for a brief instant their eyes connected.

"Thank you for a safe flight," Lilli's soft, almost inaudible voice.

"Yes, thanks," added Frank.

"*Ahlan wa sahlan, you are welcome.* It 'twas my pleasure," comes a deep throaty answer.

So very masculine. I am impressed, her mind ponders as she leaves the plane.

Totally fascinated, Tariq Rashudi watches this beautiful alluring woman make her way down the steps to the tarmac. *What a figure and those huge green riveting eyes, the likes of which I have never before seen. And her smile is extraordinary. Wow! Not a typical westerner— American. Stunning, stunning, my kind of woman.*

"*Insha'allah,* God willing, we'll meet again my flawless American beauty," he breathed softly aloud. The smooth landing disguised the uncertainty and chaos that came next. Their first sight upon disembarking was something they had never experienced. Two soldiers, armed with machine guns, stand on either side of the door to a large Quonset hut, a primitive terminal. Their Khaki uniforms askew and wrinkled, their manner very serious and threatening. "I certainly feel we are now in a foreign country. I'm afraid," she told an equally nervous Frank. "What are we doing here, anyway?" queried a clearly scared Lilli as she removed her blazer.

"Too late for that, Lilli. There should be someone to meet us. Look for an American face. This place has changed in a month. Probably because all the westerners are now arriving to work."

Behind them, two young clearly inebriated British men carrying wine bottles in their hands, loudly voice their displeasure at being in a "dry" country. Two soldiers rapidly push and escort the men into another building, not to be seen again.

"Do you hear that?" Frank asked. Off in a distance, a crashing of bottle glass was heard.

Upon entering a doorway, there appeared a large rectangular room ahead jam-packed with a confused mass of people. No one seemed to be in charge. Animated foreign conversations left Frank and Lilli tongue-tied. In one corner, a man in a soiled long, white shirt dress with a red-checkered kerchief hanging from his head, was kneeling on a small carpet, bobbing his head and barefooted body up and down. Lilli knew that this is a prayer ritual. She tried not to stare.

The sloppily painted and stained grey walls of the gloomy room had numerous gouges in its plaster. After waiting in a line, they came to a small counter where a very mean-looking man, suspiciously checked their passports. "You, Amerricanni? Where ees yourrr visa here?" Frank didn't have time to answer when pages were stamped and the two passports quickly returned to him. Frank detected a hardly discernible smile on the Arab's face. *'A scare the shit out of you' game from these guys, Frank thinks . . . a power play.*

Next, came a long shoddily-made counter with three men behind it. Passengers seemed to be waiting 'en masse'. There was no waiting in lines.

"That looks like the customs luggage check over there," Frank noted.

Well, at least Frank is keeping his cool . . . "I'm a nervous wreck and I know it shows!"

There are four torn, dirty low-backed leather chairs crammed together on one wall. "Lilli, you seem to be the only western lady here. Look, all those little hot black eyes sitting there are glued on you. They'd love to seduce you my girl."

She nervously looks around. *These fellows never get to see a woman, I know that. The few Arab women in the terminal squatted in a corner, covered in black from head to toe, some with only eye slits.*

Finally, they hear baggage come dribbling in on a noisy conveyor belt. Quickly, the counter is full of luggage being opened, inspected and clothes pulled out and rummaged through. There were no lines, no organization. It was simply push and shove with clothes left in a rumpled heap for the owner to put back inside. The search is for pornography, liquor, religious articles, bibles and guns. Another man before them had a bottle of liquor in his suitcase. It was thrown on the floor . . . broken on the spot. The man disappears with a worker. A white chalk mark quickly scribbled on each piece of searched luggage seems to be the ticket to getting out of this place.

"Frank, evidently you can't get out of here without a chalk mark."

"Right, so let's get us some chalk marks." Frank moves closer to the counter where he sees piles of luggage scattered, willy-nilly on the floor. Thankfully he finds their bags and hoists them to the counter when a tiny spot of space becomes available. Everyone then moves aside to allow the beautiful Americana passage. One of the counter men beckons Frank to open his suitcases followed by a harsh command, "OPEN"! Frank never had an experience like this. *Hell with this business, his arrogant personality took over. I'll make sure this doesn't happen again.*

"Lilli, get to a phone and tell my company I am here," handing her a business card. She nervously searched the room for a phone. Moments later, "There is no phone, Frank." *Fear engulfs her again as she senses Frank's panic at being searched so thoroughly by men with such hardened faces. No one smiled or spoke. Intimidation was rampant.*

The Arab finished pulling all their clothes out leaving one heaping mess. One by one, on the outside of each suitcase, he made the required white chalk mark checks.

"How will we ever get these to close again?" Lilli wondered aloud. With difficulty they straighten their rumpled clothes and shut the cases.

When Frank looked up, he couldn't believe that there was yet another obstacle. A ten foot chain link fence loomed about fifteen feet ahead. Another sober-faced guard stood at the only exit. As they approach, he would not let Lilli pass. He points to her purse. She looks puzzled and at that moment Frank feels a nudge. It was Abdulla.

"A sight for sore eyes, old boy. They won't let Lilli pass through."

"She needs a chalk mark on her purse. It hasn't been checked," informed Abdulla. "I'll do it for you." He took Lilli's purse over to the counter where it was immediately marked.

While they awaited Abdulla's return they notice several small creepy-looking barefooted men standing by the exit in red plaid skirts held up by ropes at the waist and white skull caps.

"They must be the Yemeni workers, the backbone of the work force now," he told Lilli. And then they couldn't believe what they were seeing. Men, openly masturbating through their long robes and skirts, as they stare at Lilli. She felt naked. She studied the scene with peripheral vision, trying to ignore the goings on and not appear shocked, as she truly was.

Again an uneasy feeling came over her when Frank ordered her to "Stay right beside me." Fear again engulfed her very soul, fear of the unknown riveted her being. Don't panic, she tells herself. "My friends," called Abdulla, the only familiar voice they knew, as he gives Lilli back her purse, "Just get your passport out so they can okay your entrance visa and luggage checks. It's the final checkpoint. I'll take you to your villa."

Abdulla has saved us, thinks Lilli. What a relief.

Suddenly they heard a deep man's voice call out, "Frank, Lilli, over here." They peer through the fence to see a tall, blond fellow holding a sign over his head . . . Boxwood President, Ralph Perkins. WELCOME TO SAUDI ARABIA, FRANK and LILLI MARTINEZ

"Thank God," whispers Lilli.

"Thanks for your offer, Abdulla, and your help. You will never know how much I appreciate it. We'll be in touch," Frank smiled. "Let's get the hell out of here, my dearest."

Their fears abate somewhat just knowing someone from America was there and expecting them. The company had said they would be met in London; but, no one showed up there. They boarded the Saudia plane to Riyadh anyway.

At that moment, several little, wiry Yemeni bag boys surround them in a court yard, shouting and pointing to their chests, "Me take" and before any acknowledgment was given, the bags, like they were feather pillows, are hoisted up on the shoulders of three skinny boys.

Strong little guys, thought Frank. Just before exiting, a loud noise, sounding like the breaking of glass again, caused them to turn around. They see bottles of liquor being smashed. A man trying to smuggle in liquor was being whisked off between two guards, drunkenly exclaiming in a thick Scottish brogue, "I'm terribly sorry, I didn't know." His voice trails off.

As they exit the fenced area, a guard checks everything for chalk marks. Lilli feels the crush of dry heat meeting the expiring hot air from her lungs and then . . . a friendly face, "Alhamdu'illah, (*Thanks be to God,*)" she says under her breath.

"Hey Frank and Lilli, I beat you here by two weeks," greets Ralph Perkins, President of Boxwood International of America in Saudi Arabia. Welcome to Riyadh, the land of sand and sunshine, not to mention heat. Hi Lilli." He gives her a big hug.

"Really good to see an American, Ralph," Frank, with some relief shook Ralph's hands. "You're the first B.I.A. employee we've seen since we left London yesterday."

"I know what you mean. There aren't too many Westerners here yet. Only twelve of us with our company and most other companies are much smaller. For the Saudis, this airport is busy."

"What an ordeal," commented Lilli. "Thank God, we made it . . . but so hot already!"

Little did she know she will be asking God to will all things (Insha'allah) for the next twenty plus years. Nothing here will seem strange; in fact, her own country and people will become strangers.

— 12 —

Odors, Heat, Dust, Urination, Masturbation

The putrid stench of urine aromas fills Lilli's nostrils. She observes dirty smelly men mulling around the parking lot, urinating and masturbating. She tries to tell herself to relax. The myriad of odors coupled with the heat and dust is almost asphyxiating.

"It's still hot," interjected Ralph. "But you should have been here earlier. It was up to 105 degrees today. It gets so hot that you don't feel your body's perspiration. It quickly evaporates before your clothing gets wet. We are nearing the beginning of summer on the edge of a desert, the Rub Al Khali. Ramadan begins on the seventeenth of September this year."

Soon Lilli was feeling much better. The cool station wagon veers precipitously to avoid large potholes in the bumpy road. They left the not to be forgotten airport adventures behind. Ralph was taking them to a company villa, all the while instructing them as to what they could and shouldn't do, and what proper Saudi etiquette was. "Don't drink any water unless it's bottled Sohat water. Women who do not cover up are considered loose and infidels." Lilli looked at Frank in disbelief, "I thought I had studied up on this culture, but apparently not all of it, for sure. "

Ralph continued, "And don't pay more than 2 Saudi riyals for a ride to anywhere in the city. By the way, did you bring some long-sleeved, high-necked long dresses? If not, there are men here that sew. By the way, to make a phone call you have to go downtown to the only post office."

"Yes Ralph, I did," she gulped. She knew an ancient backward culture was in existence here, but she now wondered what she was getting herself into. *Maybe Frank should have come here alone.*

"Good. Most local women cover their faces when out in public. You won't be expected to do that yet, but you must definitely cover your head. Now, it is important to wash all fresh fruits and vegetables with a soap and chlorine solution. When you get dysentery, which will be soon after your first meal out, take one of these Lomotil," he handed Frank a bottle of tiny white tablets.

"In fact," he continued, "all drugs can be purchased at the downtown drugstore without a prescription. And finally, try to remain as inconspicuous as possible. These people will be entering into a culture shock soon enough when more and more westerners arrive, especially women. We are the first. They like us now and are curious, but that may turn to resentment later if we don't respect their customs."

Driving along a short unpaved, roughly bumpy road to a paved circle and intersection, a turnabout with trees in the middle appeared. On the road's edge sat a very small wooden hut with, of all things, a PEPSI sign. "Look Frank," exclaims a surprised Lilli, "They have Pepsi here. It's the first English script I've seen. My goodness, I feel more at home now."

Riding past the American Mission and then the Ministry of Petroleum, a very impressive building, Lilli comments on the

Arabic motif. Her tired eyes focus on as much as the night lights make visible. Feeling lightheaded with excitement, she feels the need for sleep. The city is bathed in eery yellow street lights bestowing dusty trees with a grey, ethereal glow.

"We're on *Mataar* Street, meaning airport or as the Arabs say *Shari Mataar*," Ralph points out. "There is no room yet in the decent hotels, the only ones comfortable and clean enough that westerners could possibly stay in temporarily. So you will be housed in the nice company villa for now. It hasn't been refurbished yet but, it is still better than the three best hotels. General employee housing is not complete so our other few employees will be staying at the magnificent Palace Hotel. Ahem, I am joking. You were there overnight, Frank, so you know. You will join the others there hopefully soon, before our villas are ready," Ralph chuckles with sarcasm.

Continuing, "They tell me, in the 1960's, the then beautiful Palace Hotel was a residence for a King's large harem, luxuriously complete with imported Austrian crystal chandeliers over each bed . . . and bidets, European toilets to bathe one's private parts. Frank, you know what I mean. The hotel has passed its heyday however, and is now run down from the dry sandy, hot climate and lack of maintenance. But, it is the best, by western standards, of the few hotels in the city."

"All these concrete-looking houses we are passing are circled by high walls, piles of rubble amassed all around, goats eating garbage. Unbelievable and unimaginable, certainly not American-style," Lilli exclaims. "This really is a third world country . . . but not for long."

Finally, Ralph abruptly stops the car in front of huge iron gates. The sandy walls, covered with climbing fuchsia bouganvilla, don't conceal the dusty grey, top story of the villa. Ralph rings the doorbell.

The gate opens by a grinning Yemeni boy, immaculately dressed in a green plaid skirt, a beige shirt and white skull cap. Barefoot, he welcomes them, *"Ahlan wa sahlan, Welcome."* They enter. An illuminated weeping willow tree comes into view, its boughs laden with tan sand and dust. They walk over a sandy, marble-tiled courtyard. *Many shrubs, but no grass, notices Lilli.*

Inside, the huge villa is void of a phone or furniture, except for a dining room table and chairs, living room sofa and upstairs, a bed. A filthy bathroom, a damp earthy smell from the kitchen, an old, worn and dirty carpeting. This all causes Lilli to wonder, *what on earth are we doing here?*

"I'll be back tomorrow afternoon, Frank. There is cooked food in the frig. This villa is not very old even though it appears to be well used." Going down the few front stairs, "All dwellings in this desert age quickly. The cement used is mixed with the highly mineralized local sand and erodes quickly. With no maintenance, buildings deteriorate in five years or so. Have a restful night. I'll check on you tomorrow, ma'asalama, *good bye.* Friends, westerners learn that word fast."

Lilli notices cracks in the wall, many areas of peeling paint. Her immediate impression is one of barrenness. It probably had been a luxurious mini-palace, but now it is shoddy and rundown. The heavy living room sofa is overstuffed in gold, drapes are a heavy brocade. Sneezing continuously, Lilli feels dust floating everywhere.

But the worst is yet to come that night. Much to their chagrin they find the plumbing doesn't work. They can't flush the toilet, let alone take a shower . . . there is no water. "No water! Oh, dear, we should have never come here. Much worse than I ever dreamed."

"At least the sheets are clean," Frank sighed peering at the thick dust painting the bedroom floor a shade of brownish-orange.

Jet lag has caught up with their eastern sleep pattern. It is pitch black and they are still wide awake . . . it is 3 p.m. at home. No water, dust everywhere, exhausted, Lilli is miserable and begins crying softly to herself. She wants to go home . . . to the luxuries left behind. "We don't need this life, my socks," Frank's occasional intimate nickname.

Finally, still exhausted, lying on a strange bed in a mysterious but exciting country, they fall asleep. Oblivious to any noises, they, in some way, dream of the free USA homeland left behind.

In the morning, Lilli, very successfully, tries her Arabic on the Yemeni houseboy.

"*Mush moya, no water.*"

"*Mush moya?*" he answers and immediately runs outside. Lilli and Frank follow. There, he turns on a water pump, allowing water from a holding tank to be pumped into a cistern on the roof. Then, by gravity, the water runs down pipes into the villa. He rushes back inside the house to turn on the faucet. "*Bitshuf-see.*" He points excitedly to the running water, pleased with himself.

"So that's it. The pump has to be turned on every day and when the roof tank is full, it turns off," Frank tells Lilli. "The holding tank must be filled periodically. Really back-woodsy."

"Well, maybe when we understand how things work here, we'll feel less anxious and more comfortable in this society," she added.

"Let's take our first shower in Saudi Arabia."

While Frank is showering, Lilli peers out the bedroom window. Across the street the sun shone on what looked like a dump; but on closer inspection, she realizes it is a shanty-town. Rippled aluminum roofs, the sides of the shacks are cardboard or tin. Dilapidated huts but all have T.V antennas and cars parked outside. T.V. screens are seen from many open doors.

"That felt great. The water's hot. Take your shower, Lilli. You'll feel better."

"These poor folks, like slaves, live right beside the rich . . .

no zoning regulations here. I bet all are foreign laborers, Frank. I know, the physical aspects of this country will change, but never Sharia law . . . its inner soul.

"All women are wearing black from head to toe. Even young girls are in long, but brightly colored dirty dresses. Boys, too are wearing dirty white long thobes *(male shirts),*" she observes.

The goats are baaing, dogs and cats lazily resting on the perimeter of the settlement. Two donkeys used to transport goods to the suqs *(bazaar)* are tethered together by stakes and tied to a pole. Sand is everywhere. A camel lies under the shade of a date tree. Ten dilapidated huts stand in this run-down community. One home for each family. It all amazes them. What a backward country. No wonder they need help to become modernized.

That evening, Ralph briefly stops by with food and drink. Seeing all is well, he quickly leaves.

~13~
Salaat—Call to Prayer

The next morning, they hear moaning and wailing from across the street. Lilli runs upstairs to peek out a barred window. Everyone is scurrying around, carrying belongings in several cloth bags. Eventually all sit in the front yard. Mattresses pile up in a center circle like sand dunes. Animals and children run around in a frenzy. Darting nervous goats baaing, he-hawing donkeys bolting up on two legs scrambling to be set free, crème colored desert dogs barking and growling, a yellow desert Lynx cat with pointed ears, sadly races like the wind, away from its food zone.

Suddenly, huge smoke circles pour skyward. No men are visible, apparently they are at work. *Maybe the fire department will be here soon?* Lilli feels helpless and saddened for these poor people. Before many minutes pass, the wailing and moaning stops, the shanties are nothing but hot ashes and melted aluminum. This sight upsets Lilli immensely, but to her amazement, the next day the settlement is being rebuilt.

Ralph brought more food and explained, "I believe the government periodically demolishes these places to keep disease and pestilence at a minimum. All of these workers are from foreign countries . . . none are Saudi. These poor folks live outside till their home is ready."

Lilli recalls the second night. She is awoken from a deep, deep sleep, the kind that one can barely lift their eyelids. She fights to wake up because she thinks she heard a voice calling out. She hears it again and then again. It sounds like a moan. She bolts upright. It was four forty-five, the sky is beginning to glow with the first signs of sunrise.

Was someone being murdered or in trouble? Anything could happen here. She nudged a snoring Frank. "What, what is it, Lilli? Is something wrong?"

Again the wailing, and then the realization, "*Salaat,* Socks. Morning call to prayer by the *Muezzin* chanting, 'There is no God but God and Mohammad is the Messenger of God'."

"Bet the *mosque* (place of worship) is right down the street," Frank says, soon asleep again.

She keeps listening. She knows the words from her lessons. *How inspirational to think Muslims awaken at this hour to pray. Then again at noon, afternoon, sunset and evening. Does everyone?*

Suddenly she hears that first voice again. Jumping to the window, she sees a man with a red henna-tipped beard wearing a long white robe, red checkered scarf over a white skull cap. He is going from villa to villa rattling the heavy iron gates with a long crooked stick, calling out:

"*Salaat, Salaat.*" His voice reverberates down the street. Doors begin opening. Men exit and rapidly head down the street, each carrying a book under their right arm. She presumes it to be a Koran. From another window, she sees the mosque steeple's minaret . . . a round dome on top with two small balls connected to a half moon rising into the heavens. She can't see the loudspeaker that is somewhere on the steeple. She hears the Muezzin's (caller to prayer) magnified calls to prayer, a single voice joining many now, echoing throughout the city, like a harmonious sing-along chorus. The calls, not recorded, are the most beautiful because an actual male voice echos and floods the city.

She would live through many *salaats* in the years to come. They will always inspire her.

Lilli notices some men are praying by the road-side. No women are seen. She knows women are not allowed in mosques, so they must pray at home.

I am amazed that so many men stop what they are doing, lay out their carpets to pray wherever they are . . . five times a day. She thought, these prayers are similar to a Christian or Jew thanking God by praying over the meals they are about to partake in, three times a day.

The fourth night, Lilli awakens with fever and chills. From that moment on, she has the "Riyadh runs," as foreigners call it. Even with a daily dose of Lomotil, the dysentery does not subside until months later when they live in a company villa and Lilli cooks their meals. She was ready to call it quits many times before that.

This morning, Ralph brings his wife Joan by to pay the new employees a visit.

After general conversations, Ralph tells them, "I need to inform you what little more I know about this country. One important thing is . . . are you aware that Mosques are an integral part of the backbone of Arabia? A Muslim's daily life revolves around them and calls to pray. This is a 100% Muslim country with no other religion allowed . . . only Islam."

Lilli already knows this.

"And, Lilli, ex-patriots hold their religious services in private homes or in the American Military Mission only," Joan adds.

"And no tolerance here for proselytizing. We would be immediately excommunicated. Some Christian ladies have already been deported for doing that."

"I know, they are fearful their culture will be perverted by westerners. So guess we have to live with that while we are here? Joan, maybe we can hold our private prayer meetings in our homes, when we get settled, that is."

Ralph adds, "Probably not a problem if you can get a bible in here, which is doubtful. Good, you understand. I'll stop by tomorrow morning with Joan. She can show Lilli the town. Frank, your first day of work will begin tomorrow. See you then."

—14—
First Work Day

In Saudi Arabia, exploring and speaking Arabic,
We ask our friends, Keifel Hal, Keif Halik? (How are you?)
They answer, Kuwayes Kateer. (Very well.)
Here to help a third-world country prepare
Their ascent into today's modern world.
Silently we exude our culture . . . while grasping theirs,
With pleasure west meets east, Insha'allah. (God willing)
By Lilli Martinez

Ralph, with bubbly Joan, arrive promptly at eight to take Frank to work. "Come on Lilli, today is a day of excitement and fun," Joan smiles.

"Hey Frank, the latest news here is this truck driver with a passenger was speeding last night on the road east going to Aramco in Dhahran. A camel stood alone in the middle of the road, too frightened to move. The guy hit the poor beast, lost control and the car sped off into the desert sand. Luckily no one was killed but the camel. Poor animal did summersaults into the air and died in the sand. The driver had to be cut out from under the steering wheel by a passer-by. Luckily, he and his passenger are okay."

"Can't wait for us to have a T.V. to keep up with the news. See you later, Lilli," no usual good-bye kiss today.

"The first tour of Riyadh, Frank. I wish you could come with us," says Lilli with a frown.

"I'm here to work and that comes first. You know that my dear." He clearly wants to impress his boss. "See you later."

"Maybe one evening we can all go out," she adds hopefully.

"Definitely," Ralph answers.

Ralph and Frank drive off to "the office." Ralph is talking incessantly while driving.

"I know you realize I am number one man here along with the Saudi head, Salah abu Bayatri. You met him already. But, remember, you report to me, not Salah, at all times."

"Yes, indeed, Ralph. No problem there." *I know I also have to report to Salah.*

Ralph is a medium tall well-built man in his middle forties with greying mousey blonde hair. Good looking, clean shaven, handsomely dressed. He definitely stands out in a crowd, Frank surmises.

"We are here to help the Saudis help themselves, but to be perfectly honest, our company policy is to stay as long as possible with no rush for cross-training the Saudis. To be sure they can learn. But here lies a virtual gold mine until other companies find out and decide to get on the money bandwagon. Right now the competition is not overwhelming because no one really wants to come to this 'rectum of the world'. Course, we feel Saudi Arabia is and will be more wonderful in time. We are genuine in our respect for their ambition, ancient culture, religion . . . stopping all business transactions five times a day, no work on Thursday or Friday . . . all to please them."

"Those aren't serious problems, are they Ralph?" Frank queries.

"Well, knowing these intelligent folks are not capable of

managing on their own yet, it would take them many years to fulfill their plans by themselves. With us here, the changes could be faster, but with their societal religious rules of days off, our work will be much slower."

"There are a few Saudis, like Salah Bayatri, educated in the west and sharp. Salah is a clever asset. He facilitates and compliments companies in completing Saudi goals," Frank answers.

"Yes, but we are more clever than big honcho Bayatri, huh Frank?"

Frank listens to Ralph during the entire ride over bumpy back dirt streets.

"There are no street signs or addresses here as yet. Mail and phones for public use comes through the post office, until you have a company addresses. No personal house phones, either. You see, no organization, that's why we are here. This will all change." Finally, Ralph stops in front of sandy cement walls, the gate tightly latched. Appearing old and crumbly, a sign hangs on the wall, "BOXWOOD INTERNATIONAL OF AMERICA, Inc."

A small dirty barefooted man in a colorful over-shirt, white pantaloons and skull cap opens the door. His brown-stained toothy smile is as wide as the Gulf of Mexico. Ralph introduces him, "Hello, Muhammed, this is Frank, our new vice president."

"Hello, Meester Frank, *Sabahul Kheir,* good morning . . . *Ahalan wasahlan,* welcome. Frank shook the calloused hands and felt they were used for doing manual labor. Frank knew this man is of the masses . . . the masses of Yemeni who come here to earn a living for their families back home, where jobs are hard to find. All their earnings are sent home.

"Anything you need, you call me, *Na'am,* yes?"

"*Aiwa, shukhran*, Mohammed. (Yes, thank you.)"

Mohammed's residence is at the right of the entrance door. A

4 x 8 foot room with a gas butane portable burner. He sleeps on plastic mats with a blanket rolled on the bottom, for his bed.

Frank is thunderstruck . . . a multi-million dollar company with a multi-million dollar contract and an employee housed in this? We could do better. Many times in the next years, Frank would visit this man in his primeval living quarters, until they built him a larger place.

⸻

Frank, entering a low-ceiling meeting room with just enough space for a huge, oval exquisitely carved inlaid solid rosewood table. The sixteen high-back burgundy leather chairs are elegant dinner table chairs. Plush carpeting quiets the room's noises. All goes silent as Frank enters.

A pretty young secretary introduces herself as Sharon, "I'm from Memphis, Tennessee. I will be working with you, Frank."

He introduces himself to the American and Saudi employees. . . . "I am Frank Martinez, Vice President and assistant to the International Executive Director, Ralph Perkins. We are lucky to be here, and we will not be strangers in this room again." Walking around the table, he shakes all hands and smiles.

A chuckle sounds throughout the room when the door in back of Frank swings open ever so quietly and someone places a hand on his shoulder. He turns and sees a familiar dark-faced man. Salah abu Bayatri in his white thobe and red-checkered ghutra (headscarf). Executive Director, Salah abu Bayatri, kisses both sides of his cheeks and Frank returns the same to Salah.

"So good to see you again, Frank. I was waiting for you. I welcome you, Ahlan wa Sahalan. The employees have been anxious for your arrival so you could help solve problems . . . which will be your sole purpose in these first few months, Frank. We'll meet again in a few days."

Salah arose. He places his hand on Frank's shoulder again, "Let me show you to your office, it's adjacent to mine. Ralph's is opposite. Remember, you report to me, too, Frank."

Ralph hears Salah as Frank replies, "I'll be happy to do anything you want. You just name it."

— 15 —
First City Tour

Nervous in a floor length, long-sleeve dress and head kerchief, Lilli asks Joan, "Am I dressed appropriately?"

"Dahling, you are most certainly." The southern drawl is unmistakable. "I have nevah seen anybody look quite that good in ah baggy dress. Your beauty cannot be hidden, deah." She stares at the full bosom, slim hips, the elegant, manner. *All eyes will be on Lilli,* she thinks. "And remember, no religious jewelry can ever be worn in public."

Joan's hair is a bleached pale blonde, cropped short. "We are not supposed to attract attention. All Muslim women cover up, you know. Men heah are not used to seeing female faces, let alone their bodies. All Arab entertaining is done segregated, women in one room, men in another and nevah the twain to meet."

The suffocating May desert heat envelopes them, as they walk out to Airport Road, *Shaari Mataar,* to hail a taxi. One driver stops, but Joan motions him on. "His taxi had a few bad dents in it; he's not a good driver."

After a few minutes, another stopped. Joan gave him a look-over, she bargained for the fare by holding her fingers up through the open passenger side window of the dusty car.

"Two *riyals*."

"*La*, no," the driver answers. *"Talata,"* with three fingers held up.

"Itnayn wa nos—two and one half," bickers Joan.

"Quais, yella, imshi—Good, let's go," the driver beckons them to get in.

They amble into the back seat. Smiling, he asks "You Englesee or Americanee?"

"Americanee," replies Joan, whispering to Lilli, "That is the extent of my Arabic. We do not converse with the drivers. They think western women are sexually permissive. They do not respect them. Some have been abducted into the desert and raped. Never take a taxi alone and be sure you know the city well enough so you know where the driver is going. And never sit up front."

Lilli answers, "Perhaps this driver is just curious about Westerners with only a few of us here right now. I imagine we are an oddity to some of these people. Others may resent our invading their country, not realizing we are here to help them into the twenty first century and beyond. I see a water tower up ahead. Its saucer-like top resembles a UFO."

"The Royal Family dines in the restaurant on the top. It's theirs exclusively," Joan adds.

"The view must be spectacular. This city is so small. Bet you can see the surrounding desert really well from there. When this place grows, the desert close by will be obliterated."

Now on Shaari Wazir, "Over theah is a King's Pink Palace taking up a complete city block. A Princess's huge, sand-colored mud palace is next to it."

"Joan, the white crenelated roof resembles a castle in King Arthur's time."

"It sure does. Opposite is another Princess's palace, the only mud edifice in that huge field of sand."

"Further on are the downtown shops. We have a few hours before merchants will close for noon salaat. Shops close every afternoon at noon for prayer and lunch. Some folks take afternoon naps. Iron- gated doors over the shop's entrances open again after prayers."

Streets are overflowing with litter. The air is hazy with sand blowing in on a gentle wind. No Saudi women are on the sidewalks. Buildings look dilapidated from Lilli's western modern perspective. Clothes hang from windows of upper apartments. No dryers here yet.

Turning right on *Shaari (street) Thumari*, she notices a building. "Riyadh Museum. How nice, they have a museum," she says with some surprise in her voice.

"Not a museum, dahling. It's a department store and the only place that has a john for westerners to use . . . dirty, but usable in a Riyadh Run emergency. You have been forewarned."

"I guess so," mumbles Lilli, unbelieving this was no museum.

Joan points out, "At the end of this street sits a clock tower in the center of a little round about. On the right is the Grand Mosque, there since the turn of the century. Punishments, such as executions, decapitations, and hand chops are performed here in 'chop-chop square' at noon after mosque services on Fridays, their holy day. Maybe one day you can see one with Frank? I warn you, it isn't any fun to witness."

"Yes, we will definitely do that. I know we must be knowledgeable about every aspect of this intriguing culture in order to understand it. I came to learn a new culture."

Near-by they pass the Ministry of Justice, a more modern building with pink lace-work circling the top perimeter.

"Lilli, please tell the driver to stop here."

"*Min fadlack, Wa qif hina, Please Stop here.*"

~16~
Ancient Gold Suq (Bazaar)

He stops at the entrance of an alleyway between the Justice Ministry and some money changers. As they cross the dirt alleyway, everything has the look of old . . . smelly, dirty with some areas reeking of old urine. One man is squatting in an empty lot, relieving himself. Lilli looks away.

"Phew," comments Joan. "Let's move away from here quickly."

Men walking around in long thobes and red-checkered *ghutra* head scarfs, seem to be in no hurry. Sitting on the sidewalks are scribes and tooth brush salesmen, whittling the point of mangrove sticks to make tooth "stick" brushes for their clients.

Lilli gulps, "I feel like I have taken a step back in time without a time machine. Time has stood still here. What a marvel to see all this now before this country changes. We will make history here. I hope they appreciate us."

"Hmmmm," sighs Joan. "Ralph and I see no reason for being here except for money and travel. I do not intend to linger very long."

Further on they approach four corners.

"This is a first come first go situation . . . no traffic lights yet in this city. Quick, let's run across now. To the right is the covered *Suq* (marketplace or bazaar*)."* Joan leads Lilli.

"Looks very old, in need of repairs. Feels like it is in imminent collapse. I hope we are safe." Following the bumpy, sometime puddle-ridden dirt pathways they pass terribly unpretentious variety shops that seemed to have their merchandise displayed in a helter-skelter manner.

"I am not prepared for what my eyes are now beholding, Joan. This main passageway is quite a shock. We definitely are in the Gold Suq. I am stunned – unbelievable."

Gold is everywhere on both sides of the path, shops overflowing with gold follow one after the other. "This feels like an incredible antique store. Is it all really gold?" Lilli asks Joan.

"It sure is and it's all twenty-one or twenty-four carat."

The glistening, glittering yellow metal is dripping from walls, hanging from ceilings, amassed inside glass top counter cases and piled high on counter tops in numberless stacks. Exploding and bursting, gold flows out of semi-closed jewelry chests. Ubiquitous sparkling gold bedazzles the two western ladies.

Lilli glances around casually pretending its old hat walking through billions of dollars of gold within arm's reach. She recalls reading that one ounce of melted gold can stretch fifty miles.

Incredible if true. *I rather like being surrounded by this wealth. I am mesmerized seeing this parade of people buying and selling.* The merchants are pouring the golden trinkets out of plastic bags, allowing the buyers to touch and sort through what they want. *I don't see one policeman. Such trusting people.*

"I am thankful we are dressed in floor-length dresses, Joan. These Arab men holding prayer beads are staring at us like we are naked. Thank the Lord we are covered properly."

"Let's try to ignore the stares and enjoy what we are seeing . . . so different from anything we have ever observed in our lifetime."

Suddenly, a small man wearing a little white beanie-type cap comes running by. He grabs onto Lilli's breasts as he passes, squeezing tightly with both hands. With lighting speed she gives him an elbow and quickly kicks him in the balls. He continues his swift run, limping and is gone in a minute, disappearing into a cheering crowd.

"Oh my goodness!" said Joan. "What was that all about?"

"I don't know, but that little jerk had a good feel. All the shops are attended by men here, no women. This guy came out of nowhere to do his dirty business to a Western women." An exasperated Lilli comments.

"Yes, we are immersed in a man's world here and we can never forget it."

In one shop, they pass a tall Bedouin in a white *thobe*. His red checkered *ghutra* headdress is held on by a black rope, an *agal,* wrapped around his head. He is buying gold bangles for a diminutive vision of all black standing behind him, probably his wife. Timidly admiring the many bangles her husband is buying, she seems uncomfortable.

"Lilli, she is wearing a *Nigaab,* a Saudi *burqa* covering her body from head to toe, her face is veiled with many thicknesses of black gauze, a *hijab.*"

Lilli whispers to Joan, "Probably very rarely comes into town. In the desert, she doesn't have to cover her face unless male strangers stop by. The bangles she chose are extremely tiny. I wonder how she will ever get them on over the palm of her hand."

Fascinated, they watch as the merchant places a heavily greased plastic bag, greased side up and open at both ends, over the woman's hand and wrist. One tiny bracelet is subsequently placed over the grease-laden bag. Then the finger end of the bag is pulled while the woman's palm is squeezed excessively. Quickly and one by one, the child-sized bracelets are pushed and worked into place. But the woman shows no emotion.

"That was not possible without some discomfort," Lilly whispers. "Let's buy one, Joan."

"An amazing feat," Joan, shaking her head. They both buy two bangles. Lilli is addicted.

The clearly happy lady walks away with bangles worth a great deal of dollars based on the days gold prices. Gold glistens from beneath her ultra- thin black cloak as she walks by.

Lilli and Joan, at another shop, step up on a narrowly slanted cement step to peer through the glass-top counter. They find themselves beside a Saudi man who removes a stack of Saudi 100 Riyals about one inch high, out of his *thobe* pocket. He is looking at a gorgeous sapphire and diamond set: necklace, earrings, ring, bracelet and tiara—a dazzling ensemble costing a probable twenty thousand plus dollars. He purchases it. The recipient of this lavish gift is waiting nearby accompanied by a female companion. Both wear Burqas with eye slits flaunting beautiful dark eyes. Lilli thinks they are very pretty, very young ladies.

Further down a second dirt path of this amazing gold *suq*, another shopkeeper is rubbing some gold pieces on a black stone that resembles pumice. Intrigued, Lilli motions for Joan to follow her.

Upon closer viewing, they see the gold come off as dust on the stone. The man then applies a drop of clear solution on the spot of gold dust. Subsequently, he announces to two women, "These pieces are *wahid 'ishriin, twenty-one carat.*"

"The women are selling their pieces, probably bought when gold was much cheaper," observes Lilli.

Beneath one of the large glittering shops at the main cross-road of the paths, several crouching women are clustered together in black, long loose gowns, a*bayas* with *hijab* head veils; only their dark eyes peer out. Haggling and bargaining, they carry on animated conversations in spite of their veil. They are selling their jewelry to one another and seem to be having a wonderful time.

"This is how some women find excitement and pass the time of day, Lilli."

One little lady holds up a pair of golden earrings as they pass by. The lady's *henna,* red-stained hands have a ring on every finger. All are for sale.

"Her earrings have a turquoise stone in them, Joan. They are pretty, aren't they?" She asks, "*Kam hadie,(How much?)*"

Joan whispers to Lilli, "Here is where the art of bartering is effective providing you know what the piece is worth."

Lilli and the lady begin to dicker a little. Her black eyes are outlined with kohl, or powdered antimony that is used as both an eye cosmetic and a medicine. The palms and base of her fingernails are stained with *henna,* of a dark, reddish-orange color that reaches to her fingertips in lovely geometric artsy designs. Henna, is used for weddings and celebrations. It is considered beautiful. Religious men, especially, stain their beards with it.

A spicy incense aroma of sandal wood and rose water wafts from the little lady's person. A smile shows through the crinkles around her eyes. Finally, the price seems fair, so Lilli buys the earrings with the turquoise stones. "*Taib, nishtri,* Good, I will buy," she tells the woman and walks off with her purchase . . . the second one in the land of sand with many more to come.

They continue along the "golden" path. This New England/Southern gal is satiating her golden appetite. Suddenly a clamorous noise emanates from where the ladies sit. Glancing back, an Arab, stately in his long, flowing tan robe edged in braid, a checkered *ghutra headdress* hanging loosely from his head, stands over the little women in black.

"Over there is a *Mutawa,* Islam's morals police. See, the end of his beard has a touch of henna," comments Joan. The man uses a crooked stick cut from Yemeni mangrove trees to tap and prod the women in black away. The Mutawa sits back down beside a khaki-uniformed security policeman to insure the women do not return to block the aisle again.

Lilli adds, "So they do have at least one security policeman here after all."

— 17 —
Taxi

Walking away from all that gold, Lilli is dumbfounded, in a state of exhilarating shock on her first suq adventure in Saudi Arabia. There was so much gold jewelry to discover, she couldn't think of anything but gold and gems. Clearly in a daze, "This is a fun country, Joan."

Joan flags a taxi. "Call to prayer now, so the shops will close until afternoon *Salaat.*"

The return ride was less than pleasant. The young driver, driving recklessly at high speed despite both their warnings of "*shway, shway,* slow, slow." He ignores them and keeps singing loudly while pressing on the gas pedal, scrutinizing his cargo by way of the rear view mirror. At one point he turns around and they see he has a cataract in the right eye, so his vision is not without a flaw.

"I know eye problems and blindness are the result of many fly infections here called *trachoma,* a disease carried on the feet of flies, jokingly called the pesky national bird of Saudi Arabia," Joan whispers.

"Yes, and the sticky, light footed insects are everywhere; however, the disease is totally curable with the use of antibiotic ointments, unknown to the primitive medicine practiced here. Many, many people blinded because of ignorance and lack of medical care, especially the desert Bedouins," Lilli adds. "Frank tells me, when the new modern hospital medical center is open, there will be no more *trachoma*. Medicine here is still in the dark ages, but not for long."

"Westerners are building the new hospital. There are many areas of study needed here. The reason why the government has its five year plans," Joan answers.

The distraction of the *trachoma* problem lessened their driver apprehension somewhat. Lilli demanded the driver to stop. "*Wa qif hina*—stop here," and stop he did, with a screech and a skid.

Walking to the house, "I'm sorry that your first taxi rides were so bad, Lilli. Generally drivers are very courteous; but as anywhere, there are always a few bad ones. You know they tell us there is no drivers test as we know it. The new applicants line up, one after the other in their cars and follow a leader. If you make it to the finish, you have your license. Sometimes there can be a dozen cars following with twelve and fourteen year old boys behind the wheel. No women though. They are not allowed to drive . . . yet."

"The way they drive here, I wouldn't want a license," comments Lilli. "I noticed many wrecked auto skeletons dotting the highway edges when Ralph drove us from the airport. I think the *Insha'allah*, God-willing attitude prevails here over God's common sense, even in driving."

"You are right, Lilli. And Frank will have his license soon. That will be comforting. Westerners who have licenses from home get a license immediately with no testing."

The men surprise them and are waiting at the villa with lunch for all. Frank explains to Lilli, "Ralph says, we must work Saudi-style. All companies are on Saudi hours which means prayer at twelve with lunch siesta then prayer at four p.m. and return to work until eight, with a prayer at six. So here we are . . . back to work at four." After a recap of the morning's activities and a quick nap, the guys are off again.

— 18 —

Ramadan

SEPTEMBER 1974

The night is black. Many eyes scan the eastern horizon of the almost always cloudless sky above this desert capital . . . the perfect canvas for a rising, slimmest of moons, the crescent New Moon.

A *thobed* (full length shirt-like garment) man sitting high on a *jebbel* (rocky outcropping) on the outskirts of Riyadh, Saudi Arabia, sights the orange sliver as it peeks above the red sand's periphery. His discovery reaches the many cannon keepers via loud proclamations. The cannon's fuses are then lit. Resounding booms and explosions from ancient grey cannons left over from the 18th century Turkish Ottoman invasions, give forth clouds of grayish-white smoke throughout the city. Reverberating echoes float skyward permeating the sandy city streets, bouncing off the mud and concrete walls of old, ancient mud houses and some newer hotels and homes being built today.

Ramadan, the ninth month of the Islamic year is here when Muslims worldwide celebrate God's gift of the Koran to man. The dawn to dusk yearly holy month of daytime fasting has begun. Each day for the next 28 days, Muslims must complete the day's fast. The cities cannons will herald in the sun's rising and setting . . .

the signals for Saudis to begin and end fasting. No food, drink, cigarette or sex–not a drop of water, no cigarette puff, not even a chew on a stick of gum — from that time each morning when *the white thread of dawn appears to you distinct; complete your fast till the white thread becomes black at sundown,* so states the Koran, the Muslim holy book. The fast begins as soon as it becomes possible to distinguish between a white and black thread at dawn and continues until sundown when both threads are no longer discernible. Each sundown, cannons "boom" again. A concert of chanting by Muezzins can be heard for the fourth of five daily prayers. The calls to pray echo throughout the city from mosque minarets. (Places of worship with high slender towers and a balcony where Muezzins call.)

A lunar Islamic year is 10-11 days shorter than the solar Gregorian year of 365 days. And an Arabic day begins at sunset while a western world's day begins at mid-night.

"Frank, Ramadan is ten days earlier each year and this year's September is still hot, hotter even than August. Being outside at this time is dangerous because body fluids are rapidly lost via perspiration leaving no trace of dangerous dehydration."

"Dearest, not to worry. We will take our salt tablets if we leave home. You know if a non-Muslim inadvertently takes a sip of liquid, chews gum or lights a cigarette in public and is seen by a Saudi during the day, the Saudi may come up to him and point to that person for all to see, till he stops."

"I know, and during this month especially, Muslim women are requested to refrain from wearing perfume, and must wear their *burkas, covering everything except eyes.* Western women need to adhere to modesty also and cover up with long dresses and head scarfs. Government sanctions can be imposed on those not complying."

"My love, let's take a walk through town tonight," Frank tells Lilli.

This particular Ramadan night is still warm. With fasting and suffocating heat during the day, most folks remain inside . . . businesses, banks and shops close at noon. But tonight, the bustling night-time city streets reveal a city alive. People are everywhere shopping for things they would normally purchase during daytime.

"Lilli, our Muslim employees say they regain physical strength with the breaking of the fast at sundown. They eat and hustle out of their houses with renewed energy acquired during the meal. Most are out and about until midnight. Unless they have to work, they sleep most of the next day. They tell me that Ramadan leaves them with a sense of rejuvenation and vitality for faith and spirit . . . a revival of the relationship between Allah and man that generates happiness for all. In spite of the fortunes or misfortunes in life, everyone receives the same blessings," Frank says. "By the way, Abdulla invited us to celebrate 'Eid Al Fitr at his home."

Days continue while nights become hours of merriment. Fellowship builds in anticipation of '*Eid Al-Fitr*', (the great three day holiday festival of the year that ends Ramadan) when the silvery moon crescent appears once again and cannons explode for the last time until next year The next three days of Eid are for sharing with the poor, feasting, visiting, partying, children receiving presents of money and clothes, and salary bonuses given to celebrate the end of fasting.

"Sounds like a good custom, almost like Christmas with gift-giving, too. I heard that a few leave the country to avoid the heat. But still this Muslim holiday time is refreshing and brings folks together, especially families," Lilli adds. "Our first Ramadan in this country."

"Yes, Lilli my love, and I am sure we will be here for a few more Ramadan celebrations. Hey, do you recall the five Precepts of Islam, the rules for Muslim daily living?"

"Frank, I know them by heart. The daily fasting during the month of Ramadan, Believing there is no God but Allah and Muhammed is his Prophet, Praying five times every day, Annual gifts to the poor, and Al Hajj . . . making the Pilgrimage to Mecca once in a lifetime if possible."

—— ——

Lilli's curiosity about this country has grown. She is pleasantly surprised by the genuine smiles of shopkeepers. Every effort she makes to speak Arabic, is encouraged by all of them. "You speekee Arabee," they glow delightedly with amazement. The days are ones of Riyadh Runs, body regulation to jet lag, adjustment and settling in. No easy task; but Lilli finds it all exciting and energizing. She loves this country already. Little does she know what the next twenty plus years will divulge, how the growth of this third world country turns into a beautiful, architecturally diverse city, overflowing into a desert. Frank's efficiency and accomplishments are beginning to be counted by Salah, Ralph, employees and Boxwood. His ability to get along with all nationalities employed was uncanny. It did not go unnoticed by Saudi boss, Salah. He encourages Frank to learn Arabic so Frank takes lessons and is able to practice and talk with Lilli at home. But finally, he can converse with the Arab workers in the office.

—19—
True Love

"Abdulla stopped by the office, to remind us Eid Al-Fitr is tomorrow, Oct. 18th. I told him we'd come about six p.m. I forgot to tell you we'll be moving to the Sahari Palace Hotel soon."

"That's wonderful. I am so anxious to learn more about these people and their culture."

She finishes drying herself and is studying her curvaceous figure in the mirror as Frank comes up from behind, encircling his arms around her full breasts, turning her body to face him. "Not bad for a twenty-five year old. How do I look, Frank?"

"You look spectacular, honey." And then, "Shit, you're gorgeous. I'd almost forgotten just how exquisite you were. I have been so busy adjusting to a new job and new life." It had been awhile since he noticed. He was noticing now. Her huge elliptical eyes caught his attention. The white conjunctiva seeming to take up all the orbits space were like delicate, lustrous pearls. The sea-green irises, flecked with gold, stood out like islands in a turbulent sea. These eyes could be soothing and spiritual, yet at times, penetrating and riveting, questioning and romantic. Frank decides they are definitely romantic now and he was feeling ready for romance, a la Frank's style. "Frank, it's been so long," she murmured, her arms encircling his muscular neck in response. Together their hearts melt.

"Hmmmm, never again so long," he whispers as he lifts her off her feet with a long, deep kiss. He loves Lilli, he has no doubt about that. And right at this moment, he loved her more than ever. "I love you, Lilli." He had never told another woman that, ever. But he felt guilty because of other women he had in his life, before Lilli. He knew she suspected extracurricular activities, but there were none since Lilli. He could never be unfaithful to his wonderful Lilli.

"I love you, Socks, my Frank," she sighed in between the long osculation's. She had been thirsting for attention for quite a while.

"Me, too," was all he could manage as he rapidly became aroused. In a manner of minutes they were in bed, Frank's lust satiated, and Lilli finally fulfilled. Lying beside this huge bulk of a man, she felt his maturity made a positive change in his sexual play, and it was wonderful.

⸺ ⸻

His mother had possessed his father and she really was the head honcho of the family, as most Spanish women are. The Martinez family had a saying, *Que Isabel dice, Jorge hace*. What Frank's mother Isabel says, George, his father, does. It was a matriarchal family life and Frank was determined no woman would rule his life as his mother had his fathers. Jorge was miserable, trodden upon, made fun of and sat back taking it all. More than once in a while Isabel was overbearing, so Jorge became inebriated frequently, trying to escape from her oppressive moments. Frank would never let that happen to him and so far it had not.

⸺ ⸻

Hours later more passionate sex, "Honey, that was great," as he rolls out of bed.

Wow, she thought. *What a change in my man*, as she stood under the shower for the second time.

~20~

Eid Al-Fitr and Ahmed

Tonight, October 18th, Lilli and Frank hear cannons explode for the last time this year. The next three days are for celebrating the Eid Al Fitr and they are on the way to Abdulla's home to have a feast. They ride in a Cadillac with Lilli's new driver, Ahmed, one of many Pakistani's working in Arabia. Frank left his new Suburban at their company villa.

Before leaving Frank told Lilli, "Ahmed tells me he sends most of his pay check home every month. He has a wife, four children, plus aging parents. Once a year he takes a month's vacation. Probably brings another child into this world."

"A sad life, not able to earn a living in your own country, ever—not to be with family to watch children grow, no life to mature and love together as man and wife."

Ahmed, darkly mysterious-looking, a mustache frames ultra-white teeth. His impeccable manners are always willing to please. Ahmed can't do enough for the two handsome Americans. He will be Lilli's driver for many years. She learns she can trust and rely on him.

"I want to live in the United States one day," he repeats every so often.

Tonight, Frank sits up front while Lilli watches and listens sitting in the rear. *This is Arab-style . . . women always ride in the back.* Ahmed flashes a smile as he holds the car door open for her. Lilli liked this fellow immediately. His good nature and pleasing ways endear her to him through future years.

He speaks English so well, having learned it in a Pakistani school, and he is a cautious driver to boot. After some of the hair raising taxi rides I've had, I appreciate Ahmed in this city where wrecked autos dot the street edges. I cannot explain the sense of pleasure and safety I feel.

Driving through town, it is obvious a boom city is now developing. Ahmed points to some of the landmarks. New buildings are under construction everywhere. Tall cranes dot the skyline. On their topmost tips red blinking lights warn Saudi aircraft. The old mud edifices begin to look ancient and out of place.

"Still a small town, a five minute drive in any direction takes you to the desert. I can't understand why cars are speeding all around us—there is nowhere to go—the nearest big towns are a desert ride, miles away," Frank states. "Most of these drivers are youngsters, boys."

"But many small ancient mud villages and historic Al Kharj district are close by," Ahmed tells them. "Just a short drive away. I will take you there one day. After that there is not much but desert and the Rub Al Khali *(Abode of Emptiness)* desert until you get to Taif, where the royal family vacations. "

"That is the largest red sand desert in the world," Lilli adds.

Tonight, all is quiet. Everyone is home preparing for the end of Ramadan festivities with a grand meal, gifts, camaraderie, and visiting friends. Celebration of the most important Muslim holiday, Eid al Fitr. The festivities will soon begin.

"Look there, a new Intercontinental Hotel being built," Frank points out to Ahmed, "This country is in its oil boom years and beginning to blossom into the twentieth century. We are on the ground floor to help it into its Golden Age of the twenty-first century and beyond."

Lilli feels an excitement she could not have anticipated—like missionaries discovering a culture that needed to change and they were there ready to help it progress.

The two know the religion of Islam will never change. "Westerners coming will promote rapid development and advancement. Change in many areas is needed; garbage is all over the place, heaps of rubble on street corners, a dry canal lovingly called Batha is a garbage dump in the center of town—the stench and flies, bringing eye trachoma is suffocating, goats are still herded through the streets, men defecating and masturbating wherever they want, marauding bands of wild desert dogs run through the city. To top all this off, their health delivery systems—hospitals–stinks. They are the worst. Some modern equipment is here which no one knows how to use."

"What if we got seriously ill? Where would we go?"

"If it wasn't serious, we'd go to one of the under staffed and under equipped local hospitals, but if we needed hospitalization, we'd be flown to Germany."

Lilli ponders this explanation. "I don't feel very comfortable about not having good medical facilities right now. Pray we don't get sick, Frank."

Frank continues, "I understand the King's Specialist Hospital in Nasriya will be ready soon. They will admit western ex-patriots and locals referred by other hospitals, Salah told me. We can hope can't we? But, it may be exclusively to care for the Royal family for a while with the goal of researching unusual cases. Currently, the Royal family goes to America or England to receive treatment.

The new Specialist Hospital is hailed to become the best equipped hospital in the Middle East."

"I have been here many years," Ahmed adds, "and it has already changed a lot. Did you know that Riyadh means 'the gardens' because there is a great underground water supply so date palm gardens flourish. Several old palaces are in this area, too. We are passing the new soccer and football field over there. Youngsters play on Fridays. No women allowed to attend, though."

Proceeding along, they suddenly cringe when a loud cannon "Boom" . . . an explosion, is heard. Just ahead, an enormous massive cloud of smoke glides across the road. They park on the road side, waiting for the smoke to clear. An ancient gray cannon poised on top of a sand dune comes into view.

"Someone will get a money reward for having been first to spy the new moon. The fast of Ramadan has ended. The Eid Al-Fitr festival is here once again," Ahmed explains.

After making several turns to avoid potholes in the dirt roads, they come to a stop at the bottom of an incline. Ahmed parks in front of an impressive, albeit sandy looking, villa. Heaps of garbage and rock rubble invade the front wall. Cars rest on both sides of the street heading in any direction. Ahmed quickly gets out, runs to open Lilli's door, "Thank you," she says softly.

"*Ahlan wa sahlan*, welcome." he answers with an engaging smile. "We are at Abdulla's villa."

— 21 —

Abdulla and Fatima

The beautiful villa is lit by numerous round lights on top of the entrance wall and gate, casting mysterious shadows against the building. The gate opens. A small Yemeni houseboy appears barefoot in long white pantaloons. A white *kaffiya* skull cap perches on a full head of semi long curly black hair.

"Ahlan wa sahlan, *welcome.*" hospitality exuding in his voice.

Lilli notices the lovely garden has a panorama of reddish vegetation, flourishing shrubs and flowers, lovely roses, gardenias and bougainvillea, all warming the front yard although covered in dust. Her cryptic feelings are replaced with a warmer curiosity.

"This garden attracts butterflies, Frank. Look, at that pretty black and purple Swallow-Tail butterfly cruising around. Unbelievable, in this desert country."

Ahmed, waits in the car as is the custom. Lilli and Frank follow the houseboy into a large foyer. The aroma of sweet incense floods her nostrils. A spectacularly large, gold Incense Burner, covered with carvings and Arabic words, sits gracefully on an elegant mirrored table next to the door.

Charming Abdulla, grinning with jubilation, rushes to greet them. "Ahlan wa sahlan. *Bayti, baytec.* (Welcome. My home is your home.) I am so happy you could come. *Al'hamdu'illah*, (praise God). I just finished skinning a lamb, as is the custom here at Eid. We always share so I have sheep meat for you to take home. Fatima will give Lilli a recipe."

His round, chubby face beaming with exuberance, Abdulla is clearly delighted to share his food and home on this special day with his American friends.

"Happy Eid," the two guests tell their host. Lilli knows *bayti baytec* is only reserved for the closest friends and family and they must share with friends and the poor at Eid. She feels privileged.

An exotic aroma of foreign spices and food permeates the room as Abdulla's wife, Fatima comes forth with welcoming warmth even though they had never met. "Happy Eid, Lilli."

"Happy Eid to you Fatima. This is our first Eid. Thank you for having us."

"Abdulla has spoken a great deal about you both. He did not exaggerate your beauty though. I hope you are enjoying being here. Come meet some of our family and friends."

There are two rooms side by side. Lilli is escorted into the back room and Frank into the other one. Women in black sit around the perimeter, smiling, waiting to meet this lovely American lady. Lilli is introduced to about twenty women. A busy conversation ensues by all.

Both room's ambiance are one of antiquity. As it turns out, the home is indeed a museum of sorts. Fatima explains, "Abdulla's collections are remnants from king's palaces: Kings Abdul Aziz, the kingdom's founder Saud, the squanderer and lover of women, and our present very humble and religiously good king. These treasures contain artifacts and old Bedouin jewelry. The Kuwaiti chests here are beautifully decorated with brass nail designs." She points to several ancient swords, "*Kanjars,* used by Bedouin tribes many years ago. Here are old brass *Qahwa* coffee pots of varying sizes and carvings for coffee-making. Over there is a Russian *Samovar* tea pot for tea-making." Lilly notices it is a beautiful tall brass artistically-designed pot.

Seeing carpets on the floor, hanging on the walls, Lilli admires them all, "Your magnificent collection of Persian carpets is very beautiful and impressive, Fatima."

"Carpets are Abdulla's livelihood, but being Palestinian and preserving the history of the Middle East, is his hobby. He travels a great deal on buying trips, especially to Iran and Lebanon, sometimes to India, Afghanistan, Pakistan and Russia, too."

"Then you are alone a great deal like I am?"

"Yes, we will have to do lots of things together. Do you like it here so far?"

"I really do," her contagious, happy smile warms the room. "I find your culture fascinating and I am excited to learn and understand. It is so different from my country. The friendliness of the people is a great surprise, especially when I speak the little Arabic that I do."

"Do you mind wearing long dresses and covering your head?"

"No, I respect the ways and customs here; even if I don't agree and don't plan on spending my life engulfed in them. We hope to be here a long time so I want to learn as much as possible. I pray you will visit me one day when I vacation in the states, so I can shower you with our hospitality, as you are doing for us."

"We will be close friends, I can tell. I like you already," Fatima says sincerely. She announces to the ladies, "Dinner is ready." Taking Lilli's hand, she guides her into a dining room and gives her a beautiful English Blue Willow plate. *Maybe I am a guest of honor? But why are some dishes of food on the table half empty and in disarray?*

Fatima notices Lilli studying the table. She speaks English perfectly, "The men in this country always eat first when we have a mixed sex group. It is the custom. Women make the food, but eat last. Not fair, I know. In my country, Palestine, this is not the case. We all eat together. But while I am here, it has to be thus."

None the less delicious, there is an grand assortment of middle-eastern delicacies: squash stuffed with ground meat and a rice mixture peppered with crunchy pine nuts and chickpeas; chicken, grilled to a golden perfection sitting on flat Arabic bread that is broth-soaked; flavors of cinnamon, garlic, allspice, mingle into such a delectable taste with a yogurt sauce ladled over all.

"What is all this?" Lilli asks, "Everything tastes so delicious."

Another lady sitting beside her answers, "This one, Saleeg, is a most delicious Arab lamb dish with rice. This other one is *kouskous* with chicken, beef and chickpeas. These triangular pies, *motabbag* from Mecca and Taif, are filled with meat and spinach, my favorite. If you like it, I'll share my recipe. By the way, I'm Nancy Al Rasheed from Arizona. My husband will be the C.E.O. and Administrator of the new Specialist Hospital that will be ready for patients soon. I noticed your Arabic, Lilli. You speak it very well."

"I majored in Languages at University of Massachusetts and got a Masters in Archeology at University of Chicago. Languages come easy to me. Arabic seems easier than even Spanish. Yes, I would love the recipe. Thank you Nancy. This is delicious. Are we the only Americans here tonight?"

"Yes, we are. I have been here several years and I am still struggling with Arabic. My maid is from Ethiopia, speaks little English. I do practice Arabic, but it is futile." Lilli feels the sincerity and openness of this warm person. She is overflowing with curiosity but she must be careful not to offend this American married to a Muslim.

"How did you ever meet your husband? Was he a Saudi?"

"We met at the University of Arizona. His major was Business and Hospital Administration, mine History. We met in History class and fell in love. A member of the Royal Family, Faisal loves this country so much, that he could not consider living in the states or anywhere else. Opportunities for him were better in Riyadh. Life here can be problematic for women, but it has its advantages, as you will discover. I have a driver, money and travel the continents. I want the children to know the other side of their heritage, too so I spend summers in the states, another world, so to speak. Faisal is wonderful and understanding. I am a Muslim now and legally a Saudi but I have dual citizenship. Even though I am under thirty-five, I can travel alone with Faisal's permission. I will never give up my USA citizenship, though."

After a long conversation, Lilli feels they have much in common, both husbands somewhat aggressive, power-seekers, rather chauvinistic. They are both Americans away from home in a country pro-men. She sensed Nancy misses America more than she admits.

"I hope you don't mind my asking questions. You're the first western woman I've met that is a Muslim and married to a Saudi. Maybe you can help me with the customs here."

"I certainly can. I am immersed in this culture. Sometimes I find it hard to be an American again. If you have any questions or need anything, please, give me a call." She hands Lilli a Faisal's business card. "I do have some lonely times. Faisal is usually very busy, especially now when this country is changing and growing so quickly. Our hospital, an example of growth, will be beautiful and modern. "

"Yes, I heard and hopefully we Ex-patriots will be able to use the facility when we are sick."

"According to Faisal, you will."

With that, Nancy rises when a tall, handsome Arab man catches her eye from another room. He motions for her to come. Wrapping herself in a black thigh-length *abaya*, she winds a scarf around her head, says a few words to Fatima and then "*Fi Aman 'illah,* Go with God" to the Arab women's group.

Before exiting, she turns to Lilli, "Shall we get together soon? I will call the desk with the day I am free to have lunch and leave my phone number, so please return my call."

Lilli shakes her head yes, "Oh yes, we will be moving into the Palace Hotel very soon. I so look forward to that, Nancy. Thank you very much, *Shukran, Mashkoor, Thank you, thank you.*" "*Ma'a As-salama. Good-bye.*"

The room is emptying out. Several husbands stand in the open doorway. Fatima beckons to Lilli, "I hope you're having a good time. Nancy Al Rasheed is married to a very wealthy Royal family man and is very, very nice. Come with me. There are young people in the back room."

Lilli peeked into the room and was surprised, "I can't believe young Saudi girls wearing scrumptious, cute, sexy dresses are dancing with boys and are in the same room together. A few, on the sidelines are smoking and drinking. What's going on, Fatima?"

"Well, they can never get together in our society, no social dating you know. But Abdulla and I believe older children should be allowed to mingle, but under strict supervision. So, we sometimes help them move the choosing process along. The youngsters get to know each other and gather under our careful watch. The poorer mothers have no choice; they meet on "women only" days at the Zoo, bring their children and arrange the marriages for years ahead. Of course, many girls and boys marry without seeing one another until the day of the wedding . . . the family chooses and approves the partner. A friend of Abdulla's flew to Baghdad, Iraq to approve one of five girls his mother had selected. He was too busy to see even one girl. He told his mother to choose the one she wanted to be his wife. He did not see his wife-to-be until the wedding day."

Fatima continues, "When Abdulla and I have our adult parties, our young people have theirs. The children are family friends." She points to a beautiful girl in the pink dress. "That is our daughter, Aida. Our son Ramzi is the tall one there," pointing to a very handsome young man.

"I see pilot Rashudi looking over here," Lilli mentions.

"Yes, Tariq told us he had met you both on his plane. He seems to admire you a great deal."

"Two of these girls here and our daughter will be in the first class of women college students in the kingdom at our University, soon. We are very proud that girls can also attend college here now. Still, male lectures for girls are only via T.V. We can't wait for this to change one day. Right now, it's sometimes a tough life for females."

Frank approaches, "Are you ready to leave, Lilli?"

Lilli felt a great camaraderie with Fatima, "I do hope we will get together again soon," she said after thanking her hostess.

"Our friendship is only beginning. *Fi aman illah.* Go with God."

"*Ma'a As-salama.* Goodbye. "The new friends embrace warmly.

At the front door, Abdulla embraces Frank with a kiss on either cheek. A hand shake to Lilli. Lilli spied the tall, good-looking Capt. Rashudi coming towards them. Again, their eyes lock into eternity. Only Frank's booming voice releases their gaze, shattering another odd moment.

Frank turns to the Captain and says, "We'll see you Friday next week." To Lilli, "Capt. Rashudi has volunteered to show us the city and surrounding areas."

"*Taib,* good, I look forward to that. Maybe Fatima and Abdulla will come along. *Ma'a As-salama,* good-bye," the captain calls out softly as he departs.

Lilli mumbles a good-bye as Frank guides her down the front stairs, out into the garden and into the waiting car. The conversation during the ride home was totally about Captain Tariq Rashudi. He had impressed Frank.

He whispers so Ahmed can't hear, "We've made a good connection. This fellow is affluent and a friend to the Royal family, via Nancy's husband, so I suspect he undoubtedly has some clout. I may need him someday. We'll have to be especially nice to him. That won't be hard for you, my dear. Our Captain already seems smitten with you. Arab males love beautiful western women like you, you know."

"You are terrible to think that way," she admonishes Frank.

"Darn, it's the truth. And western women like the mystique of these handsome Arab men."

Lilli ignores that last proclamation, "I will not help you in this ridiculous climb for power and position; because I believe you will do anything to attain your goals . . . and stop analyzing Arab men and western ladies. You haven't lived here long enough to really know anything."

"Sweetheart, forgive me. I was just kidding." Ardently, he places his arm around her shoulders and hopes no one will notice. That is taboo in this country, "Love you!"

"You are being overly smug, vain and conceited, not to mention over confident. We are here on the Kingdom's terms and I intend to honor that with no strings attached." She felt a confused flush envelop her. The ride back was quiet.

In bed that night, she pulls up the covers and turns away from Frank, but he pulls her over to him with a kiss.

Contemplating his strategy for success, Frank chuckles to himself before visiting dreamland, the land of Nod. Sanguine and utopian, he feels eternal promise surround his spirit. He slumbers off to never-never land . . . *the best is yet to come.*

~ 22 ~
Palace Hotel

After living months in a dilapidated, neglected villa, sharing the living room with many company executives using it as a meeting place every night, the word comes that there is a room available at the Palace Hotel.

Returning their clothing into suitcases, they excitedly pile their few possessions into Frank's new suburban. Following Ahmed's lead back down the nameless bumpy dirt road, they travel to the main intersection. A left turn on Airport Road and soon they arrive at their temporary hotel home.

Directly across from the airport, the still impressive old-looking three story sand-colored building stands in the center of a circular drive . . . the famous Palace Hotel.

"Look, Frank, this big hotel is surrounded by a tall cement wall, a grassless yard sparsely propagated with greyish, sand covered trees. Across the building top PALACE HOTEL is written, surprisingly in English. Beside it, the same words are written in Arabic script."

"We are about to be residents of an infamous hotel where a past King and founder of this country resided." Frank whispers.

Upon entering the hotel lobby, they stroll over the sand-infiltrated blue carpet to the check-in counter, noticing two suspicious looking men sitting on a sofa. "Religious police I'll bet, Lilli."

Lilli feels uncomfortable. "Why police in a hotel?"

"It's close to the airport with people coming and going. They don't trust all the foreigners. Some resent the Western invasion. They want this country to remain status quo, but it won't."

Keys in hand, they go up the stairs to a second story room. They enter. Ahmed leaves the suitcases. He returns to his car to watch the airport traffic across the street while awaiting the arrival of darkness in a sky soon to be aglow with sparkling bright stars . . . the usual beautiful desert night. The day's end and his driving is over. His small living quarter is close by.

Lilli is immediately impressed with the sparkling crystal chandelier suspended above the bed. "It's more gorgeous than I thought. This still beautiful hotel room was for the King's harem. He had several concubines, kept lots of ladies and had many children . . . probably to enhance a needed population of his time."

"But look what we have here in the bathroom, Lilli . . . a bidet to bathe our private parts!"

"How unique. I liked the one in our London hotel room. I wish America used them more."

"This room is cleaner and nicer than the one I stayed in."

That night, Frank and Lilli are finally somewhat settled in. "I feel special here. So romantic, Frank." They snuggle close, "Maybe we are finally on our way to a great experience."

The next few weeks brings a multitude of workers from various companies and countries. Constantly arriving, many are accompanied by wives and children. Each expatriate will share talents and knowledge for this oil-rich third world country to grow. For some, these highly paid jobs are tax free.

"Arabia's first five year plan will be promptly fulfilled in four years. Then they will zoom into their second five year plan. There will be several more five year plans to go until this civilization is ready to welcome in the twenty- first century with a new modern life for its citizens." Frank prognosticates, "Spectacular changes are imminent."

Lilli's life in the land of sand becomes more interesting every day. Twice a week, she prefers walking 4 blocks down a dirt laden street to a Lebanese Arabic language teacher's home. Within a few months her Arabic is perfected. She becomes fluent. She joins the only western Ladies Club consisting of twelve ex-patriot members. She is number thirteen. As the weeks pass, the growing club swells with women of many different nationalities, but mostly English and American. *All very interesting characters*, she notices. *This camaraderie is special, like family away from home, maybe girl-friends forever? Some I like, some I do not.* Everyone brings a treat. They discuss books previously read and any unusual incidents happening to them in this land of sand. The gals share many stories, such as this one:

One day Lilli and a Ladies Club friend, who also had a room at another hotel, dress as they have been told . . . head covered, a long sleeved, high neck, long loose dress. Curious, the two decide to walk to a nearby grocery store.

Inside, all the meat hangs from a rafter. It looks like it's been torn off the animal, not sliced. It's impossible to tell the cut or what animal it came from.

"A meat market in total disarray it seems," Lilli says to her friend.

While concentrating on shopping, something Lilli never expected to happen . . . happened. Suddenly, in the narrow store aisle she feels a brush across her lower back, a very soft rubbing against her buttocks. She quickly turns around. Her gaze meets piercing black eyes. A tall Arab man wearing a long crème colored summer thobe is holding a fully erect penis. Realizing he has rubbed his body part on her backside, she is furious. Yelling, "Hey! Get away! How dare you?"

He sees her reaction and runs like lightening, flying down the aisle, out the door and quickly disappears. *As they all do when this type of harassment occurs,* she presumes.

Immediately, a shocked Lilli complains to the store owner at the counter. He answers in perfect English, "I am very sorry, madam, but sometimes the men here do funny things."

"Funny? That is disgusting. Can't you report him?"

"The boy speaks no English and has no money for a *dowry* to purchase a wife. He thinks western ladies are sexually easy."

"Sounds like your young men are probably woman-starved. A dowry should be less money."

Lilli explains to her friend what had just happened.

"I am speechless," she says. "That's happened to me several times, not just here either. I saw this one roaming around the store just now and wondered. Figured, maybe he was up to no good."

Exiting the store they walk back toward the hotel. In the middle grassy area of the street, the same Arab fellow is walking in the reverse direction, headed toward them, calling out in English, "Help me! I need help." His thobe up, his pants unzipped, he is masturbating. Not daring to look at him, they keep walking as rapidly as possible.

"Thank God the hotel isn't far away," her friend comments.

During her years with the ladies group, she learns many crafts from this international talented group: Turkish macramé . . . knotting thread into a coarse fabric in geometrical patterns for belts . . . knitting . . . quilting . . . and her favorite, oil painting.

~23~
Nancy's Villa

Nancy Al Rashid's driver, Saud, arrives at the hotel to take Lilli to Nancy's villa. Saud drives a Mercedes Benz. Sitting in the rear, Lilli closely studies the route. On the outskirts of Riyadh, a dirt road leads to a stark white-walled grand villa, enhanced by bright green roof tiles. Nancy is anxiously strolling around the courtyard when they arrive, "I've been waiting for you, Lilli. I am so anxious to see you again."

Lilli feels Nancy is thirsting for friendship and probably some Western dialogue, too.

Nancy guides her new friend into elegant, furnished rooms. All have very high ceilings, immaculate mosaic beautifully-designed terrazzo floors. An inside patio flower-garden overflows with expensive European-looking furniture and multiple Persian carpets circling the center.

"Lilli, would you care for a cup of *Shahi* tea and delicious sweet *Tamr* dates?"

Immediately a young Ethiopian girl-servant enters, pushing a cart laden with dates, meringue cookies and a lovely English floral-designed tea pot steaming with hot Arabic tea. "The cookies were my Mom's recipe. She is English."

Nancy begins pouring tea. Her manners are impeccable Emily Post.

Lilli asks, "I am so curious about this culture and especially how a young woman like yourself is happy tucked away in a country where women are treated like second-class citizens."

Nancy laughs, "Well, I take a summer-long vacation with my children and visit with my parents. Both on the way to the states and back, we stop in Europe or the Far East to shop and tour. All of this, and I don't have to worry about money. I spend as much as I like. As an American Muslim woman, I leave the country by myself with Faisal's permission, unlike most Saudi women who must have a male accompany them. I have a diplomatic passport and go through customs unimpeded . . . so I can bring anything into the country without scrutiny. I have a driver to take me any where I wish and a maid and a nanny. Does all this sound so bad?" she questions. "It's a real comfortable life without the hassle that many Western mothers, with jobs and lack of money, might have. And here, there is very little crime, it is safe; but if a crime is perpe-trated, it's taken care of immediately. No waiting years for justice."

"Your life is intriguing. Oh, these Meringues are delicious, Nancy. May I have the recipe?"

"Of, course. I would be honored to share it. Yes, and many women are happy with their lack of freedoms and want it all to remain as it is. Time will tell if they reconsider having more freedom to choose."

"Nancy, don't you yearn for Thanksgiving, Christmas, Easter, 4th of July, and all our holidays?"

"We have two big Muslim holidays . . . Ramadan's Eid al Fitr and the Hajj's Eid al Adha. But, I do get a longing for a Christmas tree. Christian paraphernalia has been prohibited here, but Faisal lets me have a tree. My driver Saud drives east to the American

Aramco compound in Dhahran to choose and buy me a beauty especially for the kids."

"He is one special man, isn't he?

"Yes, he truly is. Most Arab men who choose to marry western women are not the Orthodox Wahabi Muslims. My Faisal is one liberal-thinker. As long as the children go to Arabic schools and are Muslims, he is satisfied. He doesn't insist I wear a full body covering including my eyes. I wear the *abaya* to cover my clothing and a *hijab* head covering, but no face veil. With more Western women here, dress will soon be strictly enforced by the *Mutaween*, religious police."

Nancy has on a lovely sapphire ring and diamond necklace ensemble. *A pity, she is a bit overweight*, Lilli notices. Too much inactivity. The life-style for women here is so sedentary and after bearing three children in three years, it must be hard to lose weight yet.

"Nancy, may I ask you a very personal question?"

"Yes, sure."

"Did you have to undergo a female genital mutilation? I understand all Muslim females must have that done by puberty?"

"I did, Lilli and it was not pleasurable. Hopefully they will stop that soon so my daughters will never have to succumb to that brutal practice with no positive results for women. I had a bleeding and infection problem. I understand many Muslim countries cut the genitalia of young girls and sometimes babies. "

"Awful. Nancy, thank you for answering truthfully. I am so curious about the customs for women here. Another question I have is what happens to a girl who gets raped? Can she ever marry? I heard she might be stoned."

"Yes, she could be stoned, depending on circumstances. Also, she might never be able to marry because a girl raped is no longer a virgin. Girls must prove their virginity before being wed. But between you and me, there are ways they get around that if the husband-to-be desires . . . he can pick his finger to place some blood on the marital bed."

After socializing and more tea drinking, Lilli decides it is getting late, "The guys should be done with noon "salaat" and ready for lunch. I had better head back to the hotel."

"I certainly enjoyed our afternoon together, Lilli. Let's make it a routine every week and we can go shopping, too. I'll copy my Meringue Recipe for you."

"Sounds good, Nancy. Thanks. I can't wait for next week. Thanks for a wonderful day."

Nancy beckons to a waiting Saud and he drives Lilli back to the hotel.

~ 24 ~
Jewelry

After that first visit, Lilli and Nancy see each other frequently. They shop everywhere together. Immediate soul mates. One special day they visit the most popular jewelry store in the city. As they enter, Lilli notices a woman in all black waiting in a car parked at the curb. As they enter, the woman's driver is completing a jewelry purchase. They see him giving it to the waiting lady.

Wide-eyed and astonished by the dazzling display of extravagant jewelry, Lilli remarks, "This is nothing like the ancient gold suq. This looks like an expensive modern western store."

"It is very, very expensive, Lilli. It all comes from Europe and India." Nancy introduces Lilli to Gumar, the jeweler. He knows Nancy but he is clearly astonished by the beauty of this new American lady with the radiant smile.

"Just a minute, I'll show you some of what I have." He brings out several beautiful pieces of gold and silver jewelry to show Lilli. "This is all twenty-one or twenty-four carat. The silver is pure."

"Everything is gorgeous, Gumar. I am impressed and I promise to return with my husband."

Gumar, a Palestinian originally from India, is clearly startled by this American beauty. He gallantly kisses Lilli's hand as she is leaving. And then, as if he can't resist, he pulls her towards him bestowing her with a smacking kiss right on her lips. Shocked, she slaps him. "How dare you!" *I will never forget your rudeness.* She promptly follows Nancy out the door. Nancy hadn't seen the flagrant action of this jeweler. Lilli remains silent as they drive off.

Their special friendship grows during the following months and years. Lilli discovers Nancy's greatest fear . . . "Confidentially, I am petrified Faisal might take a second wife some day or that he would divorce me and keep my children. Men can have four wives, you know and also concubines with many women for sex." *Lilli senses this is a situation Nancy secretly expects could happen someday.*

"Men in Arab society can divorce and marry women of other religions, but to live in Saudi, the wife must become a Muslim. Children must be reared in the Islam faith. In a divorce, they live with the father from a young age. My children are sort of half breed in the sense they praise Allah and celebrate all Muslim holidays, they attend Islamic Schools, speak Arabic; but they eat western as well as Arabic food and love both. They celebrate Xmas and spend summers inhaling the American culture. I have my own bank account here and in the states so I frequently buy expensive jewelry and gold to place in my USA safe deposit box. I recently purchased a home in Arizona in my name, with Faisal's approval, so the kids and I do summer vacations alone instead of staying with my parents. They stay with me."

"Faisal visits us for thirty days during the summer, but the kids and I stay from June until September."

"How nice, Nancy. I would not have a problem doing that." *Nancy is wisely preparing for her future.*

Two weeks later, not telling Frank about Muslim Gumar's aggression to her, she takes Frank to meet him. The two men became fast friends after this visit. From then on, Lilli is rewarded with many free beautiful pieces of expensive jewelry. They are invited to Gumar's home where it becomes evident he is more and more enamored with this lovely archeologist who is well informed about gemstones. Frank did not seem jealous. Many times through the years, he made a special point to stop by and make a purchase for Lilli. He always enjoyed the offer of a cup of *shahi* with Gumar. Gradually, Frank learned more about Gumar, the ins and outs of how a jewelry store operates in this God forsaken desert country, where all this beautiful stuff came from, its value and how it was shipped. He finds out that the royal family and ex-patriots are the principle purchasers. The jewelry business is exploding for Gumar.

One day he visits early on his way to work. Waiting for Gumar to open up, he notices a few keys hanging hidden in back of a rose bush. He tries one. The door opens. Quickly locking it again, he replaces the key.

～25～
A King Dies

Lilli is waiting in the lobby for Nancy to take her on a shopping trip to a suq. All of a sudden chaos reigns as little Yemeni workers, waiters, janitors and the security police are yelling and crying, *"Malik maiyit*, our King has died." She quickly goes to the check-in desk.

"Sir, what is happening?"

Sobbing, the fellow answers, "Our King has been shot. Our beloved King ees dead. We don't know how it happened yet. Everyone must stay here. You cannot leave."

Nancy did not show up. Lilli sat in the lobby waiting. *Maybe Frank will arrive soon.* She fearfully waited and waited. Frank came through the doors at one p.m.

Frank explains, "Nancy's husband just phoned the office. He told me that the king's nephew, whose brother had been previously killed by police as he demonstrated against having a T.V station in the country, approached his uncle on the pretext that he wanted to request a favor. Suddenly, he pointed a gun at the King, shooting him several times. The King was rushed to the hospital where he died. We are not to say anything yet until the news breaks from

London on Voice of America. For now, everyone is under house arrest."

TV announcement and the Security Police sent everyone home to their families. They were told not to venture out for the next forty eight hours. Families with children were frantic to safely retrieve their kids from school, bring them back to their villas, apartments or hotels for protection. The uncertainty of what was going to happen next in this third world country was nerve wracking and scary.

Lilli felt frightened, too. "Why are we here? Is all this worth it, Frank?"

"Lilli, this King is responsible for us being here. He and his Queen wanted more than anything, to take this country forward, into the twenty-first century. They always encountered stern opposition from the Ulema, the radically strict religious Wahabi men. This King was a conservative, pro-western leader–a voice of reason for a prolific oil-rich country."

"I know he was loved and respected by most women. He and the Queen wanted them educated, to be on an equal plane with men and have freedom of equality. What a loss for the women here."

A security policeman announces, "To all who have children, it is okay to pick them up at their school now, but return right away to wherever you are staying."

Ralph stops by the hotel. "You and Lilli may have to move out to make room for all the visiting dignitaries who will be arriving for the King's funeral very soon."

Packing, they hear a knock on the door. Frank talks to a Saudi from the Palace management. "Lilli he says, if we move to a smaller room, they may let us stay. Dangerous as it may be, we cannot leave the country at this time." Ready to leave, they wait for the word to move . . . the word never comes.

Finally, twenty-four hours later a local TV announcement comes, 'The King of Saudi Arabia has been murdered . . . shot by his twenty-seven year old nephew. A speedy trial and public execution is expected.'

Sitting in the lobby the day after the assassination, they see numerous dignitaries with their entourages arriving. Those from Yemen are particularly impressive with sabers hanging from their belts. One older man has a beautiful baby blue turban twisted elegantly on his head.

Even the Crown Prince of Morocco walks by, briefly stopping in the hotel lavatory just long enough to freshen up before paying his respects to the royal family. Many dignitaries did this only to return home the same day as their arrival.

Later, sitting on the hotel roof watching planes from all over the world land and take off, they remain a little frightened. Four red jeeps with whooping sirens, red lights flashing and police bearing machine guns rush to pick the dignitaries up to take them to their destination. "This city is a beehive of activity," Frank comments.

"I realize now, we are captives in a police Monarchy country. Passports were confiscated on arrival via Mustafa, the travel agent. There is no getting away from here without proper government papers, Frank, and we have none on us. The only path to leaving is for Mustafa to apply for an exit visa for us which must be government approved."

"No getting home on the next flight as in the USA. I will never again take my American freedoms for granted, Lilli. What if this becomes some kind of government take over?"

"You'd better believe that one. It is scary and I am one nervous American."

Frank and Lilli continue watching many dignitaries continuously arrive and depart the Riyadh Airport after expressing condolences and respect for the deceased King and imparting confidence to the new leaders . . . a King and Crown Prince.

"I hope the new King and Prince will carry on and act moderately, Frank."

"Look Lilli, here comes Egypt's Anwar Sadat and the King of Jordan. I recognize them. So many delegations from every country passed by here."

Nancy's husband, Faisal, stops by for a few minutes to explain, "The King will be taken to a cemetery outside the city where all Muslim dead are buried . . . rich and poor alike . . . in an unmarked grave. The funeral procession is all men. Even the queen may not attend. He will be buried just as he is, his cape mummifying his body. The mourning continues for forty days because the King did not die of natural causes. And, because he was shot, Muslim belief is that he goes directly to paradise, therefore no need for clean clothes, make up, etc. Had he died of normal causes, he would have been prayed over with new clothes and helped to go to paradise."

On the fourth day, Nancy phones the hotel desk to speak with Lilli. A Saudi knocks on Lilli's door, telling her to come downstairs to receive her call. "Will you come with me this afternoon after salaat to the Queen's palace to express our condolences? We must wear a long, dark abaya and heads covered with hijab, no face veil needed. I have both that you may borrow."

That afternoon, they enter the palace. Nancy mentions to Lilli, "Do you see this lovely marble table top? It is a replica of the Holy Mosque in Jerusalem. The King referred to the mosque as his hope, dream and prayer that he could enter it one day when peace will reign there."

"I hear he was a moderate man, wise and good, the most

beloved of all the monarchs." Tears and great sadness fills the room. All ladies present, shake the Queen's hands, expressing condolences.

Life in the land of sand resumes in a hotel room where a beautiful crystal chandelier hangs over a bed and a bidet sits in a bathroom. This memorable adventure will continue.

Three weeks later, the nephew murderer is beheaded in Chop-Chop (Justice) square.

～26～
Exploring a Cradle of History

A year later, Lilli and Frank move to a beautiful two story, furnished villa with a 'local calls only' phone. President Ralph with twenty other employees also live in Boxwood compound.

Fatima invites Lilli to her friend's Egyptian-style wedding, "You will hear *Zagreet*, a tradition for women to celebrate a happy occasion. The bride's father is Ambasador to Myanmar, a multireligion country, mostly Buddhism, east of India. Used to be known as Burma."

They arrive when the all-woman Bride Party is in full swing. "We are hearing *Zagreet*, Lilli. Women's tongues rippling on their palate, pour out loud sounds. Screaming trills accompany shivering tambourines. See those Dervish dancers carrying candelabras on their heads over there? And guests tossing gold coins to the bride. Shall we throw too?"

"Let's do! The atmosphere feels mysterious to me. I don't see the groom."

"He joins his bride here later. They signed legal marriage papers before this party."

Another Friday, after prayers, Faisal and Nancy invite Abdulla, Fatima, Lilli and Frank to a desert adventure. They ride in Frank's brand new six seater suburban.

"Frank, let's stop periodically. First, we'll drive close by to the oasis settlement of al Dir'iya in the Wadi Hanifa, a most important Saudi historical site. Nancy and I were there years ago."

The history of Dir'iya is well known here. It was the first Saudi state capital from the mid- eighteenth century until Turkish Ottomans, who ruled Egypt at that time, sent an Egyptian army to burn and destroy the town. Mud houses were ruined, wood ones burned. A few remained.

Finally Saud and his army defeated the Turks."

Heading northwest, Faisal asks Frank to stop beside the road. He points out, "This is the new Kings Hospital."

Further on, enormous walls, huge iron gates and armed guards wearing red berets appear to be protecting numerous ostentatious palaces. These palaces belong to princes and the Crown Prince. Mosque minarets are seen in each courtyard. They reach the city perimeter where the desert claims the land.

Turning on a small road they descend, following a dry river bed, the Wadi Hanifa, one of several desert wadis. Faisal continues, "It collects flash-flood waters when it rains. The road is then impassible until the waters seep into the ground. There is a bridge ahead."

The view down the wadi is spectacular. The terrain is slowly going from reddish and rocky to flat and tan. Leaving the hills off in the distance they travel this plateau. A great green mass of palm and date grove tree-tops comes into view, a breathtaking sight after miles of colorless sand.

They stop again, "Here are many old adobe, mud and brickhouse settlements and watchtowers," Faisal explains. "At times, flowers grow in the wadis."

The remnants of this primitive town take the form of geometric, irregular, eery shapes protruding skyward above the green groves lining the dry river bed. Trees, sand, mud buildings and blue sky compliment the feeling of serenity only interrupted by a strong wind blowing into the hollows . . . and echoes of distance sounds from old water pumps that still extrude water.

Faisal adds, "The first Saudi King became Amir and founder of the ruling house of Saudi Arabia. He wanted a religious teacher for the tribal peoples of the desert, so he got a radical Shaykh, allowing him to promote a strict religious reform called Wahabism. This sect of Islam became very successful and still exists today."

Dir'iya became a prosperous town until the ruling family of that time moved and built Riyadh as their new capital. Dir'iya did grow again and today several Riyadh workers live there.

Faisal explains again, "We are passing the old Palace fortress rising from the wadi bank . . . all made of mud."

Driving up the winding road, past inhabited mud houses they notice front wooden doors, carved in geometric designs and colorfully painted. These people seem shy. They are turning and running away. Clusters of goats try to hide, too, rapidly scattering behind houses and trees.

Stopping in front of an old empty house, they enter. The door is colorful . . . painted with beautiful geometric designs. Stepping onto mud floors, they are captivated by the multi-color artwork surrounding them.

Returning to the car, "Hey, I found this . . . looks like a piece of iron," Frank yells.

"Probably a piece of cannon ball left over from the Turkish invasion," Faisal concludes.

Continuing their drive south, Faisal points out, "The Kings Arabian horse farm over yonder, by the mountain escarpment. Arabian stallions, one of earth's oldest breeds are grazing there."

For years, on Thursdays or Fridays, when Frank isn't away, they with or without friends, continue exploring the geographic landscape of this undiscovered land. They find deserted ancient mud-house towns with wells, watchtowers and mosques reaching for heaven, topped with typical minarets. "Amazing that mosques still sit in old, small, deserted towns," Lilli comments.

On another exotic trip, Frank drives along one of many oasis towns north of Riyadh, "What about that mud-walled date palm grove way out there? Let's go see, my darling."

Strolling through the grove, chirping birds are abundant. A Bedouin in a *thobe,* long shirt-like man's garment and red- checkered *ghutra* headdress, holding prayer beads suddenly exits a tent close by. *"Ahlan wa sahlan, Tatakallam Inglizi?* Welcome, do you speak English?"

"Aiwa-yes," Frank answers. "We are Americans. Your palm garden is prolific with dates."

"Shuf huna, see here *tamr* dates," holding up a handful of dates. *"Akhad akal,* take to eat."

"This is exemplary Bedouin hospitality at its best, offering food to strangers," Frank says.

"Shukran, thank you," Lilli to the smiling man as they chewed on his offering. *"Atakallam Arabi.* I speak Arabic. My husband works for Boxwood International of America."

"Ahh! *Kwaiyis,* fine, good. We hand-pollinate these palms at different times of the year so the *Tamr* date trees will have sweet dates just in time for Ramadan's Eid al- Fitr," the Bedouin's excellent English surprises them.

"The most delicious and sweetest I have ever tasted. *Barak allah fik*, God bless you." Frank shakes the Bedouin's hand as he motions for them to enter his tent. For an hour, they sip *shahi*, tea and cardamom-flavored coffee, munch on delicious *tamr* dates, warm khubz bread and halwa dessert.

"Halwa, my favorite wonderful sweet. It is made with sesame paste, aiwa yes?"

"Aiwa yes. Here, my hunting companions are my best friends." Pointing to a camel, a handsome crème-colored Saluki dog sitting quietly at his feet and a hooded Falcon, perched on a rope line. In perfect English, "I take the Falcon's hood off when he flies. They like to chase rabbits and gazelle for us to eat. They all get along and travel fast, like the desert winds."

"Frank, I would love a Saluki. They are beautiful."

Finally Frank tells the Bedouin, "*Saudiki,* my friend, we must leave now but we will return some day. *Shukhran* thank you very much." He gives him a Boxwood card with their address.

Fi aman illah, saudiki. Go with God, my friends."

Appreciating the gracious Bedouin, they are off waving, "Ma'assalaami wa Shukran Goodbye and thank you."

On the return drive, Frank explains, "Salukis are of the Greyhound family. Remember the Greyhound races at home? They are fast. That species is thousands of years old. The long hair on its tail, ears and legs makes them really elegant-looking, huh Lilli? Bedouin companions for centuries."

"I saw women peeking out from tents. Wish I could have spoken to them. Oh, Frank, what fabulous adventures we have had these many years. Did we ever think we would be here this long?"

"Never guessed or thought it. Darling Lilli. I also think we are the closest to each other we have ever been. I love you for letting me pursue this job, this exploration. I now love this country. I think you and I have fallen deeper in love. I love you my dearest with all mi Corazon, my heart."

One morning a few weeks later, a surprise knock on their door. The same desert Bedouin appeared, holding a beautiful Saluki dog on a rope-collar and leash, "For you Americanee," he told her . . . and quickly turned to leave.

"Shukhran kateer. *Thank you very much*, how nice of you." she called to him.

So now Lilli had her *Arab Greyhound* dog. Frank was not happy about that. "We will have to give it to the King's farm. They will hunt with him."

— 27 —

Adventures Continue

The adventures don't stop. Another drive for the two takes them way past the Ecarpment cliffs. "For me, this mountain resembles the Grand Canyon, doesn't it, Frank?"

Miles further, "Oh my goodness, look at the farms and colorful gardens. I never dreamed there would be farmers here. Must be some underground rivers nearby for water," Frank comments.

"Frank, I read that the sea once covered this desert. Later, when the water retracted, it became a desert leaving numerous sea life artifacts. Then animals roamed Africa and Arabia until the Red Sea divided the two countries, leaving animals behind. God must have planned His earth this way so human civilization could discover its past."

Walking up the hills, they find pieces of ancient fossilized bone, what looks like yellow topaz, and sea artifacts encased in ancient limestone rocks. Stops on the return trip reveal desert animals grazing and wandering about–goats, rats, a snake, an ostrich and . . . a Bedouin truck caravan on the move, traveling the sands. Their trucks are packed high with tents and personal possessions. Two Camels sit regally in the rear truck-beds, facing backward, their heads taller than the truck's roof. Frank comments, "Probably moving to try to find water."

⚊ ⚊

Their next trip, takes them to a small forest of Acacia trees growing in a dry wadi bed. Close by they detect a few camels grazing. "Look, Lilli, rare black one-humped dromedary camels . . . never seen black ones before."

"I didn't know they existed. Let's watch them and have lunch here, Frank. It is so cool under these shady trees for animals and adventurers like us. Oh, my, I see a horse grazing over there."

After lunch they wander through the pathway of a dry wadi river bed. Frank calls out, "Lilli, come! There are some fossils . . . sea shells, sand-polished stones, and I found a shark's tooth here, too."

"Look at this limestone, here. I see coral, a sea urchin and sea shells embedded in it. I think I just found some fossilized desert roses. Such an adventure, my darling."

Frank squeezes and hugs Lilli giving her a sexy kiss, "Mi amour, let's head for home."

"Yes my dearest Socks, let's go. Mind-boggling to be in a desert country whose proof of a living history goes back millions of years and we are here, free to explore it. I am truly amazed at how old this country really is and how, through the centuries, it's changed."

"The Saudi's are ending the second fifth year of development and my job is secure for another five to ten years or longer. The city is mushrooming and ballooning into the surrounding desert. Totally changed from years ago. From the center of town, you can't see the desert anymore. So, my dear Lilli, as long as I am needed and liked, I will have this fabulous job and we can stay. We can continue future investigations and fun, our rewards for being here."

"I love it here, Frank. You know, when we return to the USA, we must explore New Mexico and our American south-west. I'll bet it holds a similar history." They jump into the car.

Riyadh, on the *Najd* (highland) plateau, surrounded by three desserts: the Nafud to the north, the Al Dahna to the northeast, and the Rub-al-Khali Empty Quarter to the south is the largest desert in the world. The flat plains and mountains are to the west.

Addicted, Frank is as anxious as Lilli to continue periodic caravans investigating mysteries hidden in the rippling sand dunes, wadi beds, plains and mountains. Faisal advises them, "Carry plenty of water, auto emergency supplies, salt tablets and head coverings and tell me where you and Lilli are going, the route, and how long you will be gone. Frank, you never go by yourself."

— 28 —

Desert Jewels

Today they travel North East to the Al-Dahna with Ralph and Joan. Leaving the road, parking on the edge of a carpet of sand, hills ascending in the distance. An early morning sky is clear as usual, the hot sun rising. Air currents are calm today. As they gaze over the flat sand bed, they see this area is covered with an overlay of unusual sparkles never seen in the desert before.

Lilli wonders aloud, "What is scattered and sparkling all over this sand? Do you suppose these are desert diamonds? I've read about desert diamond fields near Riyadh; but never expected to see any, what with the winds and sand occasionally blowing to cover everything." She finds a good-sized stone glistening from the sun's shining rays. "These definitely are rare desert diamonds. Search away, Ralph and Joan," she yells. "This is our lucky day! We'll give some to the museum and hopefully be able to keep a few."

Ralph and Joan are ecstatic. The Americans fill their pockets. All sizes of stones lay at their feet, some are clear, some opaque.

The group sits under an umbrella examining their surprising finds while they eat lunch. Lilli says, "These are natural stones. When cut, they may resemble expensive diamonds. These here are a little amber in color, aren't they?"

Frank smiles, "Let's send a few to India with Jeweler Gumar. He can get them cut and polished cheaply and verify exactly what they are. Bet they will be worth a lot of *fulus, money.*"

Back on the road towards the city, Frank muses, "Maybe we'll get rich with these stones. I can't wait to take some to the States next week, perhaps sell them. Let's return when I get back in a couple of weeks. We can pile up more."

Frank takes the jewels to his friend Gumar, who gives them to an Indian friend who takes them to India. He returns with fabulous cut gems, sparkling like expensive diamonds.

A month later they arrive at the "diamond" desert again only to find every grain of the whole desert span is overflowing with at least a hundred small Yemeni workers. Forming a horizontal line across the desert plain, each one carries several satchels and is busy filling them.

"So much for desert diamond Friday. Word gets around fast with so many ex-pats here. Guess we'll have to search somewhere else," a disappointed Frank sadly whimpers.

Joan adds, "I am happy Omar, the museum curator, let us keep the ones we found last time."

Lilli queried, "But, more undiscovered fertile deserts with diamonds must lie here somewhere, don't you think? Maybe not as conveniently located for us, though, but we'll have fun searching to find them!"

"We will continue the search," remarks Ralph with a chuckle.

He continues, "Say, guys, did you hear that they are continuing the ban on movies here and also the censoring of T.V. and newspapers? I thought there would be more freedom in those areas by now. Unfortunate, isn't it? Hopefully that will eventually change."

~ 29 ~
A Desert Picnic
1986

The years are quickly passing. The Ministry of Information has prepared its third five-year plan for future progress. The country is trying to deal with the necessary invasion of westerners, by controlling any possible changes in their sharia law culture before their society gets out of hand. The rules are reiterated on the one television channel, 'foreign females are instructed that their clothing must not show off legs, arms, breasts or hair and no hot pants or shorts be worn. It is forbidden that men see those thigh parts of women or that women see hidden parts of men.'

This desert picnic takes them west of Riyadh to Wadi Huraymaia. Nancy and Faisal in their Jeep. Frank, lover of autos, drives a newly purchased Land Rover.

Wadis casually flow when it rains, stretching and sculpting these dry beds to reveal ancient alluvial deposits of stones, pebbles and shells.

Nancy explains, "Colorful flowers and bluish-green shrubs grow and multiply on the edges during the winter rainy season from December to April. There are too many westerners here now taking desert artifacts so a new law says all our finds must be given to the Museum director, Omar, for display and identification. Wonder if that means flowers, too?"

"Look at this! A nautilus shell," Faisal calls out. "This may be a dry river bed right now, but it will be filled with water to be absorbed into the sandy bottom. Let's keep looking. This is March, there will be plenty to see in all the river beds. Guys, place your finds in your bag."

"Hey everyone! A petrified Sea Urchin shell is embedded in a small stone." Frank holds up his find. "I've only seen live ones in the Florida Gulf. This place never ceases to amaze me."

"Nomads lived in this desert area until all the wadis dried up causing Bedouin *Nomadism*—traveling tribal nomads leaving their tents to find water elsewhere." Faisal adds, "Wadis are dry most of the time now and *Nomads* are few."

"Oh, my, look! Beautiful, colorful flowering plants growing all over. All different species." Lilli picks up a plant that looks like a brown fist. "This must be the famous 'Virgin Mary's Hands.' There is a story about it. After blooming, it dries up, becomes brown, breaks off, and is blown across the desert sands like a tumbleweed. Wherever it lands, it lives again and drops its seeds, reproducing. Story has it that Mary held these in her hands as Jesus was being born."

Traveling further along another mountainous area, they park. Faisal had told them to bring small shovels. They begin searching the desert's edges with their small shovels. Thrilled to discover some ancient tools–a hand ax, flint, a knife, some arrow heads, interesting pieces of petrified tree wood, and shiny chunks of quartz stone.

Lilli mentions, "These must be at least a million years old. We'll ask Omar."

Faisal asks, "Did you read yesterday's Saudi newspaper? A male foreigner in the gold suq was caught peddling low caret gold ornaments as twenty-one caret, but upon inspection the gold was found to be only thirteen carat. The fraud team immediately destroyed it all and the man was expelled from the country after paying a stiff fine. Also, Bedouin women are now banned from selling their gold jewelry in the suq. They can be jailed."

"We did see that, Faisal," Frank answers.

Archeology has helped Lilli a great deal to appreciate the history of Arabia, a strange and interesting land with an ancient past that has survived a desert existence.

The four friends pack their bags with treasured findings for Faisal to deliver to Omar, head of the Museum.

"Faisal, a few Bedouin still use camels to this day, don't they? I understand they have camel races here. Can we plan to see one?" Frank interjects.

"Absolutely. I'll check on the big October Kings Race. We can plan on that."

Faisal and Frank have clearly grown to like each other after all these many years. Both oversee big businesses, Faisal the hospital and Frank a building and supply business. Faisal loves America, too. Their wives are best of friends. The foursome are so compatible and respectful. A couple times a month they all have dinner at one of the new fancy restaurants and then go shopping at the new mall. And of course, their travels throughout the countryside are mesmerizing and unforgettable. If it wasn't for Faisal, their adventures would be minimal.

"It's a deal," replies Frank. "Speaking of the camel race, I hear a roaring sound."

Out of this forsaken silent desert, comes the noise of camel hoofs. In the near distance, camel riders suddenly appear coming towards them. Two Bedouin dismount, walk rapidly towards the group. Frank and Faisal look cautiously at each other. One man, dressed in a dark thobe has a pistol in his waistband. The other wearing white, looks modern.

"Arabs carry guns, ex-pats cannot," Faisal comments.

In broken English, *"Min Fadlak*, please take photo." Milking their camels, they pose. Then, *"Yella, itfaddel, come with us please. We hunt desert animals,"* motioning to Frank and Faisal, *"Oomi, itnayn bani bess."*

"They *only want the two men* to go hunting with them," Faisal translates. "We'll leave you girls the car keys to one car in case you have to go for help. I'm praying we come back safe."

"Let's go," Faisal says to Frank. "With me here speaking Arabic and being an Arab, this should be interesting and fun."

They are both helped onto the camel's back. Off they trod, bareback. They hold on tightly to the Bedouin sitting in front of them for needed balance.

Waiting in one of the cars, Nancy and Lilli lock the doors. An hour later, galloping camels return. *"Al Hamdu 'illah*, Thanks be to God.*"* Nancy says.

They stop close by. The Arabs and the guys jump down. The Bedouins hold up two dead rabbits they had pistol-shot. With a slight bow and a *"Ma'assalama, shukhran*, Good-bye and thank you.*" Off* they gallop.

Frank tells his story to the ladies, "A herd of camels were waiting for us. Those two guys rode the animals bareback into the distant sand and hills, leaving us standing there waiting . . . alone. We wondered if they would return or would we have to walk back? A little worrisome predicament!"

"Al Hamdu 'illah, All praise to God," they did return carrying two dead rabbits hanging together on ropes. A meal, I am sure.

What an experience. Arab Bedouin hospitality to the extreme. They wanted to impress us so we could see what good hunters they were," Faisal added.

"Well, we were alone in the locked car, scared out of our wits," Nancy exclaims. "So thankful to have you both back."

"I prayed that having Faisal with you, there was no danger. But, we were two women all alone here in this vast forlorn desert. Phew!" Lilli didn't hug Frank for she knew Nancy could not hug Faisal in the presence of anyone. Rules of Sharia law—Affection can only be expressed in private. Both ladies expressed relief and happiness that this particular life's desert episode was safely over.

"Well, girls, do you want to continue a little further in this desert," Faisal asks?

"Yes, yes! I've heard about rock carvings at Al Quway'iyah," Lilli answers.

They quickly jump into their cars and continue on the Riyadh-Jidda road. Descending down the escarpment between red sand dunes, a large mountainous rock looming skyward appearing in the distance, on the right.

Parking at the mountain's bottom, they work their way around and up the rock face, discovering rock carvings of many animals and human figures everywhere. With paper and wax crayon in hand, they make their copies of these Petroglyphs.

"I have here an ostrich and a scorpion," Nancy exclaims, holding her art-work up.

"How about this? A fox and cow, *ma hab'bi*, my love," Faisal shows Nancy.

"Well, I have a fox and donkey," Frank says to Lilli.

"Here is a camel, horse, and a dog. These carvings were probably made at least 5,000 years ago. Can you believe it?" The finds thrill Lilli. "Shukran, thank you Faisal for being our constant tour guide."

On the walk back to the cars, an animal darts past. "I do believe that is a desert Fox!" Faisal calls out, "*Shuf huna*, look here!"

"I never saw a fox with such big ears and large furry tail. We have lots of black foxes in Florida," Frank comments.

"The ears are huge because they hunt at night and need to hear the animal sounds in order to hunt. A bushy tail shades its body from the summer sun and heat. It hunts desert snakes, rats and birds," Faisal adds.

Nancy picks up a bone with teeth in it. "But, what is this, Faisal?"

"Looks like the fossilized jaw maybe of a camel or horse," he exclaims.

"This unimaginable adventure can never be repeated," Frank assures Lilli.

In the distance, they hear Bedouin music, with drums, tambourines. "Unreal. I think I hear a mandolin," Nancy says. "It's the Oud, an oval shaped guitar-like instrument with eight strings. They are part of an ancient Bedouin musical culture still carried on today."

Another exciting day of desert discovery comes to an end.

~ 30 ~
Ralph Perkins Departs

Frank worked hard through three five year plans. He did not go un-noticed with the Saudis, especially Salah abu Bayatri. Frank's work record in assisting Ralph to run Boxwood International was brilliant and phenomenal. He saved the company millions of dollars by astutely working and dealing directly with Salah.

Frank confided in Lilli, "With Arabs, once a friend you are his friend for life; once you're an enemy, you are that for life, too. But you'd never know it, for their custom is to treat an enemy royally, get to know him, to know his strengths and weaknesses so as to deal with his downfall."

Frank didn't have to worry because he was respected member of Salah's Saudi inner clique and he does his best to stay there. Salah was, in reality, Frank's sincere friend. Frequently, he was invited to Salah's all male parties.

He visited the airport customs folks often, too, most of whom were Bedouin coming into the city to work, enticed by the government. They all loved this friendly American. He took the time to sit and enjoy tea with them. He had taken a liking to one particular nice fellow, Akhram, a language translator from Jordan, who was helpful in searching and finding deliveries of materials for Boxwood. They also became close friends. With this man's expertise, Frank was certain all materials were received on time, swiftly cleared customs and gathered up promptly. Akhram knew the customs procedure inside and out. A beautiful new modern airport had been built, but the non-efficient customs situation was slow to change. Products delivered could sit outside on the hot tarmac for days if the company trucks didn't search and pick them up expeditiously. Storage buildings had yet to be constructed. Akhram became a storehouse of pertinent generic knowledge for Frank.

The years continue rapidly flying by. Yearly vacations in Florida with family and twice a year, Lilli and Frank visited a different European or Middle Eastern country . . . Athens, Greece and Cairo, Egypt were among Lilli's favorites. Lilli felt like a real international traveler, honing in on each country's history. Now, they mostly stayed at home in the desert, resting, socializing, and exploring. Ahmed, Lilli's driver leaves for yearly vacations in Pakistan and she misses him.

Life for them couldn't be better. They have no intention of leaving this remarkable, growing modern city of diminishing sand, any time soon. All the technical advances of home were at their fingertips here, except for many choices from the few TV stations broadcast five hours a day and two radio stations. We still use video casettes . . . no movie theaters. But mail delivery is good.

Frank and Salah abu Bayatri travel on the pretext of business, but in reality, Salah enjoys these few trips in the company of American Spaniard, Frank Martinez. Their travels are mostly to Spain. Madrid is Salah's favorite vacation spot.

This night in Spain, they are on the tenth floor of a Madrid hotel overlooking the city lights and star-lit sky. A first quarter moon outlined in full is reminiscent of the top of a Mosque. Frank wishes

Lilli was there to share this stunning, possibly romantic night. He makes a mental note to bring her here on their next vacation. In Spain for only a few days, it brings needed relaxation and camaraderie for both men. Salah personally pays for all expenses.

———— ⸺

Lilli and Frank enjoy entertaining friends, including important government people and some royalty. At one party they had sixteen guests of many nationalities . . . none were Americans. "Americans are boring," Frank commented to Lilli.

Boxwood International is making billions, because of Frank's astuteness, public relations, marketing skills and intelligence. He qualifies for a promotion to International Chief Executive Officer, C.E.O. of the Saudi/American enterprise . . . the head honcho of B.I.A, Inc. for Saudi Arabia. Ex-International CEO Ralph Perkins, is returning home to the main office. He is aware that his former position awaits him. With his Saudi knowledge, he will be needed.

"You have been let go, old boy," Frank tells Ralph. "We will miss you here. Salah gave me your tickets and passports. You leave in two days. I'll see you at your old job, in the states."

Frank advances to a much larger private villa in a Saudi resident-gated compound.

———— ⸺

"You'll probably be traveling out of country much more now, Frank. I'll be left alone quite a bit, won't I? Not going to be fun. Maybe I should see if I can get a job back at the University of Chicago?" she queried. "By the way, Joan tells me they are moving back home very soon."

"Yes, they are. I am CEO now, Lilli. And, you will have more money and time here to do whatever you wish with Nancy and Fatima. And dearest, we are due our yearly vacation soon, so let's visit Spain on our way to Miami?"

"I'll give it a try Frank . . . see if I can cope without spending too much money on jewelry. Spain would be great place to explore on our way home."

"Say, did I tell you that one of our fellas is in jail for participating in a Hashish party? The company sent his wife home, stopped his pay and he is awaiting sentence. Another guy, whose wife was working in our office, was made to quit because of her smoking. Her husband had to go to court and sign that she would never work in the kingdom again. Also several women, new arrivals, were arrested for prostitution in one of the western employee compounds. They and their husbands were sent home. Bet they made some big bucks, though! Kinda ignorant, not knowing this place is not a woman's world, but they sure tried."

"I don't think it will ever be truly a woman's world, Frank. However, progress is being made. Girls are now graduating from the several Universities here. The University of Riyadh now specializes in science, technology, English and poetry. More women doctors are training inside Saudi Arabia. Many still travel abroad to continue with internships, though."

Frank answers, "I also think ex-patriots bring their problems and faults with them, thinking life will be better and solutions found. Truthfully, I now know, if you can't resolve marital problems at home, you are lucky to solve them here. You made us lucky, Lilli."

"I agree, living in a foreign country is difficult in many ways, but here it is especially so for women. There are many temptations for both sexes with men and women from all over the world. This life takes real love. It certainly does not solve psychological problems. Money is the root of all evil and most enticement for westerners comes from that," Lilli expostulates.

She continues, "I am thrilled we love it here and appreciate its

culture. Hopefully we helped this country grow socially and mate-
rially. For us, we've had access to experiencing a different culture,
the good parts with the bad. I pray all American women here who
have experienced and know this type of life exists, are humbled by
it. When they return home, I hope they will have more apprecia-
tion for the freedom given us by the constitution of our American
homeland. There is no country equal to America for freedom,
liberty and the opportunity to better oneself . . . the American way
has beckoned folks to our shores from all over the world."

Frank, "Say let's go for a ride next Friday and take some photos
of the sights around Riyadh. We haven't done that in a long time."

～31～

A Drive for Photos

Driving past the murdered King's palace, Frank gets out of the car, takes a photo.

He proceeds driving, turning into a gas station. A young Arab who had been following demands he hands over his camera. Frank shows this guy his business card, which the Arab promptly grabs and places in his pocket. The fellow seems extremely angry and tells them they may get their camera back at the police station and "Follow me." The next stop is the police station. No one is there. The hostile Arab makes a phone call, yelling to Frank to get back into his car. The two cars wait until a taxi arrives with three more men. The three pile into the first Arab's car.

Frank follows again. Stopping in front of a huge house with green trim. Lilli asks in Arabic, "Aysh bayt hena? (*Who lives here?*)" The Arab answers, "Al Emir" (*A prince*).

"It is a Prince's house," she says to Frank.

Waiting on the sidewalk, they are finally escorted into a nearby building. The men sit on the floor. A friendly conversation ensues when they discover Lilli speaks Arabic. "The Amir will be here in five minutes," she is told. The men keep reassuring Lilli, "Ma

Laysh. *Never mind,* it's nothing." They offer water from a communal aluminum water bowl. The two accept.

Upon his arrival, they are escorted into the Emir's office . . . A room with a desk, one phone and a chair. The Emir speaks to them briefly, takes the camera and tells them, "I will look at the film and return it to you at Boxwood office on Monday." Taking the film out, he hands the camera to Frank. Exiting amid handshakes and smiles, including from the once unfriendly Arab who originally took his camera away, they jump into their car. Frank can't believe they avoided bad trouble. "Phew, that was no fun. Don't ever take a photo of the King's Palace."

"Quite scary and really a nerve wracking experience. Hope we never go through that one again. I thought for sure, we would be jailed. My Arabic did come in handy, though. I think it relaxed the situation. Wonder if we will ever get our film back?"

Hugging his wife, "Your Arabic sure did sedate them Lilli. Most westerners do not speak Arabic. I noticed they were impressed and immediately calmed down."

The film was never returned. They knew post-haste that no photographing of people without permission, was allowed in the Kingdom, but hoped photos of things were okay. So Frank purchases a very tiny camera that fits in his pocket. They secretly use it on occasion, praying each time they clicked. Now, if people were involved, they always asked before photographing.

They continue taking many photos, especially of the topographical features of this desert land, the desert artifacts, minerals, animals, plants and Bedouin. "A once in a lifetime experience we cannot ignore has been at our fingertips Frank," Lilli rationalizes. "We must take images to reminisce one day."

Frank's new CEO position involves periodic flights back to Chicago. He also continues his travels with Salah, mostly to Madrid.

"You're a real professional," commends Salah to Frank before a Dept. Head meeting one Monday morning. "When dire emergencies for building supplies arise, you handle the situation in an expedient manner. Being here more than fifteen years, Frank, you have proved your worth and performed outstandingly. I am proud of you. From now on, everyone, when you see Frank here and he gives an order or direction, you see me. I am he and he is me. His orders are to be followed as though they are mine. We are well into our fourth-year plan."

After the meeting, Salah takes Frank aside, "I want you to continue heading this company. Do you mind if I call you Francisco?"

"Certainly not. My father does and you are like family to me, Salah."

"Francisco, I have inquired into your work. Everyone has nothing but good things to say about you. You are the type of American we like to have help us. You knew our five year plans were auspicious and that we needed good workers until the time came when our own are fully cross-trained and able to take over. Our young boys are becoming better educated in schools here, instead of going abroad. The University is accepting more and more students, women also. King's Hospital is one of the world's most modern and best equipped hospitals. And now there are several hospitals throughout the country's big cities. Our National Guard is training to be the best. In agriculture, we are experimenting with irrigation processes to make our south western soil areas fertile and able to produce enough food for our population, which is growing.

Our goal is still to be self-sufficient. We are almost there. We still need people with honesty and integrity, whom we can trust implicitly. You are one of those, Francisco."

"I am honored you feel that way, Salah. I certainly will do everything in my power to continue being trustworthy to you and the Kingdom. My wife and I love living here and love the people. Our Muslim friends are our family. Thank you for your kind words, Salah."

~32~
Ancient Batha Suq

E njoying Frank's promotion and their new ultra-modern villa accommodations living beside interesting Saudis and a few expatriots, Lilli spends much of her time with Fatima because Abdulla is frequently traveling out of the country, purchasing carpets.

And, dear friend Nancy calls every week for lunch and shopping.

Her dependable driver Ahmed, takes her anywhere she wants to go. He always surprises her with her favorite Pakistani sweet, *Jalebbi*, a pretzel like candy.

Today, Lilli and Fatima, wearing *abayas* and scarfs are in *Batha Suq*, the original antiquated shopping market not modernized, still standing as it was years ago. Sadly, the other ancient market, Dirraah Suq has been slightly modernized. Always intrigued, they traverse the pathways, stopping here and there exploring ancient-looking arabesque shops adorning each side of the paths.

Fatima decides to purchase some opera length Bahraini pearls, "They say these are the most beautiful and have more orient than any other pearl. My beautiful Ooloo-LuLu's."

"They impart such beautiful shining colors of blue, pink, and a tint of green. I know after many centuries of diving, the best divers for pearl oysters were the Arabs of Bahrain on the eastern coastline, in the Arabian Gulf. Amazing that a pearl can be formed when a grain of sand lodges between the shell and its insides? "

"Yes, so interesting, Lilli. Pearl diving has dwindled now because the divers prefer taking on regular jobs with Aramco Oil Company in Dhahran. They earn more money, probably. Sad though, these beautiful pearls are few now."

Continuing their walk down the muddy pathway, Lilli suddenly feels a very light something . . . a touch on both buttocks. *What?* . . . She turns her head, stares down. There she beholds a big hand on her left hip and another on the right . . . both hands silently moving in rhythm to the cadence of her hips and steps. Quickly turning around, she yells to the Yemeni man, *"Wagguf hada.* Stop this! Please, not another crazy sex-idiot here." She quickly hits him with her purse. He rapidly turns, takes off like a rocket and disappears into a crowd of smirking, white thobed Muslim men with skull caps, sitting around the path's edges. They are watching, clapping and chuckling at the *Inglisi,* English woman's solving of her dilemma.

"They tell us, it's okay to hit those men with our purses. I had only one second to take a deep breath and swing. Incidents like this make me aware of my surroundings now. Some of these men are still perverted from lack of female affection. This problem isn't as bad as it was."

"Lilli," Fatima says, "I am always sorry the men here have to do such things. We don't have that in Lebanon or Palestine. By the way, we are going to our condo in Jidda soon. Do you suppose you and Frank would like to be our guests? We can tour Jidda, and snorkel in the Red Sea. The Hajji's will be there after performing the once in a lifetime Hajj in Mecca and Medina, celebrating the holiday of Eid-Al-Adha, Feast of Sacrifice. Abdulla and I frequently do just a *Ziyara,* visit to Mecca to rejuvenate our spirit. Other times we make a lesser pilgrimage, called the *Umra,*"

"Sounds wonderful. Let me talk to Frank when he returns tonight about his schedule. Thank you so much for the invite. Did you know that black coral only comes from the Red Sea?"

"I did not know that. I would love a piece of black coral. Maybe I can purchase a piece of black coral jewelry when we are there," Fatima adds.

"Maybe we will find you a piece in the Red Sea waters when we snorkel."

"Wouldn't that be wonderful. You are a precious friend to me, Lilli."

"And you to me, Fatima."

A call from Frank before he takes the plane to return home. "Salah just called my hotel room and wanted to know if I can take care of his family a few times during the year while he is out of the country on business. Says I am the only one he trusts with his wife and family."

"And what did you tell him?"

"I didn't think you would want me to be caring for another man's wife and kids."

"You are so right! No way, my dear. I know he trusts you but this is a very strange request."

"He understands, my Lilli. I'll see you soon."

~ 33 ~
The Hajj

While awaiting Frank's arrival home, Lilli watches the T.V. news. 'Today the right hands of two Pakistani thieves were chopped off. They confessed to thefts.'

She knows punishment for the few criminals here is swift . . . in a matter of days. Once the judgment order from the Mutawai'n religious police agents enforcing the laws and regulations are approved, the sinner goes before sharia court, the verdict is then endorsed by the Supreme Council of Judicature, and Sharia Court rules for the punishment. Lastly, if the King approves, the penalty is carried out after Mosque prayers on a Friday.

Unbelievable this drastic, horrible and inhumane kind of punishment really exists anywhere, let alone in a country I am beginning to love. I wondered why the two men I saw in the suq had no right hands. A reason crime is almost non-existent here.

She always delighted in the eight o'clock, after work, evening walks around the city with Frank, feeling so safe, aware that no guns were legally allowed into this country. They always eat in one of the new fast food restaurants. Favorites are McArabia or the Cheesecake Factory. The food anywhere is delicious. No alcohol available, of course.

Finally, Frank arrives home. Lilli immediately tells him of the invitation to Jidda.

"Wow, am I anxious to snorkel in the Red Sea. A plethora of unique fish make their home there. Fishing and snorkeling in those waters will be unreal. This Florida fisherman can't wait."

Having adventuresome spirits, they know this will be a memorable experience. The next month, after sunset *salaat*, the two board a Saudia plane. They will meet Fatima and Abdulla in forty minutes. Heading east to Jidda, Mecca, Medina, and the Red Sea, the sun slowly begins its disappearance under the earth's umbrella.

A magnificent starboard sunset comes into view. Skyward, where earth's horizontal plane of blackness and horizon meet, a bright blaze of orange, deep and rich, briefly appears. Further toward the sky's zenith are brilliant hues of luminous yellow and iridescent blue interspersed with wispy darker purple. Traces of lustrous pinks and glowing light orange give way to a beautiful ethereal Arabian night, clear except for the brilliance of twinkling heavenly bodies.

This beautiful and thrilling night takes Lilli's thoughts to the ending festivities of the three day holy pilgrimage, the Hajj, the last of the five pillars of Islam. "Frank, as Westerners, we are in for a rare encounter. The holiday of Eid al-Adha is beginning."

"The Hajji's are there now, thousands of them, I'm sure. I can't wait to witness this, to take an outsider's part in observing this celebration is a privilege," Frank exclaims.

Also anxious to visit the magnificent wonders of the Red Sea's coral reef north of Jidda, she is suddenly overcome by an overwhelming anticipation pervading her senses. *Is this exciting event a preview of what is to come in this land of sand with unknown mysteries?* Her anticipation heightens.

They land in Jidda. In the race with the setting sun, they had lost. Night has set in, but the lights of this coastal, most modern of ancient cities, illuminate the streets. Welcome humidity envelopes their bodies as dear friends sweep them away. Moments later they drive past ultra- modern villas and sculptures standing in silhouette against the sea. A giant cement *qahwa (coffee)* pot, about three stories high, is splashing, its imaginary coffee contents into the sea. The condo is within walking distance to downtown. After unpacking, the four friends become immersed in the crowded streets of Jidda, engulfed in throngs of Hajjis exploring the streets and *suqs*. "These Muslims strolling the streets have already made the pilgrimage to Mecca and Medina, as the Koran says they must," Abdulla explains to Lilli.

"I wish we could share in visiting these holy shrines. Being a non-Muslim, I know I will never be allowed to view these historic places. But, I vicariously feel the remnants of a religious fervor that brings millions of people here every year, just by being side-by-side with them now."

"These Pilgrims come from the ends of the earth; Afghanistan, Iraq, Egypt, Pakistan, Mongolia, Sudan and many more. Remember, Lilli, two weeks ago they passed through Riyadh selling carpets. Some sell everything they own to make this journey, stopping in towns along the way, bartering their hand woven carpets to pay for the trip here. I really liked those beautiful red, black and white Afghani carpets we bought, and by the way, so did Abdulla," Fatima says.

Hajjis are everywhere . . . permeating stores, alleyways. The convergence of different languages, cultures, customs, colors, and races gathered here tonight is awesome. The realization that their profound belief in Allah brings them to this distant land is even more inspiring. A once in a life time religious experience for the Muslims that can travel here.

A Muezzin is melodiously calling the faithful to prayer. His words reverberate throughout the seaside city. Hajjis, en masse, face north toward Mecca. Placing their small carpets on the ground anywhere, they prostate themselves, bobbing up and down repeating their prayers.

Abdulla and Fatima do the same. Afterward, Abdulla leads the Americans into a Jidda picturesque "suq", another ancient trading bazaar. "Although a modern city now, parts of this bustling place appears centuries old and unchanged," he comments.

Lilli notices the attires. Men and women both wear *Ihram,* long white, flowing garments for the pilgrimage. The men's are of white cloth in two lengths. One goes from the waist to ankles, the other piece of seamless material is thrown over the shoulders. Women wear all white gowns and head covering . . . no facial covering. Some Yemeni men who have already made the Hajj, return having changed to colorful plaid skirts. Others from Pakistan wear long free-flowing pantaloons. The exotic array of color and dress is bright and vivid. "What a sight," exclaims Lilli.

Abdulla explains, "Some Hajji's strolling about here are still in the required Ihram, the white, seamless garment of the Hajj. But, notice the colorful turbans and caps elegantly twisted and coiled. Some turbans are hanging long with one or both ends tossed up or wrapped so only nose and eyes are visible."

Fatima adds, "Women worship in Mecca with their men. After performing the Hajj rituals, they are still all in white with a head cover. A few women wear the black *abaya,* body covering cloak with the black gossamer hair cover, *hijab.*"

"Well," says Frank, "My allergies are kicking in . . . we are inhaling a variety of suq odors . . . food, incense perfumes. Just listening to the accents of hawkers enticing folks as they stroll into calling distance, is a decoding lesson. Lilli, look here, an antique incense burner, really nice. And tins with "Frankincense" and "Myrrh" written on them in English yet."

"Oh, my," says Lilli, "This burner is a work of art. A silver-looking metal with a wooden handle and bowl-like container on top to hold the spice. The cover has graceful openings when closed so the sweet smoke's aroma can circle into the atmosphere. I want it and some of both aromatic spices, Frank. They are resins from tree bark and plants grown in southern Arabia." Frank makes the purchase.

Walking along, Lilli explodes. "Another glittering gold suq! The windows dripping with gold -necklaces, belts, chains, brace-lets and rings are similar to the old Dirrah suq in Riyadh. Look at the semi-precious stones here," pointing to dishes and cans full of coral, lapis lazuli, malachite, topaz and turquoise. "Fatima, it still takes my breath away to see gold glistening so garishly under these night lights. Let's buy a few of the gold bracelets here." They each buy four beautifully carved bangles.

"I would like to visit King Solomon's mines in north Arabia where they say the first gold mines were active," Frank mentions.

"We'll do it, but let's browse the carpet shop here. The sign above ... *With Thread of Their Soul, They Weave Their Warp,* explains a lot. What hand-woven beauties hang before us! This one is a Persian Naim made from wool, silk and cotton," Abdulla says.

A spectacular-looking carpet. Pretty blue interspersed around a central medallion design of leaves and flowers. The border is intri-cate in its design.

"I'll buy it." Lilli feels she is in a time past, a time within the pages of the Arabian Nights, a time of caravansaries in ancient Arabia Felix when Jidda was a rest stop for camel caravans of the Hijaz (the western province) transporting frankincense and myrrh from the land of Sheba in the south to the Fertile Crescent in the north. This is a return to the merchant adventurers; Nabateans, Babylonians, Jews and Romans. Many of these ancient people passed through Jidda, some stayed.

"Fatima, this is an exciting and historic adventure. I am so lucky to be here. Thank you very much. She hugs Fatima with gratitude. I hope you will let us repay you one day in America."

"My dear friend, I look forward to visiting you there."

~34~

The Red Sea—
A Polychromatic Rainbow
of Color

The next morning, after morning prayers, Abdulla answers a knock on the condo door that reveals Tariq Rashudi. "I was on my way to Rome with a three day stopover here. Thought I could swim in the Red Sea with you."

"Great, Tariq, I was hoping you would have time to join us. We are getting ready to make the drive north along the Mecca Road, following the Sea."

Lilli is comfortable sitting in the back seat between Frank and Fatima, Tariq in the front with Abdulla. She reflects on the history of the second holiest city in Islam as they pass a road sign off to the right pointing the way, 'To Mecca' in English and Arabic. Several miles further north, is Medina, the sanctuary of the prophet Muhammad, where a grand mosque marks his resting place. Lilli is also aware that Islam gained much from the Jews and Christians, for their Koran.

Continuing up the coast, spectacular rolling mountains and long cliff-like ridges of sand and rock (escarpment) run parallel to and follow the coastline.

Lilli remembers, all the great monotheistic religions of man emerged from desert areas such as this. The Arabs say the footsteps of Muhammad can be traced here and the distant caves are where he prayed in 622 A.D.

"I think we will stop on this sandy beach area," Abdulla announces as they approach the seaside.

Lilli's meditation is interrupted. The scintillating azure waters of the Red Sea now encompass her being. Her thoughts return to the magical excitement of exploring the coral reef. The five leave smooth footprints in the orange/pinkish soft sand along the water's edge. The sea of cobalt blue waters lapping over the reef resemble Florida's ocean reef waters.

Frank utters, "This creamy sand is a haven for sea shell hunters; but Rashudi, you Arabs don't seem to like the water. This beautiful beach is void of anyone fishing or swimming."

Tariq replies, "It's true, Frank. It will soon change though. Arabs are just beginning to appreciate their unique country. But I have done much snorkeling in the Caribbean and the Keys in America. It is a favorite sport. I so enjoy the beauty of the colors. Let's put our special eye-glasses on, shall we?"

If there were people here, the men and women would have to separate. But with a deserted beach they can all enter the azure waters together dressed in long thin pants and loose shirts. Snorkeling over the first four hundred yards of the reef, they head out a little further west. The sun's rays sparkle reaching the bottom of shallow crystal—clear, sandy pools. Pale brown and green plant life, bright yellow golden and red staghorn coral colonies are spectacularly illuminated. Lilli and Frank cannot believe the spectrum of colors their eyes are absorbing.

Lilli points to a tiny tropical fish. Fatima sees it, too. It alternates emerging and backing into a sandy-bottom hole. It covers itself with sand and disappears. *Amazing!*

"The thrills are yet to come," Abdulla yells out. "Wait until you see the last few feet before the formidable seventy-five foot precipitous drop-off . . . breath-taking and spectacular."

Frank and Lilli are in a trance. They all stand in the deeper water before going further. "Spellbinding! This is the most fantastic natural sea aquarium I have ever seen. Can't compare with any tropical aquarium we have at home, Lilli. This is virgin water. Not many have had the privilege of visualizing such beauty."

After a few minutes, Lilli's mind settles to interpret the visions. Everything in sight is swaying to and fro, in rhythm with the ebb and flow of the tide. A multitude of great reddish-orange coral Sea fans gently wave, and congregations of brightly colored tropical fish silently float in harmony—back and forth. Minuscule sea life darts in and out of gigantic Brain Coral convolutions. Oversized jet black Sea Urchins crawl slowly about the sea's sandy floor.

"Nothing here seems to fear us, Frank."

"Incredible, Lilli," he replies.

Within arm's reach are huge radiant blue and yellow fish pecking each other and two lovely pale green fish with warm pink and yellow stripes, swim side by side.

There are so many colors floating below and around them. It is mind boggling to all. An elegant ink-black fish with spots of aqua coloring on its mouth swims by, along with a red and white fish with feathers. "Looks like a chicken," Lilli exclaims as a small vivid blue fish darts by.

"There is a fish only found here, in the Red Sea . . . the Surgeon Fish. It carries a scalpel spine near its tail that swishes to slice its enemies," Tariq explains. "Hope we can see one."

Abdulla comments, "I have never seen so much coral. Looks like Sea Slugs are just hanging on."

Frank replies, "Seems like all species and color of coral abound here. There's a Starfish walking on the sandy bottom. Living in Florida prepares one for this. We have most of these fish there in the Gulf of Mexico and certainly lots of coral."

"Yes Frank," Lilly answers, "Do you see that coral with colors of pink, red, yellow, green, and purple. Notice the Coral down there where small red Crabs and fish, black Starfish and Sea Worms are crawling in and out of. Oh, Fatima, I found a piece of black coral for you!"

Now, they are snorkeling just a few inches from the coral plateaus extreme drop off into deeper blue sapphire waters. The reef's jagged edges are in view, changing the water color to a dark iridescent turquoise. The coral escarpment wall, like a tall mountain cliff, juts in and out.

"Looks perilous," thinks Fatima. "Hold on to that Black Coral, Lilli."

The most eerie fish of all glides through the water about forty feet down from the rim of the reef, close to the sea's bottom. Floating silently there are two black and white striped, poisonous Lion Fish. Schools of large game fish passing by are safely staying in the deep water's distance, away from these dangerous predators. The five visitors quickly swim back to shore.

Strolling out of the water, "Tariq, the unusual variety of fish species here is comparable to nowhere else, even our Forida reefs," Frank says in amazement. "I am surprised to find such a prodigious sea life thriving in this Red Sea. I never expected it."

Lilli's rational thoughts return, as she tries to absorb the dazzling kaleidoscope, the harmonious motion from the sea and its sea life. Surreal is the surrounding chromatic palette of natural color and design. A spellbinding encounter.

"This Red Sea has left us fascinated and in awe of its wonders.

Fatima and Abdulla, I hope you will let us return with you another day," Lilli asks.

"Our pleasure," Abdulla agrees. "Say, let's take a short trip to Taif this afternoon, a cool resort in the Hijaz mountain where members of the Saudi Royal family spend hot desert summers. It is a summer seat for the Kingdom's government building complex recently built there. We will take a city taxi instead of driving. The taxi ride climb from the costal Tihama plain of the Hijaz Mountain to Taif on the mountain top, is steep, winding, uplifting, and exhilarating. The view at the escarpment top is breath taking-spectacular. There are huge rock formations, mountains, and below are farms, palm groves, and camel herds. Interesting place."

Frank is breathless, "This is all unreal."

"There must be similar sights in the western desert of America, except for camels, that is. I know the Turkish Ottoman Empire ruled the Hijaz and also Taif, turning this city into a military garrison in about the eighth century," Lilly affirms.

"The Hijaz mountain range rises high. It has many road bends winding through beautiful natural flora and fauna." Abdulla adds, "Baboons, Hyenas, and Wolves procreate and multiply here."

The ride up the mountain is exhilarating. Arriving, they browse about the suq noticing a dozen stalls covered by black tents.

"This is an old Bedouin farmers market. Carpets are less expensive than in Jidda. Goods are hanging or tucked into tin trunks. Lots of gold and silver, too," Fatima explains.

"I see many knick-knacks. Seems people here are very relaxed, cheerful. I think I'll buy a bottle of perfume, some pomegranates and dates over there, and I see spices," Lilli says. She makes her purchases. "Let's go see that one pretty Bedouin lady in a red embroidered dress over there, Fatima."

"Lilli, the red embroidered dress means she is married. Blue embroidery is a single lady."

The friendly lady removes her face veil with a broad smile revealing gold capped front teeth. Her nose is pierced and back of her hands are covered with artistic henna designs. She holds up a hand full of purple stones. "These pieces of Amethyst are beautiful Lilli, let's buy some of these gorgeous gems for a necklace." They both make a purchase.

— 35 —
Christian Church
in Arabia?

Back at the Jidda condo after a thrilling day, "Do you suppose we can visit that old Anglican Church west of Baghdadia district tomorrow before we leave? To realize that Christian Churches actually existed at one time and had an active membership in this now Muslim country, blows my mind," Lilli exclaims.

"Absolutely, let's go to the church early. Our flights aren't until six tomorrow evening," answers Abdulla.

The next day finds them amongst the ruins of an ancient place of prayer.

Abdulla explains, "A British-built church, it was popular here especially in the early 1900's. Situated close to the city, it made attending services convient for Merchant Seafarers who anchored their dhows (ancient Arab sailboats) at Jidda's port."

"I can't believe there were Christian churches in Saudi Arabia, ever," Lilli exclaims. "I wonder if you are aware of this Tariq?"

"Yes, I have heard of it, but it is not written in any of our history books. I will be interested in seeing it, too," he smiles warmly. *Can this Americanee get any more beautiful?*

Abdulla adds, "A Christian Church was also built in Jubail, north of here. We'll visit it one day, too."

"The Wahhabi purists from the Nejid desert in the middle of the country, annexed this region and forbade public practices of other religions. These little Christian churches have been kept a secret ever since. Jidda, here in the western Hijaz, practices a more tolerant Islam. They do not follow puritanical Islam. Their rules and traditions are much like moderate Egypt, more relaxed, at least for now," adds Abdulla. "There is a Christian cemetery not far from here, too. Today, religious restrictions for Christians are severe. Religious beliefs must be celebrated in the home."

"Well, folks, let's get going home. This is so much fun. We'll all be available for another exciting venture soon. Just let us know when," Abdulla states. *"Yella! Let's go* to the airport.*"*

They all say farewell to Tariq. He gives a wink to Lilli. She smiles. Frank notices.

The return trip to Riyadh, cannot hold a candle to the Red Sea with its winds, waves, and exotic sea life color or Jidda, with the heart-warming visualization of a Muslim Hajj celebration.

＊＊＊

They land into the hot summer heat of Riyadh, a city surrounded north, south, east and west by desert systems. The city absorbs the sun's heat, baking its residents in the process. They can't wait for the colder winter to arrive.

Lilli remarks, "We will never forget this exciting adventure to Jidda and the Red Sea, will we friends? I wish I had a magic lamp to rub for Aladdin's Genie to transport me back to that spellbinding coral reef of the Red Sea and a cooler historic Jidda. Maybe another day, Insha'Allah."

"Amen, Insha'Allah, God willing," voices come from all the happy friends.

— 36 —

More Archeological Sites

Entertainment in this city is now a shoppers' paradise with modern grocery and clothing stores, the new "women only" malls . . . where husbands can accompany their wives, and restaurants. Frank and Lilli stay busy entertaining, periodic expensive travels outside the kingdom or their favorite is having a desert lunch while enjoying the search for endless surprises, and, of course the camel and horse races. Never has a country grown so rapidly magnificent . . . still no theaters, though.

So this Thursday, the four friends decide to travel back to the desert, including Pilot Rashudi. Leaving early, they caravan many miles west of the city. Tariq rides with Frank and Lilli.

Stopping, they climb a solitary rocky path up where they are pleasantly surprised to discover more ancient history. Petroglyph rock carvings of tribal hunters with bow and arrow, holding their game caught high in the air, horses and dromedary one humped camels, snakes, and prolific undecipherable pictographic scribblings and drawings.

"Discovering prehistoric rock carvings and writings is exciting. Ancient people passing by had the beginnings of written languages by drawing and carving," Lilli explains. "Here, everyone, take a sheet of paper and chalk for rubbing over a rock to make a picture. You will have a souvenir to frame. This is archeology history. The archaeological realization in this country is beginning to expand. Start rubbing everyone!"

"Look down there," Faisal yells. "Our second sighting of a large-eared desert fox. Looks like a huge dog."

"Hey, I found a carving of a horse up here," Abdulla sounds excited at his find.

Again, Lilli explains, "Yes, the Arabian horse is renowned for intelligence, beauty and endurance. I believe Bedouin still raise them. They are coveted by Arabs. When we first arrived, we purchased one for me. His name is Guidras. His most striking feature is his beautiful head and thick arched neck. He is a creamy white color and an excellent jumper. He isn't very friendly, will nip at your hands when petted. I was a little scared when I first rode him, because he was so fast and jumped very, very high. I kept him at the Riyadh Stables, rode him when I was bored . . . one of my secret pleasures. Frank has since sold him to a Bedouin."

Driving further, all three cars stop at the eastern edge of the mountains.

"This is where Camel caravans probably stopped on route to Yemen where they purchased *labbaan (frankincense) and myrrh* s and spices to sell back home," Faisal says.

"I do know there are rich grazing areas around this area where sheep, goats and chicken are raised." Tarig answers.

A few months later, on a Thursday afternoon, the whole group of six plus Tariq, take another trip heading south, down a sand embankment desert road to a gigantic deep water hole.

"There are no vital rivers left in Saudi but this water hole here must be fed by an underground river that receives occasional rainwater running off the foothills of the Tuwayq Escarpment," Faisal explains. "We used to rely on these rivers and water holes for water, but since the seventies, we get our water from many de-salinized sea water plants."

"Lilli, this is amazing. Thank Allah that you arrived here interested enough to want to visit these natural sites that we never paid attention to. Our country is so intriguing," Nancy smiles.

"Look here, a spearhead lying on the ground right in front of my foot," Tariq adds. "Another great adventure in the land of sand complete."

They are all ready to return home when Faisal mentions to Lilli and Frank, "I wish you could join Nancy and me in a swim in our employee pool . . . today is "family day". Some days are just for men, others are for women only, never for the public. Sorry."

A few weeks later, Faisal asks Frank to go hunting for rabbit using his Peregrine Falcon. "They are the fastest most perfect hunting birds. They prey on any small animals that move, like rats, lizards *(dhab)*, and geckos. Falconry is a popular sport with us." Faisal's sharp-eyed Falcon catches several rabbits and small birds that day. Frank is impressed.

The next week Faisal and Nancy invite the five to their home for a delicious rabbit and bird grill-out.

~37~

Ships of the Desert

Months later after Friday prayer services, Faisal returns home, prayer carpet folded under his arm. Of course, Nancy has said her prayers at home.

They drive to Frank and Lilli's villa. The guard at the entrance recognizes Faisal and flags him to proceed. All identical villas are situated within a walled area surrounded by high sand dunes . . . dunes positioned further away into the desert now, since the city's explosive expansion.

Nancy sits with Lilli in the back seat, Frank sits beside Faisal. Traveling northeast from Riyadh to the Dahna desert and into the sands of the great Nafud desert, they pass an isolated mosque beside the dirt road. "I know exactly where the annual King's Camel Marathon Desert Race is held," Faisal says. "A good thing because there is only one road sign. A compass is a necessity in the event of a sudden desert wind sand storm. There is a caravan of several cars kicking up sand ahead, hindering my vision a little, like a *shmali (wind sand storm).*"

"The encroaching sand dunes are beautiful. Can we stop to climb one?" asks Lilli.

Faisal pulls over. They all climb the hill of light brown golden sand. "After many years, this will be the last race run out here in the desert, so enjoy it. A great new big Stadium for camel and horse racing is just about complete. It will seem different than the races held here. We will be waiting under a roof with stands for spectator seats plus the races will only take minutes to run the track. We are growing in every aspect, aren't we?"

"The ripples of this 'sea of sand' seems to be rhythmically patterned by winds blowing, akin to ocean waves. Look at all the green plants here and flowers protruding from the rock edges," Lilli says fascinated.

Driving further, Faisal explains, "Hundreds of Bedouin riders and their 'ships of the desert', pre-historic nomadic Dromedary camels, take part. One-humped Dromedaries are the only camels found in Arabia. Racing camels can travel thirty-seven miles or sixty kilometers per hour, so it takes about one and a half hours to reach the fifty-six mile or ninety kilometer finishing line here. Some are faster, some slower. Every entrant who finishes is rewarded with money worth a very good day's work. My driver, Saud, will be in the race riding "Kama", his one humped, white dromedary. Saud says white camels give the best delicious milk."

Nancy adds, "But most camels are a light brown. I know the camel hump is all fat stored for travel energy. It does not store water as most people think."

"White camels are rare. All camels have a three part stomach holding fifty gallons of water and plant juices. When all liquid is depleted, it can keep traveling for about seven more days."

"Wow," Lilli answers Faisal. "They are truly amazing creatures. Humans, with loss of water in a desert would not survive."

Frank mentions, "I read where nomads, still today, weave camel hair for carpets, tents and clothing. They burn camel dung to keep warm."

"Yep, Camels provide the Bedouin with milk and meat. They eat the thick low-growing wadi greenery, trees and shrubs. An incredible animal. The importance of a Bedouin is measured by the number of camels in his herd," Faisal adds. "He also sells them."

"This country never ceases to astound me, Faisal."

Having seen these camel races out here many times, Faisal parks at the edge of the sandy road, close to a dry river bed. Many other parked cars line the dirt road. Waiting in the afternoon sun, the four watch and listen for the approaching cushioned-footed animals. They casually converse and munch on snacks of khubz-*bread,* hummus-*chickpea dip, and* baklava-*desert.*

Suddenly, a loud cannon boom reverberates throughout the dunes, reaching their auditory reflexes on a current of air, like a sea breeze but there is no sea, only sand.

"They'll be here soon, Insha'allah. Saud will win. Yellah, *Go,* Saud," an excited Nancy yells.

Later, they harken to a loud, disturbing sound, a train or tornado? The only thing visible is an unimaginable giant cloud of sand encompassing the whole area . . . a desert sand storm, a *shmaal?* Within the sandy cloud, a horde of advancing, roaring camels on the road now appears, heading straight toward them. Heavy hooves sound on the sandy dirt . . . whoomp, whoomp . . . the deafening, stampeding camels gallop closer and closer. A multitude of riders sitting on the one-hump rapidly move forward. Many remain in the rear forming a long line down the road.

Faisal shouts, "Quick, get into the car." He starts up the engine and rapidly pulls further into the edge of the dirt road, out of harm's way.

Five camel leaders in a horizontal line across the sandy road advance, pulsing in rhythm closer and closer. These riders, perched high on humps, pre-cede hundreds of seething, groaning, grunting dromedaries following behind, digging up the sand. An ocean of dusty waves forms. "Yikes," Nancy screams. "There he is . . . Saud is first. The one with a red turban piled high on his head. Kama will be the winner, *Insha'allah!* Oh, what a treasure to see this."

Lilly notices, *no saddles or foot stirrups on the passing camels, the rider sits on a heap of folded blankets—easy to slide off of. Some have feet and legs tucked up, others ride side-saddle. A few walk along the road's far edge, holding their camel reins. They gave up. Unreal!*

"*Yellah,* let's go, Saud," the four yell as he passes by. Kama's lower lip is frothing, undulating and drooling. His particular trot still graceful, even if tired. He passes the finish line ahead with a moan and a groan–"Arggh."

"Kama's the winner," Frank announces.

"*Al hamdu lillah*, thanks be to Allah!" Faisal shouts.

Lilly notices, "Isn't it interesting that each camel is owner identified by large Arabic numerals written in bright red on its neck. Saud's number is 1487–*wahid, arbaa, tamanya, sabaa.* Saud is definitely the winner. He is handsomely poised on Kama's hump."

"Lilli, let's ride a camel at the camel *suq* next week," Nancy suggests.

"Sounds wonderful and fun."

All riders wear some kind of headdress—skull caps, dark turbans, red and white or black and white, checkered head coverings, *ghoutrahs.* Many head coverings are all white held on by black ropes, *igals.*

"Look," yells Frank, these guys twist those scarfs around and around their faces, covering everything but their eyes. Smart to protect their skin and lungs from wind and sand, and the hot desert sun. These Bedu know how to live in the desert for sure . . . incredibly smart adapters for centuries. Man, this sand is suffocating. Handkerchiefs help some," covering his mouth.

The camels are controlled by reins held in their master's left hand. Their right hand holds tight to a long stick used to flog their steed. *"Imshi! Go,"* they shout, as the drooling exhausted camels move swiftly by, curly tails pulsating with every stomp of their long, thin legs.

The riders continue to pass quickly, white thobes resembling parachutes rising and falling with the air currents, up and down to the rhythm of the animal's cadence. Flying freely like wings in the breeze, whirling white visions of cotton cloth circle rider and camel, legs holding tight to the creature's side. Thumping of hundreds of hoofs on the sand echoes in the many spectators ears, like an army on an attack march. A few lag behind, their riders dropping by the wayside.

Gazing toward the desert reveals silhouettes of many dismounted riders holding their camel's reins, ambling slowly off in different directions. Some animals lying exhausted in the middle of the now disrupted and furrowed sandy course, mouths exuding a white froth.

Faisal explains, "These men are Bedouin living in an arid desert, competing for a yearly big prize. The multitude of those standing on the edge of the raceway are betting on their special camel rider."

The last riders pass. "Let's walk to the King's tent to see Saud," Faisal says as they walk, "The King decides the winning camel riders. He and his royal entourage sit in the shade of a white *Majalis,* king's tent, at the finish line, waiting for the last camel to pass."

Faisal points to an area where bright green flags marked with the Saudi Emblem of palm tree and cross swords blow in the breeze. Arabic words hover in a semi-circle around a white tent-top rippling in the sandy wind. He explains, "Translated the words say, *'Ash'Hadu ana la illaha ila Allah, Wa ash'hadu ana muh a madan Rassul Allah,'* meaning 'I believe that Allah is one and only and that his prophet is Mohammed.' Before Islam, the Saudi flag was black," he adds.

A carpeted area comes into view. Lilly comments, "The Persian rugs are beautiful. So are those large silk-covered arm chairs receiving the King."

"His royal family administrators sit beside him. The King and Crown Prince are in the center on throne-like chairs. Two small flags mark the finish line. The race is over. Three riders will be chosen winners."

The winners are called to the tent where the King presents the awards. Saudi riyals (money) equivalent to twenty-five thousand dollars is given to Saud, the first prize winner . . . lesser money prizes go to the other two winners.

"Kama, the winning "Ship of the Dessert" is now a very valuable asset. Occasionally, the King's own camels win the race, but lucky for Saud, not today," Faisal points out.

The King, Crown Prince and officials shake hands and kiss Saud's cheeks. Saud and the two others are presented with their winnings in a large *Qahwa, coffee* pot. Then, every rider comes up to the tent to receive their promised small stipend. All enter the longer, large tents and indulge in a kingly late afternoon feast before sundown Salaat.

A happy Faisal, "This is a fortune for these poor desert Bedouin. They can buy more camels if needed to transport family and possessions from camp to camp, whenever weather or lack of water and food supplies determine. For the most part, very few Bedu want to live even in small towns. In fact, an eight story condo in Riyadh was built just for Bedouins, free, to get them into city society. The beautiful condo is very slowly filling up. Some folks enjoy the freedom of nomadic existence. I'd say they are smarter than most. I am delighted Saud won. He is a true gentleman. I can't wait for the next races in our new modern stadium."

The setting sun shares its last reflecting glow on the dunes and distant rocky hill-tops. The sky slowly darkens while a herculean full moon and overflowing heavenly diamond bodies begin to substitute for daylight. The hot day begins to cool.

After many hours, the four sit in the jeep ready to leave, "At one time, all of Saudi Arabia was Bedouin tribal country, wasn't it, Faisal?"

"Yes, Lilli. You know, not until King Ibn Saud, hero of the Arabian peninsula, come into the picture did the nomadic tribes of the desert become unified under one flag," Faisal answers.

Traveling out of the desert toward home, Lilli mentions her desire for a job.

"You wouldn't need a secretary at the hospital, would you, Faisal? It's time for me to stop playing and be constructive in some way. I would really like to be busy now that I am familiar with all aspects of your country. Or perhaps Museum Director Omar needs some help? I could work at home for him. I know he would not want a woman in the museum."

"You know, Lilli, we can really use you at the King's hospital in the Admitting Department. With your knowledge of Arabic, you would be an asset to give tours or help in many departments including video productions. Maybe with Omar later on, but hospital admitting can use you now."

"That is wonderful, Faisal. I am so happy. When can I start?"

"*Bukrah, Inshallah,* Tomorrow, God willing and it will be for two days a week for now. We'll have Saud pick you up at eight forty-five. Work begins at nine."

"*Shukran*, Thanks. I will be ready. Thank you both for a wonderful day that we will always remember."

"*Afwan*. You are welcome. We, too had a great day."

"Thanks, Faisal, what a terrific time." A smiling Frank expresses his gratitude.

"*Masa'ul Kheir*, Good evening," Nancy replies.

Lilli ends with, "*Fi Aman-illah, Masa'ul Kheir,* (Good bye and good evening)."

That evening, Lilli and Frank hear the last "*Salaat*". In the middle of the call to prayer, Frank reminds her, "Remember, my flight to Cairo is tomorrow at ten. We stop briefly in Dammam, to pick up Westerners working north of there in those burgeoning phosphate mines. Our Florida had lots of phosphate at one time . . . providing the world with fertilizer. We ran out. Arabia has taken over that industry. I am sure your father's family is out of business now."

"Yes, I know, dear. Unbelievable, Saudi Arabia has finally discovered itself after centuries in the dark. Are you traveling with Salah, again? This is your third trip out of country this month. As Chief Executive Officer, can't you send someone else? How long will you be gone?"

"Four days for the company. Salah wants me to accompany him in two weeks. I should be back Wednesday. I'll call you. Not to worry, darling Lilli." He jumps into bed and clicks on the TV. "Please be sure my socks are packed, white ones this time, all is well. Thanks my love."

Lilli knows he is never without his socks. He believes his special 'FM' monogramed red, white and blue socks are an indication of the fact that he is a proud American. She is so happy she will finally be busy working after over twenty five years in this country, and that Frank, having less employees is still needed and wanted.

Frank gets his usual satisfaction and rapidly falls into a deep sleep. Lilli kisses him and whispers, "*Masa'ul Kheir,* good night. *Allah yubarik fikum,* may God bless you, my love."

~38~
To Cairo

Frank rises early. He hears the *Mutawah* calling the faithful to prayer, walking the streets, tapping on doors with his cane while *a Muezzin* chants a harmonious call from the mosque minaret. "There is no God but God and Mohammad is the messenger of God."

Lilli is also awakened by the call and thinks . . . *Most calls to prayer today are previously taped and played over a loudspeaker, but this call is the actual Muezzin's voice emanating from a mosque.*

Not as musical as a Chopin prelude but quite as flowing and gentle, spiritual and compelling too. It makes me feel like praying in a mosque now that women, including ex-patriots are allowed to enter some mosques if they are totally covered and remain in the rear area behind the men. They must remove their shoes and have no makeup.

"I would love to return to Cairo again one day, Frank. It's been years since we visited." Lilli helps Frank pack, not forgetting his special white socks, but she includes a pair of each, red, white and blue . . . blue underwear with white shirts, red ties, navy pants and jacket.

"Worn these colors since college days," he told her. "My good luck coverings."

"I know, you told me that years ago, dearest. I have noticed you very seldom have to the wear red ones, thank goodness."

"You are so understanding and good to me, Lilli. By the way, this Saudia flight stops in Cairo and then Pakistan. You know, Saudia Airlines used to be the only aircraft allowed to fly in and out of Saudi Arabia, but this has all changed. This country has had so many advances."

"Yes, my love, it's a different country than twenty five years ago, a beautiful place now."

With a passionate goodbye kiss, Frank is off to the airport.

⸺ ⸺

Reminiscing, he is amazed at this countries progress. *This new modern airport is comparable to any in the world today. No one could believe the primitive condition it was in when we arrived.* He realizes how far this country has advanced because of all the western technology and assistance.

Taking his seat in first class on Flight 22, he notices a Pakistani carrying a mini-butane burner with a bag over his shoulder that clunks with something sounding like glass. Frank watches the man head for the very rear of the plane.

An attractive stewardess approaches him and asks, "Are you Frank Martinez?" He nods and stands as she hands him an envelope. "This was just brought to the ticket counter with instructions to make certain that you get it. Please show me some I.D."

The sealed envelope has his name imprinted on the front, so he tears it open. "By the way," pointing to the rear seat, "What does that fellow back there have a butane burner for?"

"Oh, you didn't know? On Saudia, Middle East passengers are allowed to carry one on board, but not to actually make tea. In past times, they could, but no more."

E-gads, I can't believe this. How dangerous if he did decide to fire it up for tea.

——— ——

Thirty minutes later, the take-off from Riyadh is smooth as usual. After a two and a half hours, the flight, high over the Red sea, becomes turbulent. Over the intercom, a deep masculine voice, "We will be landing in Cairo shortly. Tie your seat belts. Prepare for landing."

Suddenly, a desperate command, "Seatbelts, seatbelts. Take your seats! Take your seats, quickly, quickly! Emergency!" Silence . . . !

An instantaneous drop in altitude causes the trembling aircraft to turn upside down. Clouds of black smoke, suffocating fumes, hot licks of reddish-orange and yellow fire slowly begins traveling from the rear of the cabin, searing and burning human bodies to a crisp.

Now in a tail spin, the aircraft begins shaking unmercifully producing scraping noises—metal clanking on metal. Fearful, dizzy and confused, passengers throughout are praying with screams to God and Allah. Shouting voices from the few remaining live first class passengers are eventually overpowered and subdued by fire and smoke from a twisting and twirling aircraft. Crying and painful moaning is all that remains of this blazing transport as it spirals head first, disappearing into the peaceful waters of the Gulf of Suez only minutes before arriving at its destination, El Qahira, (Cairo) Egypt.

~39~
A Sad Day

At nine, Faisal's driver Saud knocks at her door, "*Assalamu aleikum,* peace be upon you, Miss Lilli." Politely, he holds the door open for her to enter the back seat of his Mercedes. She misses her driver, Ahmed. He has retired . . . home to Pakistan. She wishes he would return.

"*Wa'aleikum assallam,* and on you be peace," Saud. *Yella,* let's go to the hospital."

She sits in the back seat. Women still cannot sit in the front seat with a trusted driver, not even beside her husband, for fear of being punished by the religious police. Of course, women are still not allowed to drive. So unfair to the female sex. Will this ever change? Many Saudi women travel to other countries and have the freedom to drive and live their own way.

She couldn't be more excited about her new job. *Finally, a job!* Arrival at the hospital (*mustashfa*) takes only 10 minutes because the past crazy traffic problem has subsided.

Entering the Kings Hospital lobby, her eyes immediately focus on a mosaic of the King. Nancy had told her about the king's portrait, but Lilli could have never imagined its beauty. The resemblance is remarkable, "Like a puzzle, artistically created from many pieces of Lapis Lazuli, in shades of blue and white by a famous Pakistani artist," Nancy told her.

"The diamonds sparkling from Faisal's eyes were placed there by a dentist from Egypt. This huge work of art is displayed on an artist's easel. A beautiful tribute to a beloved King."

Lilli recalls meeting the artist a few years ago during one of the many dinners they were invited to at Nancy and Faisal's home. The artist had told them, "I also have a painting in America's Smithsonian Institute." The Americans were impressed.

"He always stopped by to see Frank whenever he was in town, joined us for dinner frequently. We chuckled when he shook massive amounts of pepper on his food until his plate was covered in black, loving it hotter than how I cooked food. He was a nice talented guy."

Today, in the hospital lobby, she notices on the bottom of a mirror Arabic words written in pure gold. She translates, 'God is a great healer.'

Elegant upholstered furniture throughout the hospital lobby is of all colors: red, green, blue and pink. *This place looks like a fancy hotel.* She can't resist walking up the stunning black marble stairs to the business offices. *What a beautiful hospital to work in.*

She knocks on the office door. Carol, an American from the Admitting Department, greets her and takes her on a tour of this magnificent hospital, "The most modern medical facility in the world, it has the latest technology and expert professional staff from many countries. Ex-patriots and even Bedouin are now taken care of here." Carol proudly tells her, "You will find it a pleasure to work in this hospital's admitting department. We will work together."

Spending her first day with Carol, Lilli feels another life is beginning for her after so many years here.

At five o'clock, a serious-looking boss, Administrator Faisal, welcomes her, "I hope you had a good introduction to our King's Hospital."

"I love it here and am so excited to begin. Carol was so helpful. My first day was great."

He motions Lilli to follow him. He sits on a lobby chair and beckons her to sit opposite him.

Looking sadly sober, he whispers, "Lilli, I am so sorry to have to be the bearer of bad news, Especially on your first day here." His head lowers and she sees tears forming in his dark eyes.

"I've just received word that Saudia flight 22 crashed into the Gulf of Suez. It happened just minutes before its Cairo landing."

"No, no, no! How can this be? My Frank?" Tears roll down her cheeks, "Are they sure, are there any survivors? I can't believe this. My Frank, my only love." Her hands cover her face.

"So far, no survivors that we know of. They did say, there was a Pakistani on board with a tea-making butane burner whom they suspect might have been a terrorist. The explosion was heard with a big splash just before the plane approached the runway. Important dignitaries from Europe and the West visiting in Aramco were also on board returning to their home country with a stopover for an international meeting in Cairo."

"What will I do without Frank? He must be alive. Was Tariq Rashudi the pilot?"

"No, he is still on the ground here in the city. But he must be nervous about this, if he knows yet. I will call him and Saleh abu Bayatri now. Lilli, I know you will want to fly home. Nancy can help you make arrangements, okay? You know we want you back. The law here says, you can't work at the hospital without a work visa if you don't have a husband here, so you must have a work visa. I can help you with that. Kings Hospital will be your new employer so I will tell travel agent, Mustafa, to obtain a work visa for you."

"Lilli, I can't express how saddened Nancy and I are about our dear friend, Frank. He was like a brother, a good man. I know how sad you feel. We will miss him. But, we want you to stay here. Nancy would be lost without you. Let me get Saud to drive you to your villa and I will call Nancy to come help you."

"Thank you so much, Faisal. I must have time to think. May I use the hospital phone to notify my parents and Frank's?"

"Absolutely. Come into my office."

Salah abu Bayatri calls Faisal's office with sincere condolences for Lilli. Saud drives Lilli home. *This is surreal, unbelievable. How can I stay here without Frank? Do I really want to return? I know there are nurses and teachers here without husbands. Dear me, what to do?*

Thirty minutes later, a knock on the door. Nancy, teary-eyed, offers her sympathy with hugs. "Faisal called me. I can't believe it. I'll help you pack."

At seven, Faisal arrives. He consoles a weeping Lilli and Nancy, "We'll get you out of here as soon as possible. Tomorrow, Mustafa will return your passport stamped with an exit visa and your plane tickets. A hospital return work visa will be mailed to you in the states. You will be an official hospital employee. I am in the royal family, so they won't refuse me. Plan on leaving in three days. I'll try to get a direct flight into New York from Dhahran and then to Melbourne Beach, Florida so your parents will know when to expect you."

I am not sure I will return, she speculates.

Finally with her exit visa, Lilli is able to leave the country on the third day. After a long, exhausting flight, she arrives in Melbourne. Her parents meet her with hugs and kisses. *Funerals are always sad and this one without a body is no exception.*

Her dad comments, "Frank, a very successful fifty two year old man, still had a grand future before him. Such a pity."

The week after the funeral, she discusses her future with her parents.

"I must make a difficult decision. Either work in a booming modern country or stay in Florida.

I do have to return to collect our belongings, but in my heart of hearts, if given the opportunity, I want to stay there just a while longer." *I love my new found country and friends.*

"Mom and Dad, living there is so comfortable. Only a few relics of old Riyadh are still in existence side by side within the new city. There are modern schools and universities for women to get a higher education, women-only businesses and banks owned by women, and large hospitals. I will be working in a beautiful medical facility.

Still, no pork to eat, alcohol forbidden, women must cover up; but there are shopping malls, fancy stores, fast food and good restaurants, beautiful buildings, homes, modern streets, handsome hotels. Movie theaters are outlawed, but women are Master of Ceremonies of women only TV shows. They can't drive yet, but their life has changed immensely. I am proud Frank and I were part of the transition into the almost 21st century. The country still is not perfect for women, but it has improved immensely. And I have wonderful special friends. I will go back."

"Okay, sweetheart, we are fine here and we will look forward to your visits. We love you."

Faisal calls and he is in total agreement with Lilli's return, "Nancy will be so happy you are returning. Fatima will also be thrilled. I'll mail your ticket today for your return next month."

"I did receive my work visa, Faisal. I am honored and happy that you did this for me. I would love to return home."

"Great news! Next month, we will meet you at the airport, so look for us. Your new job in Audio Visual awaits you. And Lilli, whenever you need a driver in the future, phone Nancy and Saud will take you. *"Fi Amen'Allah*, Go with God, Lilli."

"*Shukhran* ,Thank you, Faisal. *Insha'allah*, God willing, I will be with my family soon."

~ 40 ~
The Return

Faisal moves Lilli from Frank's villa to a hospital condo near the hospital campus. She packs her clothes, including Frank's numerous red, white and blue socks. *These were his epitaph. They will always remind me of him.* "Where are you, my socks?" she cries out loud.

A first floor, lovely little place, just the right size for her. She can walk to work but, being a Female alone, it is not proper. A daily bus stops for all women employees. *At least I can sit up front in this hospital bus. Women are permitted to ride bicycles, too, but must be covered up. Soon we will be driving, God willing.*

One of her first visitors is Captain Rashudi with kind words. Nancy becomes her most frequent companion and closest confidant; but sweet Fatima, Abdulla's wife, is her dearest sister. Lilli is invited to many parties by both. Her life outside of work is busy. After six months, she is still liking life in this country, but not as well as before with her Frank.

Much to her surprise and delight, Capt. Rashudi, now Tariq, begins stopping by late in the evening when he returns from flying.

The visits become more and more frequent . . . a knock three times on her door and she knows who it is. He stays into the night, watching T.V. Lilli is becoming more and more attracted to Tariq Rashudi. She feels he is also smitten with her, big time. She needs male companionship, but knows he is married.

"Lilli, I know you are aware of how much I really like you. I want you to know that I am obtaining a divorce from my wife because of my feelings. I have had a deep affection for you ever since you boarded my plane years ago. I thought it might go away with time, but it has not."

"Tariq, I have had similar feelings for you since that time, too. But you know, here we cannot even be friends, me a Christian and you a married Muslim. If anyone were to find out, I would be sent home or worse, jailed or stoned. You would be excommunicated or jailed."

"Right, so I wonder if you would like to travel when I travel. I will pay your air fare, hotel expenses and dining. Mustafa in the Travel Agency will not say anything, I am positive. We can meet in different countries. My flights are all international and I attend many business meetings in different countries. You work two days a week, Lilli, so that leaves extra open days. We can travel during a week that you would be free for a few days."

"Yes, that would work and the contract rules say that all hospital employees also receive a week off every four months to leave this desert land, breathe some less sandy air and travel to parts unknown, if they desire."

"Will you join me in this adventure, Lilli?"

"Oh Tariq, yes, I would love to. It truly sounds very exciting and you already know I am an adventurous and curious woman. But you must promise you are divorced. Show me the papers."

"But, Lilli, there are no divorce papers involved like in the west. A man only has to tell his wife in front of two male witnesses, 'I divorce you, I divorce you, I divorce you.' three times.

But, I still have to support her for the rest of her life. She will live in a nice home with my mother. Our children are married now so they are on their own."

Yes, Lilli thought, *and the poor woman cannot contest your decision without a plausible reason. Divorced, he gets custody of the children when they reach age nine and he can take three more wives if he can support them or he can have a concubine with unmarried women. We in the west call them mistresses. This helps populate the kingdom. But, I have my feet on the ground and know this culture pretty well now. I accept that Muslim women are like slaves to men, but I can't resist this handsome man or his invitation. I will never be a Muslim woman or wife. So, I will enjoy the passing moments in this land and Tariq's generous paid travel expenses for now.*

"Tariq, I am anxious to join you in this adventure, *Insha'allah,* God willing."

"I am obsessed with you and only you, my dear beautiful Lilli. I will divorce my wife soon."

Tariq hugs Lilli for the first time. His strong muscular arms thrill her very being. The osculation lasts a long while and neither want it to end. But end it must for Tariq Rashudi is still a married man. Lilli's principles are strong on this front . . . never a partner to adultery or infidelity. Marriage is a must before sexual intercourse or fornication. Rashudi doesn't know . . . yet. *Stay strong, Lilli,* she tells herself.

"Oh, by the way, Lilli, I found out more about Frank's plane crash. Two hundred eighty passengers were on board when it crashed in Sea. Doors wouldn't open because the plane did not depressurize during descent . . . everyone died in their seat before hitting the water. The fire on board was fed by dropping oxygen masks caused by a gas tea-making machine. Such a tragedy,

Lilli. A few bodies were found floating in the Gulf of Aqaba."

"I do miss my sweet husband." *But, I am glad Tariq can be a friend.*

One day, a neighbor drops by with a Canary bird on a perch in a lovely cage. "From the Canary Islands Lilli, would you like it? We are leaving for home in England. I can't take her."

"Oh, how nice. I would enjoy having her. Being without Frank is lonely. *Shukran,* thanks."

The fluffy yellow bird spends its days chirping, singing and twittering from morning till night.

"You are a delight and make me so happy, Goldie."

By the end of the day, a tired bird flies to the top perch of its fancy home, pulls one leg up under her body, the other leg holds tightly on. Turning her head, she buries her beak under back wing feathers and closes drooping eyelids over black beady eyes till *bukra,* tomorrow.

A few weeks later, Tariq visits with a beautiful desert Lynx in his arms. He carries a bag of cat food, "Lilli, I think you need an everyday companion. This cat will make you happy." He sees Lilli flashing her killer of a smile. He melts. "Driver Saud found it in the desert and offers to take care of her when you leave on vacations, etc. What do you think?"

"Seems like you have it all arranged, so how can I say no. I love animals. Sadly, I had to give my saluki away. Come here my Cleopatra." Cuddling the large yellow cat, "You can sleep with me. Thank you, Tariq. This feels like my real home now that I have Cleopatra."

'Meow, meow,' Cleopatra's voice is shrill, saying good-bye to Tariq. Her unusual ears have exceptionally long tufts of hair that stand straight up like an exclamation point.

"I hope you and Goldie get along," Lilli tells her new pet.

~41~

A Romance Begins

Travel agent Mustafa, drops off round trip tickets for a stay of four days in Istanbul, Turkey, departure in four weeks. "You will be staying in a world class hotel. I will take you to the airport."

"*Shukran*. Thank you very much, Mustafa. Do you miss Afghanistan?

"*Afwan* welcome. No, my wife and I bought a home in Turkey. I travel back and forth. She and the kids reside there year round. By the way, the Hajis from Afghanistan have stopped at the Carpet Suq on the road to Dhahran as usual. They are traveling to Mecca and are selling beautiful Afghani carpets to help pay their way. If you are interested, go visit the site."

"I think I will call Fatima. She might like to do that."

Lilli thinks about Tariq's generosity. He is a proud handsome man—strong, virile and sure of himself. He seems to have a gentle loving nature, but masks his love because of his Arab heritage. Love is always hidden in Islamic culture, never exposed to the outside world or even family. She knows this has to be the case while here, but she is anxious to see if this aspect of Capt. Rashudi changes when visiting another culture and country. Time will tell in four weeks.

She will get an inkling in Istanbul. Right now, in this country, she feels worlds apart from him. His family are Sunni orthodox believers of Islam. She hopes Tariq may be more of the Baha'i sect of Islam . . . believing men and women are created equal. Many Farsi speaking Baha'i have had to flee Iran and the Middle East because some of these areas are governed by strict radical Islamist dictators. These Baha'i believers are constantly being persecuted. Lilli feels Tariq has assimilated much of our western culture from his Chemical Engineering Studies at Mass. Institute of Technology. Hopefully he does not follow the strict Wahabi sect of Saudi Islam . . . maybe he is more moderate in his belief of Sharia law and women's freedoms. *I will explore his beliefs with diligence. I need to know, I must know.*

Lilli answers the phone, "Hi, can you go to lunch tomorrow?" asks Nancy.

"Love to."

Nancy and driver Saud arrive. The ladies, dressed in their black abaya cloak. Heads covered with gauze scarves are a bit warm. It is late August and the temperature is a hot, dry 130 degrees. They have water bottles and salt tablets.

"*Marhaba,(hello)* Saud," Lilli acknowledges this Sudanese gentle man and driver whom she likes and respects.

"Marhabtain, *(hello to you)*" he replies.

On the way downtown, Nancy proudly comments, "The many new restaurants are phenomenal, the hotels beautiful and the diverse building architecture is out of this world, don't you think so, Lilli?"

"Yes, and all the main streets are now four lanes, back streets are no longer mud roads, the airport is ultra-modern, beautiful buildings are everywhere . . . Security police guard the numerous gorgious shopping malls and thankfully women are no longer harassed by those perverted men roaming the streets and markets. What a relief."

"Who would have expected that this poor third world country could grow so rich in a span of twenty-five plus years. A beautiful city now, but more changes for the better are still ahead. Big credit goes to Aramco oil discovery in 1964, American, English, German and other foreign personnel temporarily working in a country needing to modernize," Lilli says.

"Saudi goal is to remain uncompromising by not drastically changing the basic dogma of Sharia law and Islam. They have successfully trained citizens so the country has become more self-sufficient and independent," Nancy explains. "We are almost there, one hundred percent."

She continues, "Even after all these years, in some areas, women aren't treated as equals. A Muslim woman still can't fly alone without a man's permission, even though I can as an American citizen and Faisal always permits me. Our young girls cannot be taught in person by a male teacher. Those lectures are via video conferencing. But soon, we will have a co-ed university where men and women can study together. And more women are teachers and doctors now. Entertaining with mixed sexes is still taboo, marriages are arranged and a Saudi Muslim woman cannot marry a non-Saudi. But, female genital cutting is rare now, thank goodness."

"And you still must totally cover up, even in the summer desert heat. Phew! But hopefully good changes are coming soon, Nancy."

"Well, we are now allowed to go into some restaurants with our girlfriends without a man but we must be segregated from the male customers. We can shop by ourselves in the huge women's malls. And the best is the minimum age for our daughter's consummation of marriage will be age 17 now instead of 9. But, there is still necessary progress needed and that means, among other freedoms, being allowed to name our children whatever name we want, wear modest clothes without having to cover up totally and lastly, to be able to drive a car. This car business is a must. That time is near, ma sha'allah, my God willing."

"Nancy, last week I read about several women arrested for driving. What courage. They are in jail now. I wonder for how long? Most Saudi gals I know who vacation and shop in the west, return desiring some of the west's freedoms for themselves. I can't blame them, can you?"

"Not at all, Lilli. Being a second class citizen is not fun. I love visiting our home in America, just to feel its freedom. I pray it never changes. With my dual citizenship, I still vote in Arizona via absentee ballot. Faisal never complains. I drive anywhere I want in America."

"*Waguf hena*, stop here, Saud. This is one of the new restaurants. The food is excellent."

"Wonderful. I love going to new places," Lilli voices her excitement.

The ambiance in here is delightful, she notices.

"*Ahlan,* welcome." The waiter greets the two beautiful ladies in Arab dress, leads them to a table in the "Women Only" back room that is not quite as nice as the main dining area though.

Lilli responds, "*Ahlan wa sahlan,* welcome."

They look over the 'no pork in this country' menu and both decide on grilled "*samak*" (fish). Nancy places the orders, "*Min fadhlak yibli wa sadiki, samak, ruz, khass wa tomat, Please bring us fish, rice, lettuce and tomatoes. Wa itnayn shai, And two teas.*"

After the meal, Nancy asks the waiter for "*as-cream*". The two share a dish of ice cream.

"*Atnil hisab min fadhlek,*" Nancy instructs. "Bring me the bill, please."

On the way home Nancy stops by the Hajj Carpet Suq. Each purchase a beautiful red Afghan carpet. "Lilli, we've helped pay the way for these poor folks to make their once-in-a life time religious journey to Mecca and perform the *Hajj* as the Koran says we must do."

"Al 'Hamdu 'illah, Thanks be to God. I am delighted with my carpets. Will this land ever cease making me happy? I hope not. And you, my dear Nancy, are one who makes me the happiest. I love you, sweet friend. *Shukran,* Thank you for everything you do."

At home, Lilli's thoughts turn to Nancy . . . a wonderful human being. How could a woman live in this Wahabi ultra conservative country, married to a Saudi? She must really love him and him her, to provide her with a home in the USA so she can "go home" when she wants. That is her salvation. All marriages should be like this.

All of a sudden, she hears what sounds like a powerful loud crash echoing throughout her condo. She runs into the kitchen and there on the floor, Goldie's bird cage lies on its side, empty, the door flung open. Long, bright lemon-colored feathers are strewn everywhere, some still floating in the air down to the floor. Suddenly a little yellow flash zooms past Lilli with Cleopatra in hot pursuit of the little bird's flight, reaching up to claw at the canary's tail feathers.

"Cleopatra, stop!" After much chasing, she finally catches the precious bird, picking her up to cuddle. Goldie, is panting, her little heart beating fast, her mouth wide open.

"But, wait a minute, where are your tail feathers? Goldie, your tail feathers are gone!"

Cat Cleopatra crouching, teeth grinding and tail heavily beating on the floor, is ready for a final attack which was thwarted. "Insha'allah," *(God willed it)* Lilli cheerfully yells with relief.

Months pass. Not until her feathers begin growing back does

Goldie sings her repertoire of beautiful melodies again when Lilli turns on the water faucet as she used to.

"Goldie, you had a close call, my little bird. I am pleased you are singing once more. You make me happy every day. I've locked your cage door, so that can never happen again."

～42～

Istanbul, Turkey

Lilli boards Saudia flight 065 to Istanbul. Tariq Rashudi is the pilot.

"Ahlan wasah'lan . . . Welcome!" a familiar deep voice resonates from the intercom.

"Our traditional Arabic hospitality welcomes you on board with open hands. Delicious Arabic coffee and sweet dates await, just for your pleasure."

Tariq has such nice manners. I am totally impressed. I am to take a taxi to the Buyuk Hilton Hotel. I wonder how long before he will join me. I know he has a meeting of some sort.

The plane inside is a cloud of smoke from people puffing away on cigarettes. She can hardly breathe. The gentleman in front of her nervously rocks and rolls, up and down in his seat, like he's sitting on a rocking chair. So obviously nervous, his ears, neck and bald head are totally green. *A good thing the flight will not take long,* Lilli thought. *Poor fellow is in a panic.*

After a very bumpy landing in a thunder storm with flashes of lightening, a relieved Lilli finds her suitcase, rushes to flag a taxi. Most people speak English in Istanbul so no problem with the driver understanding her directions.

checks in. Sitting in a beautiful room,
q, she is hungry. She orders a bowl of
(lentil soup). *Delicious!*
sist on dinner at some exclusive restaurant

At four o'clock, a knock on the door awakens her from her nap. A very tight and warm hug, a long passionate kiss from a handsome man, brightens her spirit.

"Where have you been? I thought you'd be here earlier," she whispers, brushing his hair with her hand, staring lovingly into keen dark brown eyes that are making her melt.

"Beautiful lady, I know. I missed you more than life, but Gumar, Mustafa and I had an important meeting downstairs. I am sorry it took so long. Let's go to a restaurant in the city. I am famished, my darling. Let me take my shower right now and change clothes. Will you join me . . . in the shower, that is?"

Oh, no! I must stay strong, but I feel weak. "Of course, my love." *She feels he was quickly getting ready for love. This is totally against my morals, she thought. But I can't resist. Oh, dear, it's been so long.*

<hr>

They had a fantastic Turkish meal of   *Kuzu dolmasi . . . lamb meat stuffed with rice, raisins and pine kernels and Imam bayildi . . . eggplant with olive oil, tomatoes and onions.*

For desert, a delicious Baklava . . . a sweet stuffed with almonds, walnuts and pistachios.

"I have never had a Baklava as wonderful as this one," comments Lilli.

"Me neither. Okay, now I have a surprise for you, dearest,

because I know you must like music like I do. Let's go to the Opera House in Taksim Square. Would you like that?"

"Oh, Tariq, I can't believe how good you are to me. I'd love that." She hugs and kisses him. "How nice to be where we can show our love to each other," her long-lashed beautiful eyes look up adoringly at him. *I believe I have met someone I can love and who loves me.*

"Yes, my dear. But my heart is always filled with love for you everywhere. I have loved you secretly all these many years–since you were on that plane in '74. I have never seen one so gorgeous and desirable. *Mahabbi min kul kalbi*–I love you with all my heart."

"Tariq, do you suppose we can get married very soon in the states? Must I become a Muslim? I know it means believer, but I could never be all that Sharia requires. We do, of course, believe in the same God. Only our languages call Him by a different name. Has your divorce become final?"

"Yes, Lilly dear. I said 'I divorce you' three times to my wife in front of two male witnesses. But if we marry and stay in Saudi Arabia, you must become a Muslim. Your freedom will disappear. I think it best for us to have a home for you in America and keep it a secret."

He continues, "You know, no one knows I am of the Ba'Hai sect of Islam. We believe women are equal. If the Department of Justice found out I was Ba'Hai, I might be sent out of country.

Please, never tell anyone, Lilli."

"Of course, you have my promise on that, my darling."

"I am serious when I say, I would never like to see your beautiful face and body forever covered with a black abaya or chador cloak . . . like a bag from head to foot. I never approved of women being treated as third class humans and abused like what happens here. If you became a Muslim, you would have to submit to Sharia for women. You know, in Arabic, Islam means total submission to Allah, but women surrender everything to their men."

"You are so right, I could never succumb to that, as much as I love you, Tariq. And I do respect you for watching out for me in this way."

"I don't expect an intelligent American woman like you, to want to do any of these radical, Islamic customs and become a lesser human being. If the Ulema authorities (strict religious men) found out I was dating you in Saudi, I might be excommunicated, you might be jailed . . . lucky if they only sent you out of the country. A Muslim woman, would be stoned to death, if the man was married to another women. You know, sharia law is not freedom . . . more like socialism or fascism. We have an archaic totalitarian philosophy here. I am hopeful things will change soon."

Changing this confusing subject, "Aieda was just beautiful. I am so surprised to find this kind of entertainment in a mostly Muslim country. Its Christian history makes the difference, I think," Lilli comments.

"I know, but I have a feeling the Middle East is radicalizing. We will see what the future brings, my dear. Let's go back to the hotel. Tomorrow, we will all tour this interesting city, where Mustafa has a home. His wife lives here full time with their kids. The next day we will visit historic Ephesus to the south. The day after that, I have another meeting with the fellows and you will return to Riyadh. You and I can't arrive in Riyadh together so you must fly home before me."

~43~
Touring a City

The next morning, Lilli, Tariq and his friends, spend a few hours learning about the city on a tour bus with a guide and several tourists. Lilli feels uncomfortable being with three men.

The guide hands out maps. He begins with some history. "Istanbul was first known as Byzantium; then as Constantinople, the Roman creation built on seven hills by a Christian Emperor Constantine in 324 A.D. Today's Istanbul became the heart of the Ottoman Muslim Empire for 500 years . . . until after World War I in 1917 . . . when the Ottoman Turks, fighting with Germany, lost the battle against the Allies. Turkey was then given to Greece. In 1923, Turkey's independence was won under Mustafa Kemal Attaturk, the first president of the Republic of Turkey that exists today."

"How interesting. What a panorama of mosques and minarets silhouetting the skyline," comments Lilli, totally intrigued. The guys all agree.

"Istanbul is ninety-eight percent Muslim. Listen! Hear the echoes throughout the city. The "muezzins" are calling the faithful to noon "salaat" prayer. This is the second prayer of today. I will stop here." He unrolls his prayer carpet, places it on the ground facing southeast towards Mecca, prostrating himself, repeating prayers. The guys and a couple of Muslims put their carpets on the ground and pray too.

After prayers, the guide continues driving. "This is a city divided by water and connected by four bridges. The Bosphorous Strait separates the Continent of Asia from that of Europe . . . it empties into the Black Sea to the north and the Sea of Marmara to the south. Part of Istanbul is on the Asian side of Turkey, part on the European side."

"A further separation by another river, the Halic (or Golden Horn), divides the old and new cities on the European side. The southern banks of the old city rise up from the Sea of Marmara. The Asian side of Turkey is to the east of here. It is a little complicated."

"With water everywhere, no wonder the views are so spectacular," Lilli comments to a nodding Tariq.

"We are stopping here so you can see the magnificent Topkapi Palace perched atop that huge rock overlooking the sparkling waters of the Bosporous and Golden Horn that connect the Black Sea and the Sea of Marmara."

"I've heard of this palace," Lilli mused.

"This is one of the world's richest museums. It houses the famous 86 carat pear-cut Kasikci or "spoon makers" diamond along with many other priceless jewels and relics from the Prophet Mohammed era."

"Oh, my! This is just breathtaking, too!" Lilli exclaims. "What an interesting city."

"Another masterpiece of Turkish architecture, the beautiful Blue Mosque, is over there. So called by Europeans because the interior walls are of gorgeous Iznik china tiles. These tiles are predominately subtle blues, greens, interspersed with exquisite shades of red and white. Creative, artistic floral and tree designs predominate, leaving a beautiful lasting 'blue' impression, thus the name "Blue Mosque".

Lilli asks, "Why are there only four slender minarets on the main mosque? There are two others on the attached smaller building . . . a total of six. But, the holy mosque in Mecca, has seven minarets?"

"Sultan Ahmet wanted it that way when he had it built. The small building on the western side in front of these two minarets is a library. This mosque is also known to Turks as the Sultan Ahmet Mosque. And true, the holy Mecca mosque does have seven minarets."

They walk around the courtyard before entering huge mosque doors. "I am in awe of such a beautiful, cultural and artistic place," Lilli comments.

"Over there," points the guide, "is the cemetery where they say the sultan, Ahmet I, and his family are buried. One son, Osman II was put to death by the compression of his testicles, the custom of the Ottoman Emperors of that day. His wife, brought into the Harem at age thirteen, was strangled to death in that Harem. Not a pretty history there."

Entering the mosque left Lilli and Tariq stunned.

"This mosque is illuminated by windows placed everywhere. Its brilliance is spectacular."

"Can you believe this beauty, my dear," Tariq whispers in her ear.

A masterpiece thought Lilli. I see bronze work on the courtyard doors and what looks like ivory and mother-of-pearl woodwork. I am so impressed by the Turkish talents. The reflection of gentle blue everywhere is outstanding. Everyone is work of tile art. The subtle color everywhere is mind-boggling. A fantastic city.

On their return to the hotel, "I hope to return to Istanbul

another day. There is so much more to discover. Thank you so much for taking me along, guys. One more day of culture."

"Yes, tomorrow it's Ephesus, south of here," Mustafa adds. "You know, Lilli, you will fly out before us, the next morning."

"The sun is setting now. Let's stay here at the Hilton for some eats and then go to the Grand Bazaar," Tariq suggests.

"You will love shopping at the Bazaar as my wife. She lives here full time," Mustafa adds. "Next time you may meet her. She is visiting her family now, but our home is your home anytime. Omar likes to visit here also."

"Okay guys, we are getting hungry," adds Tariq. "You know, Turkish food is an interesting blend of Greek and Arab cuisine."

Devouring a wonderful Turkish meal of *doner kabob, dolmas, and baklava for desert* was such a treat for Lilli. She bought some *Turkish delight,* a soft transparent sweet with a thumb print hole filled with thick buffalo cream and *Kadafi,* a shredded wheat pastry, to take home.

Leaving the hotel, the taxi heads for the famous *Grand Bazaar* where hawkers and vendors line the streets. They leave the taxi and walk along the streets.

Stopping at one fellow's stand, Mustafa insists, "Lilli, try a taste of this popular drink, *boza.* It's made by fermenting stale bread soaked in water till it becomes sour. Then milk and cinnamon is added. Very popular here."

Lilli took one swallow, "Oh, this is awful, Mustafa. Not for me." The guys laughed at her puckering face. "I'll take some of those roasted nuts from that vendor across the street, though." She and Tariq did just that.

An exploration of the ancient Grand Bazaar in the old city encourages them to bargain for Turkey's famous leather jackets. All five purchase one. Lilli's is a beautiful red.

Walking along the many shops, Lilli spies some unusual paintings like she has never seen before. She questions the salesman behind the counter, "What are these?"

"These are famous Turkish miniature paintings. The style flourished in the 16th century Sultan's era. The most prolific period of Ottoman miniatures, show various aspects of Turkish life with the Islamic Sultans. The pigment used is mostly vegetable with egg white mixed in."

"I thought, under Islam, paintings and photos of figures were taboo," she offers.

"There is not a single word in the Koran against figure painting," he replies.

"These are so colorful and bright, I must have one, this one," Lilli points to one replicating men on horses chasing gazelle and deer. "Beautiful!"

That evening, in their posh Hilton hotel room, she and Tariq spend a lovely romantic and memorable evening. Lilli is beginning to believe this will be her next partner for life.

Marriage is not far away, I think. I wonder how this unique mixed marriage will work. I can never succumb to being a traditional Muslim wife, walking paces behind a husband and leaving behind my Christian beliefs and church. Thank God, Tariq is not radical in his faith, being of the Ba'Hai Islamic sect, so he says. Time will tell, but I love adventures, so this situation may be a tour de force. I do have the strength to give it a try, although I will never live in a Muslim country married to a Muslim man.

Before falling asleep, they hear on local television, 'A plane has been hijacked flying from Istanbul to Ismir. The pilot was shot.'

"Izmir is where we fly tomorrow, Tariq."

"Yes," Tariq answers before turning off the T.V. "We'll be fine, Lilli. Don't worry, please."

~ 44 ~

Ephesus

Rising early the next morning, the four have breakfast in the hotel. A taxi takes them to the airport where they fly south to the town of Ismir. Lilli is very nervous in this small plane.

They disembark as the pilot announces, "From Ismir you can hire a tour guide to the ancient Ionian city of Ephesus. In 2 A.D., it was the Roman capital of Asia and the center of Christianity. The car ride south to Ephesus takes about one and a half hours."

They jump into one of the waiting tour guide car. "Ephesus, please," orders Tariq.

Traveling south, "This countryside is a simple, agrarian peasant lifestyle in contrast to Istanbul's bustling big city," announces the guide. "What you see over there are fields of cotton. Did you know that Turkey's first cotton seeds came from Georgia, U.S.A.? You will also see tobacco, olive, apricot, cherry, peach groves and grape vineyards on the way."

Lilli asks, "Really? You are kidding. Wow! But, who are these women peasants working the fields? They all wear kerchiefs and their dresses are balloon-type pantaloons with blouses and vests."

"They are mostly nomadic Gypsies. Some, tend to grazing

camel herds along the roadway. You will notice buffalo dairy farms dotting the fields, too. Buffalo milk is delicious."

It wasn't long before they exit the car. The guide explains, "The ruins of Ephesus are comparable in magnificence to those of Greece or anywhere. Here are the Roman ruins of the theater where, in 53 A.D., St. Paul preached to the Ephesians against the pagan cult Artemis–the Roman goddess of the hunt, and Diana, goddess of chastity. He converted many from paganism to Christianity, almost like today's growing clash between Muslims and Christians. Evangelist, St. John, also walked here making his mark, wrote his gospel and is buried."

"Okay, lady and gentlemen, let's ride a little more to the summit of *Nightingale Mountain at Panaya Kapulu,*" he continues.

"Lilli, look at this view. It's a panorama of the Aegean Sea," Tariq quietly whispers.

"Breathtaking," Lilli replies, engrossed in what she is seeing. "I knew Turkey had much ancient history."

The guide informs them, "I am one of the few Christians living here. Down there by that huge statue of the *Blessed Virgin Mary* is Nightingale Hill. It leads to a humble Byzantine chapel nestled in that peaceful olive grove. The chapel, now a sanctuary, is said to be the last home of the *Virgin Mary.*"

Continuing their ride to the small town of Selcuk, the guide explains, "This is where, on the edge of the city, lies one of the *seven wonders of the world,* the *Temple of Artemis* built in the time of *Alexander the Great.* At the top of this hill lies *Isa Bey Mosque.* Here is where both the *Citadel and Basilica of St. John* were built by the Byzantine *Emperor Justinian* in the 6th century."

"Incredible, isn't it Tariq?"

Walking through the town center, the guide continues, "The

last place to visit here is *The Great Theater* over there. It is just one of the most interesting sites in Ephesus; there are many more to be seen in this historic city. The final theater construction was in 98–117 A.D. by Emperor Trajan. Parts of the stage and columns are in Doric architectural style and are the only remains. Originally a huge theater, it held 25,000 people."

"Incredible to think of the construction and architecture these ancient people could accomplish . . . mind boggling! These buildings are so important from an archaeological and historical point of view. I also know they were built and rebuilt during the struggle between paganism and Christianity and Islam. It went on for centuries, didn't it," Lilli asks?

"Indeed, you are so right," adds the guide.

"Well, guys, it is time catch our plane back to Istanbul. We must leave now to return another day. There is so much compelling history here that it is hard to walk away. I wish we could stay longer," Tariq announces. "I think you could spend at least a week in Ephesus and not be bored at all."

"Oh, I agree, Tariq. Ephesus exists as an archeologist's dream of ancient history. We must come back soon," Lilli exclaims.

"Our country is not only intriguing but both ancient and modern, like no other country on earth. My wife and children love it here," Mustafa adds.

Jeweler Gumar politely let the guide do his job, but now he adds, "I will definitely pay another visit to Ephesus. When I come to Turkey, it's usually for brief meetings, so my time is limited. In the future, I will make time to visit this ancient Greco-Roman town and the Roman ruins along the Mediterranean Sea."

"I think all of Turkey must be interesting. Istanbul is a very modern city compared to other Muslim countries," Lilly comments.

"Here, most women dress moderately but do not cover their faces. I saw very few abayas. But it certainly has a religious history in its mosques, churches, temples and museums. I feel that Ephesus is where the real Turkey began. I can't wait to discover everything there."

~45~
Return to Riyadh Life

Lilli's plane ride back to Riyadh was smooth, *thank the good Lord,* she mused. When the plane landed it was noon prayer time. Entering her apartment, Frank's socks were still on the chair where she left them, red on top for her fear of flying alert. Since his death, she always rotated their position once a week if indicated. She places white, all is calm back on the top—blue, all in control underneath—with red, danger, be on alert on the bottom. *Just a reminder of poor Frank and it keeps me thinking of him. I do miss him very much.*

Driver Saud arrives at the usual eight thirty. Her day at the hospital is uneventful but always interesting. On her way to the cafeteria, she passes several Saudi women patients. They are covered head to toe in black. Smiling eyes peek out from a gossamer veil. *I wonder how they approach a doctor to be examined covered like that,* she mused.

She meets a nurse and asks, "If the doctor is a male, how is an examination possible?"

The nurse tells her, "Women take their long, loose body-covering *abayas* and under clothing off but their face stays covered with a *hijab*. These are head scarfs with a black thin, delicate face veil.

Their body is naked for the exam, while the face is anonymous. Unreal, but it works for the Muslim women's modesty and culture. They believe face covering is a sign of pure virtue and keeps men away, even doctors. Covering up discourages sinning and is God's will."

"*Shukran,* thank you." She continues her walk down the immaculate hall to the hospital cafeteria.

Just before clocking out for the day, Faisal opens the office door to see if Lilli is still working. "Lilli, Nancy, Fatima, Abdulla and I are heading out to the desert on Friday. Would you like to come?"

An elated Lilli, "Thank you, Faisal. I am delighted to go with you all."

"We are going to head west to Taif near the Hijaz mountain chain again. We will spend the night in the mountains at Taif, so bring a change of clothes. Last time we didn't get to stay in the beautiful Taif hotel. Tariq Rashudi might be able to be there also."

Lilli left the office in a dream state. She was so excited to again do some exploring and discovering on the spice coast of ancient times. Her dreams that night took her on a unique adventure of tomorrow. *Maybe with Tariq, too, maybe?*

She hears sunrise *salaat* and jumps out of bed to ready herself for what she anticipates to be another fascinating desert trip. It had been several years since the last adventure from Jidda to Taif. *A cool November, yet not too cold. Now is the perfect time to explore.*

Faisal, Nancy and Lilli drive to Fatima and Abdulla's villa.

"*Assalamu Aleikum*" Abdulla smiles. "Peace be upon you." Fatima's welcome is a warm "Hi, Lilli and Nancy."

"*Wa'Aleikum Assallam,* And peace to you," Faisal replies.

"*Keif Halik, girls?* How are you?"

"Quais kateer, Fadia. Doing good," Nancy replies.

"Aren't you excited to be on this trip into the desert again . . . escarpments, wadis and the mountains of Taif?" Lilli asks as they travel to the outskirts of the city.

"We are thrilled beyond words to be accompanying our friends once more. We don't travel into the desert anymore since Frank is gone," Abdulla notices the escarpment. "Way over on the right is the Mountainous Escarpment, remember?"

The smooth road reveals mounds of red Rub al-Khali desert sand sculpting the gentle hilly landscape to the left.

"Hey guys, I see several Bedouin camel herds off in the close distance, seemingly headed north." Nancy shares the sighting. "I heard that some Bedouin live a modern life in our cities now; but a few still refuse to leave their ancient, nomadic and free lifestyle in spite of the tempting incentives of the government."

Fatima adds, "I don't blame them, do you? I am certain it is a tough life at times. After centuries, it is the only way they know, living free as the wind, stars, sky. Something to be said for that."

"This land continues to amaze this Amerikee," Lilli smiles. "It is so curiously different . . . beautiful too. She realizes now, there is beauty in everything and everywhere if one has open eyes, and looks deep into their heart. Geologically, this land has everything: mountains, vegetation, artifacts, desert, minerals, animals, ancient history, mild weather and oil. Unreal."

Now close to another large *jebel mountain* rising out of the sands, Faisal pulls off the road as far as is safely possible so as not to get stuck in the sand. He says, "Let's snack and then we can walk to the jebel to see what's new to discover. We haven't searched this one. There may be pictographic, primitive writings and drawings up there. Also a *wadi* is not far away."

Lilli is overwhelmed and delighted. "I hope there are pre-historic *Petroglyph* rock carvings here, too. I've got my black charcoal crayons and paper ready."

"Look what I found again, ladies, my birthstone! A happy glowing bright blue turquoise. Come over here, lots of *fairuz*, (*turquoise*) for you gals. I thought fairuz was only found in Taif," Fatima explains. "Bedouin women believe turquoise is good luck."

The group begins the short walk to the rocky Jebel. Reaching the Jebel base, "How can this be? Pieces of blue and red painted clay pottery here. I know this pottery must be ancient" Lilli continues in amazement. "Let's take photos.

They work their way up pebble paths noticing many caves. "Just think of the ancient people who were here centuries ago," Faisal adds.

Lilli is the first to discover rock carvings and more writings. "Oh my, luck is with us. Just what I have been wanting to find . . . camels, horses, goats, horned animals, palm trees, men with bows and arrows. Ancient inscriptions . . . perhaps these were tombs. Graffiti is everywhere."

She holds her piece of paper tightly to cover several carvings. Running her charcoal over all, "We will have many ancient stories to tell and replicas to frame. We are so lucky."

"I can't believe this is all real," Nancy exclaims for everyone to hear. "Must be where the pilgrim caravans camped out a long time ago."

Back down the rock wall, on the sand, "Hey, here is a pool of water." Abdulla adds. "There are small colorful creatures swimming around."

Lilli runs over. "Oh my gosh! I think these tiny bug-like creatures are Trilobites, extinct for millions of years. We saw Trilobite fossils in the British Museum when we visited there. I bet no one knows they exist here and are alive. We will have to stop by the museum to tell Omar where they are."

"We will, Lilli. Okay, time is up. Let's get going. Not far to go now," Faisal calls out.

Continuing on, "Looks like several Bedouin tents over there. Want to investigate?"

As they get closer, "I hear music of some sort," Lilli excitedly exclaims, "Sounds coming from beating drums and shaking tambourines, I believe."

"Bedu music always salutes the ending of each day. Their music remains un-changed from centuries ago. Sounds that may go back to the dark ages, I'm sure. Let me drive closer. Ah, yes, there are many tents here. "

"I hear loud horns. I see them, I see them. They are huge," Lilli calls out.

"Listen, Lilli. I hear clattering and knocking of thunderous drums, clanging cymbals, and horns blowing. The rhythm resembles American Jazz." Nancy is excited.

As they close in on the tents, they see mustached Bedouin clapping and singing, sitting in a semi-circle in front of the main majlis (tent), dressed in brownish thobes and different colored ghutras. Women in black are singing and dancing to the music, up and down, round and round.

The travelers stop to watch. Women quickly cover their faces and run into the tents. The squatting men beckon and wave. They continue making music, some dancing and clapping.

Visible are four loud, large tamborene-type drums struck by hand, accompanied by several big pipe-like horns. A few Bedu are working the strings of an Oud guitar while singing. Others are pounding on drums with sticks, lifting them high over their heads, rising on their haunches, bending over, returning to the ground—

boom, boom, clapping and bowing in rhythm, sitting, rising again, playing, bending. The singing is in exact unison with the music. The men with horns dance and blow. *"What a sight!"*

Abdulla comments, "Music is an integral part of Arab worlds. This is a traditional Bedouin musical performance. We don't have time to stay, darkness will soon settle in, but I am sure these Bedu would warmly welcome us with *shahi* tea and treats, if we drove closer to their tents."

Waves of good-bye with a cacophony of ancient musical sounds sailing through the air sends them back to the main road. "A memorable event to stay in my soul forever," Lilli says.

The ride to Taif is still thrilling and without incident as it was years ago. The hotel is beautiful. Tariq is waiting for them. His eyes remain on Lilli all evening. They have separate rooms, but late that night, he knocks softly on her door. The two spend a few hours talking and loving. Tariq leaves for Jidda early the next morning before anyone is awake. "I have an afternoon flight to Lebanon for a meeting."

Their adventure to Taif is over. Returning to Riyadh is not without some nervous and scary moments. About twenty miles outside the city, Faisal recognizes a wind storm heading their way in the not too far distance. The rolling light brown sand, darkish at the underside, is rapidly moving. The dusty, curly mass of sand about to reach them is traveling close to the desert ground, covering the road. Nothing is seen behind it. Strikes of lightening light up its progress.

"I think we are in trouble, gang. *Shmaali's* always build up in mid-afternoon. Look up ahead. Looks like a *windy sand storm*, a "*shmaali*", traveling fast. We are headed directly east and into it. I am going to pull over or if I can find a desert road that heads north, I'll take it," Faisal nervously announces.

There is no road other than the road they are on, so Faisal pulls
as far over to the edge with one side of the car wheels remaining on
the asphalt. With calm instructions . . . "I will turn off the air con-
ditioning so outside air doesn't enter. Block your eyes and mouth
with your clothing and try not to breath fast. It will be over in a
short time, *Insha'allah.*"

A scary situation, thought Lilli, as the growling wind and sand
turn brownish-red, whipping reddish circles of clouds, enveloping
the car. Inside, a breath of air becomes thick and sandy. And then,
flashes of lightening brighten the landscape.

Finally, lightening disappears, sand and wind still make circles
as darkness ensues.

"This is as if the lights of the earth have been turned off,"
Nancy quietly comments.

*A car with occupants immersed in the middle of an isolated desert
sand storm is like being caught in a dangerous northern winter snow
storm, only worse,* Lilli surmises.

Breathing becomes hard and dangerous. Thankfully the scary
predicament only lasts a few minutes. The rotating sand mass leaves
the coughing group and is off, heading north.

"*Alhamdu Lillah,* praise to God! *Taiyib,* good. "Everyone okay?
You've had a not unusual desert experience. I knew *Allah* would
take care of us. Now, let's get on home . . . if the car will start,
Insha'allah, God willing. "It did start up. Faisal elicits a sigh of relief.

Lilli breathes deeply and is thankful to be home with her
photos and archeological rubbings. "*Tesbah Ala Kheir,* good night.
Ma'a as-salama, good-bye everyone. *Allah yubarik fikum,* God bless
you, Faisal and Nancy for taking us on this journey."

*Not many people could enjoy an experience like this when tourists
are not allowed into this kingdom—neither are those without work visas*

or Jews. I am one lucky lady to have such friends and been happily living here for over twenty-five years. Thank you God—shukran Allah.

The phone rings. It is Tariq, "Sorry I couldn't make that last desert journey. But Lilli, I have a ticket for you to come to Salzburg, Austria with me next week. Will you join me? I have some meetings. We have reservations at the Park Maribell Hotel. I will meet you there in the lobby. Love you, darling."

"This will be a special Christmas for me. How nice, Tariq. I'll be there. Love you, too."

Spending Christmas in a Christian city that I never visited before? How wonderful! Most of past Christmases have been in the states.

⸺ ⸺

She recalls their first Christmas in Riyadh in 1974 as the most memorable. Sitting with Frank on a blanket out in the desert on Christmas Eve, they spied a brilliant star shining. It was more brilliant than any of the other heavenly bodies. They just knew it must be the star over Bethlehem. It was here that they felt they were the closest they had ever been to the land of the baby Jesus' birth. Just by sitting, gazing skyward to the west and praying on a blanket in the desert sands, they felt mesmerized. Jesus was alive . . . here . . . at that moment in this Middle Eastern world where Christianity and all religions had burst forth centuries ago. Who could have dreamed this miraculous heavenly sensation would occur in this country, this foreign desert?

~46~
Christmas 2000 Miracle

As she has always done in previous years, Lilli cuts a leafless tree branch. She covers it with homemade ribbons of red, gold and green. Several of Frank's socks hang on every branch. It's been over a year since Frank's death. She places her Christmas tree in a bowl of water. Even though, Christmas trees, ornaments, and bibles are frowned upon here, she feels better being able to enjoy thinking about Frank and Christmas when she sits alone in the evenings at this Christian time of year, in this desert land that is so close to where Jesus was born and preached.

Her day-before-Christmas Eve flight to Austria circles on its final approach to Salzburg, Austria. She absorbs the clear view of gently rolling hills surrounding this Baroque city, home of Mozart and The Sound of Music. An overlay of fresh, snow covers the countryside, reflecting opalescent from the sunny day's light. Tall Evergreens carry their heavy white burden with grace and beauty. The many Gothic and Romanesque church domes and spires reaching towards the heavens present a toy-like impression of an Old Town. *I haven't seen snow in years.*

Salzburg, the fourth-largest city in Austria is the most beautiful and picturesque, she sighs. The icy Salzach River snakes its way through the city, dividing Old Town from New Town. It leisurely meanders, emptying into the Blue Danube and finally the Black Sea, the borders of which edge Turkey and Russia.

Arriving the day after Tariq and friends . . . *How nice that the guys chose this city at Christmas time for their meeting.*

Disembarking, she hears chimes from many church bells resounding throughout the countryside…musical variations of tones, some high pitched, some low pitched, a few in unison. *This is like a fairyland–a city of music is mine to have fun unfolding its secrets.*

Collecting her thoughts, *today's snow and crispy fresh cold air suppresses the sun's warmth . . . quite different from living beside the massive, Rub Al Khali desert for so many years. The seasons, forest green pines and colorful winter flowers are very sparse in the desert, but are taken for granted here, I'll bet. But, most of all, I really appreciate being in a Christian atmosphere. Christmas trees are abundant even at the airport. I have missed all this beauty. It makes me homesick for my America.*

After checking into the Park Maribell Hotel situated beside the Maribell Palace, she notices how squeaky clean their room is. It overlooks gardens resembling a winter fairyland. A sparkling crystal carpet covers the ground, icicles cling to every tree branch. Opening a window ushers in below zero, dry cold and nippy air that swirls around the room . . . a perfect Christmas ambiance.

Early afternoon is still sunny. Feeling safe here with map in hand, she decides to walk through New Town into Old Town. Strolling across the Salzach River Bridge, the ancient character of Old Town comes to life. The atmosphere totally changes from modern to old.

The baroque Old Town's narrow streets are almost without cars. Lining the cobblestone streets are cute specialty shops, elaborately decorated, windows exuding holiday flair. Christmas carolers singing acappella, their songs overflowing into and around the town, inundating people's hearts with pure joy. An unexpected aroma of chestnuts roasting wafts through the air, around corners, up and down roads and town squares. The character of this town is unique, its elegance has endured. The cold wind is beginning to "bite" just as Lilli spies some evergreen Christmas trees and a horse drawn buggy nearby.

She beckons to the warmly attired rosy-faced driver after buying her chosen tree. Deftly, the carriage driver lifts the tree up onto the rear of his buggy. She slides into the back bench-seat with his help. He covers her with a heavy red and green checked woolen blanket. In no time at all, the sleigh bells jingle-jangle, the blanketed horses gallop. They are on their way, crossing over the icing Salzach River Bridge to the hotel Maribell. The cold day is beautiful.

A setting sun shines its remaining warmth on large white Geese huddling together on benches lining the river bank. *Poor birds trying to keep warm.*

The gallant driver carries the tree up to her suite, placing it in a corner. Lilli attaches a gingerbread angel she purchased to the tree top. The Christmas spirit fills her aching heart. Suddenly she wishes she was back home in Florida with Frank and family.

I don't need any gifts. I know I am blessed in many ways. Including having Tariq now. He is so generous to pay for my trip here. Many Christmases were spent in Florida. This city reminds me of New England in my younger days.

While waiting for Tariq, she turns on the radio, listens to caroling and sings along with them. She fall asleep. A knock on the door awakens her. Tariq rushes in and is astonished to see the tree. "I see, we are celebrating Christmas, my dearest."

"Do you mind, Tariq?"

"I love you, so whatever your wish is, it's mine also. Always remember that."

They spent a few romantic hours that night. The next day, Christmas Eve day, they did a tourist tour early, including attending a melodic Glokenspiel Chimes Christmas concert. Later, a delightful Mozart, Hayden and Shubert chamber concert at the "Salzburger Schloss Konzerte." It reminded them both that Salzburg is the birthplace and the home of Wolfgang Amadeus Mozart.

They then walk to Old Town. They investigate Mozart's home and learned he died at the age of 35 to be buried in a pauper's grave in Vienna. Mozart's life is celebrated yearly with Festivals and performances at the Mozart University of Music and Dramatic Arts. After seeing his piano, they saunter up and down the stone streets stopping at one of the sidewalk cafes for a cup of Viennese coffee.

"So quaint and friendly here, Tariq. I like it very much."

A visit to the famous Von Trapp family home, known from the movie, 'The Sound of Music' is interesting. But the last thrill that day was a sled ride down a hill close to their hotel.

"Seems the Austrian sled is steered by a person's two feet on the snow. Be careful, my dear." Never having steered this unusual sled, Lilli almost ran into a tree at the bottom of the hill, but she veered away just in time.

"Not like our New England sleds," she commented to Tariq, who had never been sledding in his life. "But it is fun."

"Yeah, but I prefer riding a camel," he laughed.

That evening, Christmas Eve, they dress warmly with scarf, mittens and snow boots for the walk once more across the bridge. Lilli anticipates attending a midnight mass in a four hundred year old cathedral. The air is cold and fresh. The brilliance of the stars in the clear sky is incredible. The bridge lampposts shine ethereally. The path is well illuminated as they follow the lights toward the ancient church's domes and spires.

Entering the old cathedral they notice beautiful wood floors dulled from the promenade of millions of feet traversing its spaces over the centuries. The rich mellow oak pews are musty and dark. A high altar looms ahead. Hanging full center is a painting of the resurrection of Jesus.

"So moving and realistic," Lilli tells Tariq. "It gives me goose bumps."

Quietly sitting and contemplating the magnificence of this 17th century architectural monument to God, Lilli feels a deep *raison d'etre,* reason for being here. These spiritual edifices and the inclination to pray is overwhelming.

Suddenly the organ loudly reverberates throughout every space. A Mozart mass is about to begin. Cello, viola, violin and organ are in harmony with a choir of heavenly German voices echoing the identical mass as it was played and sung two hundred years ago in this very same place of worship.

"Like our first desert Christmas, I feel as close to heaven as I ever will while on this earth. This experience is so moving," she whispers to Tariq. "I think a miracle is going to happen tonight."

"Beautiful girl, I don't know what to say or not say. Christianity and churches are not my thing. I just love you because you are you."

When the inspirational Mass is over, angelic voices envelope the atmosphere as people slowly begin to exit. From the choir loft comes a sensational rendition of "Silent Night" in English, accompanied by a deftly plucked version on a modern electric guitar. People begin to softly sing along, as they slowly move up the aisles to exit.

Lilli's miracle awaits as she and Tariq step through the cathedral's huge open doors into the most lovely, peaceful light snowfall . . . snowflakes silently mingling with the peal of all seven Salzburg cathedral bells harmonizing with bells from every other church in the valley. This continuous communion of music echoes throughout the land.

"I have goose bumps. Christ was born, a birth that cannot be any closer to the here and now, than it is at this moment. And with not one present under the tree."

Tariq comments, "I am speechless."

"These miraculous snowflakes are covering us, Tariq. There must be a reason."

My Christmas is complete. I am complete. I am certain Tariq is touched, having never had such an experience. Could he change to become a Christian? Only time will tell . . . Maybe another miracle will come to fruition.

Lilli departs the day after Christmas, before Tariq. He is to meet again with his business partners. She doesn't see them. She assumes they are the same guys from Riyadh.

The return flight is smooth and without incidence until her plane lands in Riyadh.

— 47 —

Surprise

Lilli disembarks, goes through customs. As she exits the terminal, she is surrounded by four Saudi *Mutawai'n*, (*religious morals police agents.*) Their long beards, semi long robes and black beady eyes indicate they mean serious business of some sort. Puzzled, she asks, "*Aysh hada?*" (*What's the problem?*)

"You are under arrest," one firmly yells in broken English before handcuffing her.

"What have I done?" In shock, she screams as she is handcuffed and escorted to an unmarked red police van. "No, no. You can't do this! What did I do?"

"Yella, (*Let's go,*)" one security policeman yells, gently pushing her into the back seat of the van.

Rapidly transported through the so familiar modern, smooth and busy city streets, the police van stops in front of a high wall. Lilly notices an electric wire follows around the top. Entering a tall gate, she sees barred windows. The front porch seems dilapidated. This is an old wooden and mud house that she had never seen before.

"*God help me. What is happening?*"

Beckoning her up the stairs, one policeman unlocks the door and motions for her to enter. He sets her suitcase on the floor tells her to stand still, *"Shuwai'ye, shuwai'ye" (slowly, slowly)*. He attaches a golden collar to her neck, like a dog's collar.

He speaks in a barely understandable English, "Theese collahh, has shock featurrre with electronic lockh. To take off you needhh computer and pahss code, so no bother try. Eff you get out of thesse house, you be shocked. We know immejeeately. Cameras everywhere." He points to several in the high room's corners.

"You stay *hena*, here. *Ulemas takal'lam ma'a mayor, Ulemas* will talk with the mayor. *Ba'd hadha*, After that, Mayor *takal'lam ma'a Malik*, Mayor talks with the King," he says in his thick Arabic brogue.

"But what have I done to deserve this, this, this jail? I demand to be taken to my villa."

The Arab smirks as he removes the handcuffs of this beautiful Americanee and slams the door shut. The lock clicks.

Crying, she wonders why she is locked in this old filthy little house. Walking around the room, she sees iron bared windows, no phone, lights, T.V., bed or refrigerator.

How long am I going to be like this? Will Tariq notify the American Embassy and my Mom so someone can get me out of here?

"No way can I escape this house, for sure," she says aloud. She feels deeply worried, scared, anxious and curious to know why this situation has happened to her. A nightmare she has always dreaded for twenty-five years, especially when Frank was here. Many misbehavers were sent out of the country, some jailed for long periods. One ex-patriot socked an Arab man for touching his wife. He was beaten by that Arab because in Saudi, it is an eye for an eye and the person hurt can decide on the punishment. The American and his wife were sent back home "toute suite."

Another incident, not long ago, happened when a young nurse, was having an affair with a married Sudanese Muslim doctor, both living in the same condo development. She was sent back to England. The good doctor was dearly needed here at this time, so he stayed, no punishment.

Suddenly it dawns on Lilli. *It must be because of my relationship with Tariq. That has to be it. I know how these Islamic laws and traditions work. I hope he told me the truth: divorced his wife and continued supporting her and his children...that is Sharia law. I know I am in deep trouble. Where are you Frank? I need you now.*

Browsing around, there is no television because of no electricity, no soap, or towels . . . nothing. There is water as she turns on the faucet. *Dear me what am I going to do?* Suddenly the lights come on. *Thank the Lord.*

Her eyes sting and tears begin to overflow like a waterfall. She is becoming very frightened. Drinking water from a soiled cup, she lays down on a dirty sofa and falls asleep, until she is awoken by several knocks on the door.

A guard opens the door and there stands Faisal and Nancy with some bags and a cup of coffee. Relieved, she cries with joy. "Oh, thank God, *Al Hamdu'lillah, (thanks be to God),* you didn't forget me and knew where I was."

"Yes, we knew, because Saud and I went to the airport to pick you up and the guards told us of your dilemma. They won't let us in. I called your Mom in Florida, Lilli."

"Thank you so much, Nancy. But, what have I done?"

Faisal answered, "I am sorry, but the Ulema, religious authorities, know all about your relationship with Tariq–your travels with him, his visits to your place, your secret getaways. A Security *Muttawa,* Morals Police Guard has been following you two everywhere. Tariq found out today that you were arrested when he tried to board his flight. He called me from Jordan where he is waiting for you. He is banished from Arabia for now. Usually the Arab man can come back after his lover has left the country, as long as he has no wife, which Tariq says he no longer has."

"How long do I have to stay here? When can I go back to the states?"

"You will be here for a while. Hopefully not too long if we are lucky. I am going to the king on your behalf tomorrow. I know your love has been true . . . it is just the religion part that is against Sharia law. You must become a Muslim to stay with Tariq. Men cannot marry a foreign woman in Saudi Arabia that isn't a Muslim. At least not now. This may change in the future, as many social rules are slowly in the process of change."

"I cannot become a Muslim, Faisal. But, I am happy Nancy could."

"Okay, then, you will be sent out of this country. No marriage."

"If you give Nancy your apartment key, she will pack some of your belongings and take them to Abdulla and Fatima."

"Nancy, thank you, and please put Frank's red, white and blue socks with my stuff. Give Cleopatra and Goldie to someone, please."

Nancy gave her dear friend a big hug, "Our grand kids will love the kitty and bird. Saud will bring you food and drink every morning until you are freed. He will pick you up when it's all clear to go."

She cried with gratitude, "Thank you Nancy, dear friend."

During her time in the bug and rat infested house, she found only one book, the Koran. Ironic to read this book after being here all these years, but she did read parts that reminded her that this book is a book of laws, telling a Muslim exactly how to live their daily life.

A week passes slowly by. Every day her friends Fatima and Nancy drop by, leaving food and all of life's necessities, including two books. Saud stops by briefly. Lilli keeps her body in condition by doing self exercises with weights that Nancy had brought her. Guards are keeping watch twenty-four hours a day.

The day after New Years a loud knock at the door resonates off the bare walls. Opening reveals a happy face. "Yallah, Let's go, Saud calls out with a grandiose smile. "Let's go! *Yallah!*"

A *Mutawa* religious police unlocks her neck collar, taking it off, smiling all the while, "You are free to go, *yallah,* Amerricani."

Her heart races as she grabs her suitcase, runs down the porch stairs into the back seat of Saud's car, leaving the Koran on the table. The guard stands watching, smiling.

"The king has freed you because of Faisal, a royal prince and man of great respect. He vouched for your integrity. You are one lucky lady, Lillee."

"*Shukran,* thank you for being my friend these months, Saud."

The next evening, Faisal and Nancy briefly visit her at Abdulla and Fatima's home. Faisal tells her of the arrangements for her final escape trip. "You must go after last *salaat* about ten pm tomorrow, Friday."

He continues, "Nighttime is the best time to get away from here. Saud will pick you up and drive you to Jidda where you will take a boat over the Red Sea to Port Sudan, then fly to Jordan. Tariq will meet you there. All expenses have been paid for. Saud will give the boat captain some Saudi Riyals money for the boat journey from Jidda to Port Sudan. Here are your plane tickets to Jordan from Sudan and some Sudanese pounds for the taxi. In this purse is more money if you need it. Tariq will meet you at the Jordan airport." Faisal hands her a small purse.

"*Fi aman allah,* go with God, Lilli." Faisal sincerely looks sad to lose this fine American lady who has lived and worked here for so many years.

"This is not good-bye, Lilli," Nancy explains. "We will see each other every summer in Arizona. I will send you an airplane ticket to come spend some time with me, you can be sure of that."

"Dear Nancy, you must promise to visit me in Florida, too. My parents retired close to the ocean . . . beaches are wonderful there and your children and grand-children will love it. I love you . . . both of you. And Faisal, I sincerely thank you from the bottom of my heart for getting me out of this awful predicament." Lilli wipes the tears from her eyes. Lilli and Nancy hug.

"*Ma'Asallama,* Goodbye, Nancy." Tears stream down her cheeks blinding her vision.

"*Fi-aman illah,* Lilli. Go with God. My gratitude is in my heart's memory," Nancy sobs softly. Faisal quickly leaves, Nancy follows.

~48~

Goodbye Garden of the Desert

JAN. 2001

Her heart is heavy and her spirit troubled. Hopefully she will safely meet Tariq and get back to the U.S.A. Gazing out the window of Fatima's home, she observes the dust and rubble surrounding old mud houses and card board aluminum-roofed shanties of yesterday. This old section of town, still populated, sits among new and beautiful high-rise apartments. Building projects completed leave a cluttered skyline of beautiful tall modern buildings. Only a few metal cranes left reach skyward. "Not a third world country any longer," she thinks out loud.

"Roads are now super highways, heavy with traffic and garbage-free. The usual herds of city goats are gone. Few browse their old haunts in search of food no longer available. But now it's a women's shopping-mall paradise with fast food restaurants. My favority is Mc Arabia."

A mental image of this changed country floods her mind. This was her home for twenty six years. What an intriguing culture. *I loved and respected this kingdom and its people, in spite of some primeval radical customs.* She questions this after her incarceration.

Now, a beautiful modern city that has changed for the good in so many ways. Life here is still a paradox, complicated yet simplistic, remaining unique. *I am so thankful to God that I've lived to explore this ancient, unusual culture. I am now certain, that to have a peaceful world, mankind must understand and respect each other . . . RESPECT all cultures and customs . . . without trying to change any other. West and East must also respect their own, regardless of religion and approve all religions—or human peace will never exist, mankind will not survive.*

Lilli realizes Ramadan is in November this year of 2001 and she will miss all the merriment and festivities of Eid al-Fitr, the last three days for partying. She looks at her gold Swiss Chaupard watch and feels a real sense of loss at her impending departure. Her evolvement took all these years; but she knows in her heart, she is leaving this experience a better person—more respectful, appreciative and knowledgeable of different cultures. So immersed was she in Saudi culture, she often thought she could easily become a Muslim and a Saudi woman of modesty . . . walking ten paces behind her man. The reality of the thought scared the pants off her now.

Lilli Martinez is still a handsome, sensuous woman, with a curvaceous figure even after years of a semi-sedentary lifestyle in Saudi Arabia. Wearing a loose-fitting, long dress does not disguise her sexuality and attractiveness, in spite of a ten pound weight gain. Lilli's absolute chic and classiness still shines through everything she wears.

Always respectful, she complied with the Saudi custom of modest dress and found it was not difficult because she was raised as an introvert of modesty.

Some Western women living here could not give up the tight jeans and revealing clothing. "Their freedom to choose was at stake," they said. They simply could not conform to the Saudi woman's world of being subservient to men . . . like slaves.

The husbands of those ex-patriot ladies, were unable to keep their fabulous paying Saudi jobs for very long. Constantly tapped by religious priests snapping mangrove staffs at their unsuspecting ankles . . . these wives could not adjust to being second or third-class citizens. They and their mates high-tailed it back to the land of freedom. If fortunate, they regained their past lives, the one they had before the Saudi adventure of money, travel and in some cases, escape from negative situations that enticed and lured them away originally.

Lilli thought at the time, *these folks are missing the greatest opportunity of their lives. To understand other people, to know and live their culture, their customs. This is living. So what if she had to cover up? There are higher and more important rewards to this life.* And sure enough, in the years to come, she thought she had found them by developing a taste for this magical, ostentatious, and unreal lifestyle. Leaving it now is the most difficult and emotionally de-stabilizing event of her life. This interesting existence she could never have experienced had she not taken that initial plane ride over the North American, European and Asia continents back in seventy-five. A life that became exciting, addictive, fearful and uncertain, dependent and insecure—a life of excesses—a paradoxical existence.

Lilli was always the perfect boss's wife, exemplary and keenly aware of the political repercussions that could be forthcoming if mistakes were inadvertently made. This gift of public relations followed her to Arabia to help open doors for Frank by befriending important people, like Faisal and Nancy.

An innate politician, she always made a point of explaining to Frank's visiting business associates, "We are guests here and happy to do as our Saudi hosts request, even if the customs and beliefs differ radically from our Western culture. We totally respect their ways," she smiled.

And she meant every word. Over the years, a quiet, gradual change took place within her being. So subtle, even she did not realize it encompassed her essence, her existence, a something addictive and growing inexplicably—it was an affection for the people. But after this jail experience, she knew she could not be happy living in the land of sand any longer, even if she was given permission to do so.

It is Friday evening. A soft knock on her bedroom door brings her back to the present. "*Ahlan, ahlan, ahlan*, Welcome, welcome," she calls out softly in Arabic. For Lilli, Arabic, was an easy language to speak, even simpler than Spanish. She turns as the door opens. Beautiful Fatima enters, her black hair encircled by a cobalt blue scarf, wound as a turban, coiling high above her head.

Large jet-black eyes, about three shades darker than her skin, sadly stare, "*Masa'il-khair*, good evening, Leahllee."

Lilli's heavy eyes follow this attractive woman as she walks across the spacious bedroom. Walking down the winding stairway, the dear friends hold hands.

An aroma of wonderful Arab spices and incense reaches Lilli's nostrils—now a familiar indicator of Arabic cooking and life she has been privy to for so long. *How I love this spicy food. It is not hot like Indian food, even though the spices are much the same. Arabs never use cayenne red pepper like Indians and Pakistanis. I prefer the simple Arab cuisine,* she mused.

Chanting of prayers from all the local TV stations ends; the women, fold their small prayer carpets just as the men of the house come through the front door. Their carpets are tucked under their arms. They had prayed the sunset prayers in a nearby mosque. The men after greeting the ladies, headed immediately to a back room where the table of food awaited them. Men, sit with men, women with women, if guests have been invited. *These men must leave the living room where they usually eat, because she, the infidel, is there. Women usually eat in the back. Only the immediate family eats together.*

Fatima explains. "The fifth and last call to prayer will beckon the men once more to mosque for nightly prayers. You will leave at that time."

Lilli knows there is some peer pressure for men to attend these prayer meetings. Mosques are usually within a block or two and neighbors know who attends and who does not.

All the ladies are sitting on the communal carpet. One says, "At knife point this man forced a young girl waiting for a bus back into her apartment where he made her disrobe. He raped her till she began screaming. The Saudi guard at the complex entrance had seen them pass by. He knew the girl, so flagged them to enter. Later he heard the screams and ran into the girl's apartment. Several witnesses saw the man jump out the broken window and run down the street. He was caught and arrested."

Lilli nodded her head. She felt the tears coming. "That is so sad."

"No mistake. He raped that young girl. A policeman caught up with him," Fatima explains. "They say, he was from Egypt."

An Ethiopian maid in her brightly colored long dress and head scarf enters carrying a tray of small glasses filled with homemade apricot juice. Always thick, delicious and refreshing. Then, a fancy French Lemoges bowl overflowing with the sweetest, most luscious Arab dates sits in front of her. "They come from the King's date grove," Fatima's mother, *Oomi*, adds.

Lilli and Fatima sit in silence while the other ladies chat in animated conversations that seem to reverberate from the ostentatiously decorated, high-ceilings. A rumbling hum of deep men's voices flow in from the other room and are vaguely deciphered.

The juice glasses are re-filled, then a huge tray is set down on the Qum Persian carpet. Ladies gather around a little closer. Lilli sees rice, piled high, laced with a delicate flavor of cinnamon, raisins and pine nuts. "It smells heavenly." Intermingling with that, chunks of roast lamb submit an aroma of delicious juices. No smiles today as she whispers, "What a meal to help my spirit!"

In the states, this would be called a gourmet culinary experience, Lilli thought. A second tray arrives . . . a whole roasted lamb surrounded by carrots, peas and potatoes. The eyes of the roasted animal stare out into space. Small dishes of chilled spiced yogurt, sliced cucumber and smashed garlic, along with large, flat Arabic bread is set on newspaper in different places on the carpet.

Using no utensils, everyone eats with their right, clean hands. The rice, rolled into a small ball is safely popped into mouths. *Khubz* flat bread is torn and used as a pusher.

How she loves these customs. There is something special and mesmerizing about living in this foreign, desert country. The people are so wonderful, sometimes naive and earthy; but, basically good, religious folks. Once I could see past the dress, Sharia law customs and the "Matawa" religious priests, I felt right at home here. Leaving now is still not easy.

After everyone ate, a huge dessert tray of fruits is placed before them. Lilli knows she will miss this camaraderie with friends she had grown accustomed to and loved. This year is the first time she would miss her favorite *three day holiday* of *Id Al-Fitr*, the end of *Ramadan* festivities. Celebrations something akin to Christmas, but with day becoming night. *Ramadan* was a welcome respite from the monotony of the rest of the year in this desert town.

I can hardly stand the thought of leaving; yet, leave I must, I have no other choice. "I am so sorry if I've saddened this night for you and your family, Fatima. You know my heart is heavy to have to leave my dear friends who are my family now. Especially, you, my sister Fatima. I don't have to tell you how I feel, you already know."

"I know Tariq's love for you is sincere, Lilli. Your smile and ways are the light of his life. When you leave, that light will be snuffed out. I don't know what he might do."

"Tariq will meet me in Jordan tomorrow night."

"You have this family's blessing, Lilli," said *Oomi. "Fi-amanal-lah*, go with God. But I do wish things were different. Nothing that has happened is your fault, we know that."

"Thank you both, Oomi, Fadia. The decision has been made and I have no choice. I do believe it is for the best. We will see each other again. You will visit America, I know."

As they speak, a muted knock from the outside villa gate causes silence. A second knock, louder, bounces off the tall cement villa walls simultaneously with one short burst of the door buzzer. The maid opens the door and there is what they were expecting.

— 49 —

The Escape

Saud, more handsome than ever, appears neatly dressed in his long white *thobe,* red checkered headdress, an *agal*-rope holding it tightly in place.

"*Ma'saul kheir*, good evening, *Assalamu aleikum,* peace be upon you Miss Lilli. We must leave just before last *salaat* prayer. The drive to Jidda is long and we need to arrive before daybreak and first *salaat* prayers. Hurry, the boat waits."

"Saud, I will join you in one minute."

One by one she embraces each woman until she comes to Fatima. With tears streaming, she deftly throws her black *abaya* cloak around her body. Fatima nervously fumbles with the folds of her glorious golden-hued turban, her cheeks are moist.

"Lilli, we will see each other again. Soon, I shall come to Amir-kiyya, *Ma' Sha'allah*, my God willing."

"*Na'am*–yes, you will come to America. *Insha'Allah*, God willing, we will be sisters again," believing as her friend did, that what God wills, will be, and certainly this relationship was exactly as God willed.

The family men come to the doorway of the room. A heavy-set man steps forward. Abu, Fatima's father. "Lilli, I leave you in the goodness and safety of God. We shall miss your smiling face." Head bent down, he turns and leaves the room.

Next, Abdullah, Fatima's husband, comes forth and shakes her hand. "We will see you again Lilli, soon. I helped arrange everything for you to have a safe trip. Quickly now, may God be with you. You know my name means 'servant of God' and Allah told me to help you."

"*Barak Allah fik,* God bless you, Abdullah. You have been by my side through this whole ordeal. You are a jewel. Fatima is so lucky to have you and you, her." *A good, honest man and loving husband and father she thought as she said,* "*Shukran,* thank you for everything you have done for me. I will never forget you both. I am eternally grateful, Abdullah. *Ma'assalama,* Good-bye."

Lilli's huge oriental eyes are dimmed by a landslide of saltiness. Fatima could not look up. Two soft hands touch briefly. One last sisterly embrace.

How I will miss my dearest friends residing in this foreign, once backward land that has been transformed into an ultra-modern commercial center, architecturally diverse and a part of the twenty-first century. A land totally constructed by foreigners, mostly westerners.

With a fleeting backward glance, Lilli flies down the stairs, wiping tears from her cheeks.

Straightening her black *Abaya* cloak, she pulls it tightly around her curvaceous body before slipping into the back seat of the new Mercedes. As Saud shuts the door she ponders, *why is this old Turkish custom of covering up still relevant? Turkish women are now free to choose their dress code. Women's modesty is written in the Koran; not this ridiculous total face veil except for eyes covering. I absolutely can never do this all my life . . . and walk two paces behind a man.*

At this moment, she feels like a nonentity . . . a black blob totally incognito. *I could be any woman or even a man whose eyes are the only windows to my feelings, my soul and the escape I am praying and hoping for.* The only skin visible is the white of her hands and eyelids. Her beautiful face is discernible by the prominent nose profile protruding from the tight cloth. Sad eyes stare into space. *"Yallah,* Saud, let's go! I am ready."

Finally relaxing a bit, she recalls her years of adventure to Saud. "I was so excited twenty-seven years ago when I first saw the Tuwaq mountain. Mountains in a desert? We traversed all the escarpment areas to find ancient artifacts—arrowheads, fossils, shells, turquoise, and in dry wadis, we discovered flowering plants, pottery, and shells from millions of years ago when this area was an ocean. Saud, we explored caves with prehistoric works of art, pictographic writings and carvings. It was all unreal."

"I wish I could have seen all that, Miss Lilli."

The pressure of the terrifying immediate past overcomes her, causing drowsiness. She feels her heavy eyelids closing. Soon, deep in sleep, the years unfold in her dreams recollecting the many times she and Frank participated in an audacious cultural experience. It gave them knowledge, friendship, respect, travel, sadness and lastly fear.

Reaching the Port of Jidda, Lilli's dreams of the past are on an interlude as she is awoken from her much needed sleep by the first beautiful, melodic call to prayer. As they pass by, musical words resonate from the tall minaret of late King Khalid's majestic guest palace, *Al Hamra Gaser,*

She knows the call, 'There is no God but God and Mohammad is the Messenger of God. *Allahu Akbar.'* This call to pray is directly from a Muezzin's tenor voice, flowing like a gentle, spiritual and compelling song.

I too feel like praying in a mosque or on a carpet . . . but to my Jesus. My prayers must be silent as I sit here in the car while Saud and many other men pray on their carpets laid on the sandy ground.

Lilli is more relaxed now when Saud returns to the car. "Saud, did you know, Jidda, is called *"The Bride of the Sea"* because at nighttime, its myriad of twinkling lights resemble a sparkling jeweled-covered bride. Some believe the tomb of Eve, the wife of Adam, may be located here."

Saud looks puzzled, amazed this Americanee should know so much.

He says, "I know Jidda, is the largest seaport on the Red Sea. It is one of the largest cities for commerce in the Kingdom, too. I don't know much about this country, but in my Sudan, I know very much."

Saud follows the shoreline to the port. Lilli cannot believe what she sees. A huge triangular sculpture appears, rising up toward the cloudless blue sky. "Looks like concrete, Saud." One particular one is silhouetted against the sea, looming skyward like a huge sail. Two concrete *dhow* sailboats are sitting on either side.

She can imagine these concrete "boats" sailing off to ports in Africa. She hears the music of waves slapping against the shore line and boat keels, while cool breezes waft smoothly everywhere beneath the beginning of the sun's daylight glow.

This ethereal scene is made more believable because of the few *Arabian dhow sailboats* docked along the water's edge. These monuments to the Kuwaiti sailboats of yore are ancestors of the modern sailing yacht. From her studies about these boats, Lilli remembers, "Saud, did you know that a thousand years ago, Arab sailors used these sail boats to trade at ports of many countries. They say navigation methods learned from dhow captains helped modern navigation."

Saud answers, "I didn't know that. I do know in my country, *dhows* are built from mangrove and teak. No power tools or plans are used. Everything is held together by wood pegs and iron nails. Today they use motors, not sails as much as they used to."

"Saud, look in the distant bay there. Water spraying skyward."

A monumental *qahwa* coffee pot stands tall, sending a heaven-reaching fountain of water from its spigot into the Jidda harbor. Illuminated by the light of a rising sun, it glows and reflects a shadow for miles across the water.

"Yes, so nice," Saud answers.

"A memorably, beautiful sight for me. The eastern sun is preparing to light the way across the Red sea to Sudan in a few hours, Saud. I will be leaving you very soon."

"I could not be sadder, but very happy for you."

～50～

Sailing to Port Sudan

Saud parks his car parallel to the water's edge. Another huge sculpture of sunflowers hovers overhead. The welcoming sun begins to glow on murmuring waters splashing loudly against the nearby shore.

"Lilli, that is your sail boat over there," pointing to a real large Arab dhow, its triangular sail reaching for the sky, blowing with the wind. You will sail. It also has a motor."

Surrealistic is the silhouette of a huge sail against a background of aquamarine sea water, Lilli thinks.

Breathing deeply, "I'm going to sail on that huge *Dhow*? My, how exciting!"

The sun, with its luminescent awakening in a cloudless heavenly expanse, is in progress.

"The last dawn I will see in this country is arriving, Saud. This is my almost final venture—an unexpected voyage across the Red Sea in an ancient *dhow* to Sudan and a flight to another historic country, Jordan. It all takes my breath away." Her spirit soars. She feels a new adventure is in store and can hardly believe this is all happening. Almost the end to a magnificent experience, but she is ready to return to freedom and safety.

Saud opens the car door and Lilli jumps out. "Saud, I'm on my way to America."

Several men sit on the boats edge, sipping shahi, *tea* and puffing on the hubbly bubbly hookah, *water pipe* filled with a fruit-cured tobacco.

Saud chuckles, "Soon, I will cross this sea too. My home is in Sudan, where you are going now." He points directly west, across the busy moving water-waves.

He helps her into the rocking boat with "Inshallah, *God willing* and *Barak allah fik,* may God bless you, Lilli, Happy sailing!"

He hands the captain a handful of Saudi *Riyals* money to pay for her trip. Lilli knows that Faisal is doing this for her and Tariq. A handsome sailor grabs her hand and guides her to a boat bench.

Waving, "Ma'a as-salama, Saud, *Goodbye,*" as the sailors detach all ropes securing the boat to the dock. The winds quickly fill the sails, and the boat departs. Standing on the dock, Saud waves a last sentimental farewell.

Saud sits beside a *Hookah,* smoking. Murmuring to one of the smokers, "I've loved this lady as a sister for many years. My friends here in Saudi help my loneliness because I only visit my wife and children once a year. They must remain in Sudan, not like West-erners who can bring their children and attend school here, too. I send most of my month's pay to my wife. One day I will be home forever in Sudan, too."

The captain, in excellent English to Lilli, "It won't take long to arrive at Port Sudan. There, I am told you will hop a plane to a Jordan destination. Tariq Rashudi will be waiting there for you." He offers her tea.

She sees a few other expatriate guests on board. Kind of scary to be the only woman though. Could anyone be a terrorist?

"Tariq Rashudi is a good friend of mine. I am Lebanese and

also know Abdulla El Bagawi, a Palestinian carpet trader originally from Lebanon whose wife is close to you, I am told."

"I know them both. He, the best of fine men and Fatima is a forever best friend."

Sailing and unimpeded, the gently blowing winds and fluttering full single sail brings a small sense of relief. Emotionally sitting on top of the world, she is still nervous. *Thank God, I am leaving this frightening situation behind and I will never return. I can't believe it happened to me. I am thankful I've had this unique experience but it is past now. I am going home to a free country . . . America! It's time.* She thinks of Frank, *I wish he could be with me now.*

History loving and intrigued by the Arab Dhow's ancient appearance, she notices the ornate carvings on the boat's stern and hull.

These historic sailboats remain resilient sea-traveling transports. Centuries ago they carried exotic cargo from foreign countries to the shores of Arabia. Camel caravans then delivered goods inland over desert sand and desert dunes. Business was good then. Bahrani pearls were also delivered to various other ports in the Middle East.

"Welcome! How do you like this ride?" the smiling captain asks all his guests. "Today's *dhows* are few, but are being rebuilt with motors by those who want to preserve their beauty and sea worthiness. We use our diesel motor when necessary. We have aluminum on board today, a by-product from oil drilling. We stay busy delivering and sailing the seas."

This classic *dhow*, now under full sail going southwest, seems to catch the spirit of yore, the simplicity of the past—a past Lilli landed into in 1975. She feels antiquity in her soul and bones. She still has an affection for this country, even though it is not perfect, especially in the freedom of women. She senses she will miss all the historic romance she has felt for the last many years. Except for the past week in prison, it was a fantastic life. But, she does have mixed emotions at this time in her life.

The motoring to Sudan is uneventful and pleasurable. The Captain helping her off, directs her to a waiting taxi. "Take this American lady to the airport," he orders the driver. He hands Lilli a handful of Sudanese pounds and her plane ticket. "Just in case you need it. One dollar equals 5.67 Sudanese pounds. I am paying the driver now so you won't have to. Safe travels, lady."

"Thank you," from a grateful lady.

At the airport, she awaits her flight by sitting and reading a magazine. Her Arabic suffices so she deciphers the information. One article gives a short, interesting history of these people.

'Sudanese are Nubian Muslim Africans who speak Arabic. Goats are also named Nubian Goats. These people invented the bow and arrow. Anwar Sadat, the late third president of Egypt, was born from an Egyptian father and a Sudanese mother.'

Her plane flight number is called. She rushes to board. A short ride, the landing in Amman, Jordan brings her relief with hopes Tariq will be waiting. And he is, "Thank God you are here, Tariq. While in prison, I had never been so frightened in all my life." He hugged her and held her tight. The tears streamed down her cheeks. "My trip here was good, though. Thank you."

"We'll talk at the hotel," he whispers in her ear. "It's only a short taxi ride and we will be in a beautiful modern room at the deluxe Jordan Intercontinental Hotel."

They made long overdue passionate love after showering. Both exhausted, they slept for a few hours before dressing to go out to dinner.

"Dinner was lovely at that Jerusalem Restaurant, Tariq. Thank you so much. I am so anxious to return to the USA."

"I know you are, Lilli. I am so sorry you had to go through that jail event. I felt the police had been following me for quite a while. Things will work out, don't worry. We will be comfortable in Chicago. I fly there very frequently and I did get us an apartment on the outskirts of the city along the edge of Lake Michigan before flying here. You have a place to live. It is in your name so no one can trace me to it. We have to be cautious for a while until the heat is off."

"Oh, that will be great. I can work again. I will apply for an Archeology teaching job at the University of Chicago. I know everyone there. I can buy a car to commute. I want to visit my parents in Florida, also. I am feeling a little relieved, Tariq."

On the way back to the hotel, Lilli notices a few Christian Churches with crosses, even a Roman- Catholic and Greek Orthodox one.

"Tariq, I am amazed at the many churches here. Unbelievable. The people and Islam are not as radical here in Jordan as in Saudi, it seems."

"No, they are not. There are several churches, but no Jewish synagogues, of course. Saudi is more purist in their Islamic beliefs." Changing the subject, "Are you up to taking a drive down to the Dead Sea tomorrow for a swim? I'd like to show you around. We'll spend the night at the hotel there. Our flight to Chicago doesn't leave until the next night at 10 pm. The airport is not far so we can go directly to the airport when we return."

"Absolutely. Tariq, to be with you is a dream come true. Thank you for helping to get me out of that horrible situation. But, what about you? Will you be allowed to return to Saudi ever?"

"I will, in time. The main thing is you are free and out of my country. You know, we can never be married unless you become a Muslim.

"Yes, I know."

Early the next morning, they take a tour bus, suitcases in tow, and follow the Jordan River south to the Dead Sea. The sun shines on the silent salty waters. "This is the lowest spot on earth, 'the Salt Sea of the Bible.' Dense waters so buoyant no one can sink in them—six times more saline than sea or ocean water," a proud guide says. "See the many people floating along the edges? The salty lightness keeps the body up. No one can drown here. Our Jordan River empties into this Sea with water from nearby Mt. Hermon."

"I remember from the bible that the Lord rained upon Sodom and Gomorrah, brimstone and fire from the Dead Sea," Lilli says. "And here we are!"

"Yes," the guide answers. "The natural minerals help skin to stay healthy. Americans have been helping us extract potash from the sea so that Jordanians can sell to the world market one of the salt compounds derived from it . . . potassium! And potash is one of the three ingredients of fertilizer."

"Just like Arabia does. That is so interesting," Lilli answers. "Amazing isn't it that farmers of the world can help the world grow food for all."

"Lilli, shall we take an afternoon swim? Let's go to our hotel room and change."

For hours, they float in the salty, healthy waters, until they see eerie cloud formations rising between the distant mountains. The dimming sun signals to the world, "Adios, *Goodbye* till tomorrow," Lilli sings out. "Look, moon beams peeking between rock clefts—a marvel to behold."

That evening, they dine at the Dead Sea Beach Club restaurant overlooking the water. They eat delicious Jordanian olives, the country's chief agicultural product.

Returning to Amman the next day, they have dinner at a local restaurant before entering the hotel lobby to await the time to leave for the airport. They see the sitting area is overflowing with Jordanian police mulling around. Several doctors are caring for wounds of visitors staying at the hotel. The moaning and groaning of injured people is horrific. *What is going on? Is this terrorism?* Lilli wonders.

A policeman tells them, that two unnoticed terrorists with pistols, shot the policeman guarding the door entrance. The two men hustled past the empty front desk usually manned by an employee, but, he had quickly ducked down behind the desk and was unknown to the two armed men. They began indiscriminately shooting at mostly western visitors sitting and conversing on sofas.

The man behind the desk subsequently crawled quietly to the right side, head down, peeking out to view the terrorists and fortunately shot them both. Quickly, he called the police, an ambulance, and stood, aiming his gun over the two.

Immediately, Lilli and Tariq leave, hail a taxi for the airport. They have a few hours wait time to catch their flight. Lilli prays. "*Insha'allah*, God be with us."

~51~
Home at Last?

The uneventful flight has a short overnight stopover in London. Arriving in Chicago the next day, Lilli cannot believe she is home . . . in the good ole U.S. of A. While Tariq is retrieving their luggage, she prays quietly to herself, Psalms CVII. "I give my thanks unto my Lord, for he has been good and I know His mercy endures forever."

"Finally, I feel a big relief from my scary ordeal . . . jailed in a foreign country" she murmurs faintly to Tariq.

Checking into a fourth floor downtown Chicago hotel room, "Let's stay at the condo tonight. I have a meeting with the guys tomorrow, so this suite of rooms will be available for them tomorrow night. You can spend the day shopping. Let's go to your condo for the night, Lilli."

Lilli phones her Mom to tell her she's reached the United States and is in Chicago with Tariq Rashudi. They talk a few minutes. "I'll be in Florida soon to see you. I'm doing great now. Love you."

At her new third floor condo overlooking the waters of Lake Michigan, they relax on the veranda. The view is wonderful. Tension lessens after her ordeal, her spirit is lifting to hope. The electricity will be turned on tomorrow, but they stayed the night there anyway. The evening was one of constant love making . . . Tariq is insatiable. Love floats high above the lake waters into the winds of celestial eternity. A still mysterious love, she has to admit—an uncertain treasure but a light from heaven shines through.

The next morning they taxi back to the hotel for breakfast, and Lilli is looking forward to shopping in America. Tariq receives the call he is expecting. "We will be holding our meeting all day on the 27th floor. If you are out and about, don't worry. Lilli, we can meet at 6 p.m. in the lobby."

A kiss goodbye and Tariq steps on the up elevator while she waits for the down. Lilli shops in the hotel gift store until about ten a.m., then investigates a few unique shops along the street. Returning to their room, she decides to find where Tariq is holding the meeting.

Into the elevator, she accidently pushes the 37th floor button instead of the 27th where Tariq said they will hold their meeting. The doors open, she exits, looks around; but this floor seems deserted. Quickly, she turns to hold the door open and punch the down button. But too late—the elevator door closes before she can hold it open. Realizing she had punched the wrong floor button, thirty-seven instead of twenty-seven, she knew, *I must go back down to the 27th floor where Tariq is. But, where are the buttons? There are no buttons here to push . . . none. How will I ever get down from here? These elevator doors are closed!*

Much to her shock and dismay, there are no going anywhere buttons to be pushed on the outside of the elevator, let alone "down buttons". Frantic, *"Oh, my God!" I am stuck on the 37th floor. The only way down is stairs, but where are they?"*

The search for stairs is on. She begins trying the many empty glass office doors. "Must have been special office businesses up here. A desk in each all glassed-in rooms. Walking around the dark floor, tugging on each door trying to find a phone, perhaps? But to no avail, all doors are locked and no stairs. *What am I going to do? No one knows I am up here on this last empty floor. I can die up here and no one will ever know or discover me. This is a dangerous isolated situation, worse than being in a prison.*

Her breathing becomes rapid, she can feel her heart beating strongly. She knows her blood pressure must be sky-high. She slowly walks from office to office, trying each locked door. *I am going to have a heart attack! I feel like fainting.*

The perspiration flows from her pale forehead and underarms. After a fearful, stressful while, she makes one more circle around the office doors, expecting nothing. *Maybe, I can break the glass on a door and simultaneously break an outside window and yell down to the street.* Suddenly, she discovers a plain unmarked exit door she didn't see before. She turns the knob, it opens. There . . . there she sees stairs going only down. Breathless now, she inhales and exhales deeply, thanking God. But, as she is about to enter the opened door, she hears voices, familiar voices. *DON'T close the door yet,* she says to herself.

Wait a minute! That voice! It's Tariq! A moment later, she clearly hears the voices of Gumar and Mustafa, too. She is elated, relieved and grateful. *I think they must be in that dark office door next to these stairs. Maybe the door is cracked open a notch because I hear a phone ring.*

But, after hearing Gumar's words, "I believe we are ready for the big Boom in Chicago, *Alhamdu' lillah.*"

What?? Lilli is bewildered and stunned. She hears Mustafa next. Seemingly excited and proud, he announces loudly on the phone, "The bomb is in place on the top of the Sears Tower skyscraper, one hundred eight stories up. In 48 hours, the Tower will no longer be standing. One million people visit its observation deck each year. The city will be a mess."

The phone clicks off.

"We will show them," Tariq adds, sounding loudly satisfied.

"Say isn't that close to your new condo apartment, Tariq . . . and Lilli?" Gumar questions.

"That really doesn't matter, but I do believe the condo is out of the bomb's reach. I hope so, because we will all be staying there whenever we come to America on business. As far as Lilli is concerned, I knew this affair with the beautiful Americana was only temporary. It had to end one day. This may be the day, but I don't think so. She surely fed my sexual drive in a big way. Lilli is terrific. She was far better in bed than that old hag I did not divorce like everyone thought I did. Lilli knows nothing of who I really am. You all know that. I had to tell her only what she wanted to hear: That I was not a radical Islamist, I had liberal Baha'i religious beliefs and I divorced my wife for her. I knew, she eventually trusted my words. I guess I really did love her."

An incredibly shocked Lilli did not want to believe what she was hearing from Tariq. She could not resist continuing to eavesdrop. *I must listen a little longer.*

Tariq spoke, "Next, we have to finish work on our Trojan Horse virus we will use for the Cyber Attack planned for next month. All electricity will be off in Chicago, New York, Houston, Seattle, Boston, Cape Canaveral Space Center and Los Angles. Our men are working diligently in each of these cities for that goal. After that, there will be a phenomenal air attack."

The deep voice of Tariq continues, "We will be able to control all of this from our hidden safe-houses positioned elsewhere. The cities affected will be without lights, refrigeration, water pumped, car gas drawn, or food delivery to grocery stores. We'll have access to bank and business records. These Infidels will be punished for not bending down to our Islam and Allah's wishes. These non-believers will eventually be killed, decapitated, all of them! We have many of our own already here in America preparing to fight for our cause, our caliphate. Unfortunately, some will be killed, but they give their life for Allah and receive seven virgins in return." Tariq looks up to the heavens. The three loudly chant *"Allah yubarik' ficum. Allah Akbar*!" God bless us. God is great.

"Our Jihad with the west is just beginning," Mustafa adds.

A soft chorus of *"Alhamdu illah! Allahu'Akbar!"* We praise Him! Our God is Great, repeatedly emanates from that office, permeating empty hallway spaces like a threatening but melodic concluding concert.

Horrified and bewildered, in a state of shock, Lilli had heard enough. She quietly enters the stairwell and softly closes the door. Rapidly flying down the stairs, she pulls on the first door she comes to. It opens. She finds the elevator, rides down to her floor. Rushing into the room, she writes a note for Tariq, 'I will return at six.' It was twelve o'clock now . . . she had six hours to make it to the airport and get to Florida. She picks up the phone and quietly places a call to the FBI, identifies herself and tells them exactly what happened, what was said. Giving the hotel room number and the Chicago condo address, she explains, "These terrorists might go there."

Taxiing back to the condo, she instructs the driver to "please wait." Incredibly, the first thing she sees is two Red Socks thrown on the floor close to the condo's door! "I can't believe this. What on earth . . . ?" She feels jittery opening the door.

Socks were not there this morning. How could it be? Frank is alive alerting me to danger, and all is not well? Only he would have done this to warn me, but he is dead. Or is he? Could he still be alive? She almost went faint. After this morning, I don't think I can stand anymore surprises. But I must get out of here "tout suite" fast. Flustered, she grabs her suitcase, stuffing the socks into her purse, takes the elevator down to the lobby and runs to the waiting taxi. "Quickly, Chicago Airport, please." Her anxiousness was not subdued in the least. So far, she had heard nothing back from the FBI.

After an hours wait, she felt lucky to be boarding a plane to Atlanta. Then two hours later she was in the air to Melbourne Beach, Florida where her parents retired.

She thought about the red socks—alert, danger, all is not well. Fingering them on her lap all the way to Florida, she smells them. These are Franks for sure. *What on earth can this be?* She can't figure this puzzle out.

Her arrival to Melbourne is at six p.m., Eastern Time. She knocks on the condo door and her Mother opens it, expecting her. Tears rolling down her cheeks, Mother sobs as she sees her Lilli, "Thank God you are here. It's been a while since we saw you last, my dearest daughter."

"Oh, Sweets, God has returned you—our love, our beautiful beloved daughter back with us in one piece. We knew from Faisal's call exactly when you left Jidda. We were so thankful to God, so we went right to church and prayed for your safe flights to us. But your Mother thought you were staying in Chicago longer. We are not going to let you leave us again, my sweets." Her step-dad always called her "sweets".

"It's a long story, Mom and Dad. We will sit and talk when I am rested. I have lots to tell you, believe me. But right now, I am so happy to be here with you both." Tears flood her sight as she gathers these faithful and loving human beings together and squeezes them tightly. She didn't want to involve them, so she told them nothing.

At last, my permanent home. I will buy a place close by so I can oversee Mom and Dad as they age . . . the least I can do for them.

~52~
"He Who Returns from a Journey Is Not the Same as He Who Left."

CHINESE PROVERB

S hocked, upset, disturbed, satisfied . . . her emotions are totally in disarray when she and her parents hear this announcement on the TV News: 'Yesterday, the Sears Tower in Chicago was in jeopardy of being bombed. But three terrorists were apprehended before they could implement their plan. They are now in jail. The Tower is still standing. Chicago is safe.'

"Al Hamdu 'lillah, Thanks be to God." goes through her mind.

A month later, she settles into a lovely condo near a gated golf community. Her porch overlooks the beach, and is within walking distance of Mom and Dad. She interviews for a future position at the local community college teaching Spanish, another of her bilingual talents.

The struggle adjusting to residing in a free country again is tough and unexplainable. She attempts to push the bad parts of the past aside. Her thinking is clear now. It was a unique cultural learning experience, but, never to be repeated or forgotten. *I so*

appreciate my America. America, the land of the free and the brave!
My home. I will work hard for you America, never again to leave.

After surviving jail, it took Lilli until then to realize the impact of living in a culture against women's freedoms and rights. A country, historically unique, and now so magnificent and modern, yet remaining archaic in its ways of dealing with women. She hopes women have more freedoms soon–if they desire it. Many Saudi women are content with their freedoms as they stand now. Some want more, especially to drive. Rumor had it that the first co-educational university is planned in the near future. But, I do believe segregation of the genders will prevail for many more years.

She feels lucky to have left the land of sand, thanks to dear friends. She felt so innocent and ignorant when first beginning that adventurous life journey. No longer, though. She wishes Frank had been with her all the way, especially at the end. *I know my bad situation would not have happened.*

The next day, she finds another pair of socks neatly hanging outside on her condo door knob, blue this time, just be on alert. No immediate storms brewing.

What on earth is going on? I can't believe what this is all about. For sure Frank is alive, but why is he doing this? Why doesn't he show himself? I must relax.

"This is too much for my psyche. I'm going out to get some air, sun, relax and read," she muses aloud.

For the first time since her arrival, she decides to go to the beach. Walking in her condo hall, she hears loud voices echoing off the walls. Stopping for just a second . . . *my gosh, I believe that's Arabic they are speaking. How about that. Some Arabs must live here. I can't believe it . . . here in Florida.* They are speaking very fast, sounding excited. *Maybe I will find some Arab girl-friends.* But she only hears male voices, no women speaking.

Breathing refreshing salt ocean air, she struts over a sand dune, passing by a large circular disruption of sand below the dune, a Loggerhead Sea Turtle nesting area. The turtles come ashore to the same specific beach year after year, to dig sand holes for laying eggs. They cover the holes to conceal the nests before returning to the ocean, never to return until the following year when they lay another egg litter. About two months later the babies hatch out of the holes and scurry down to the ocean. The lucky ones make it without being eaten by various birds and animals who wait the turtle escape.

But, how do newborns know where the ocean is, which way to run fast and why?

The warm sun shines brightly. A sparkling surf roars like intermittent thunder, splashing the water's coastline. Cute little sandpipers quickly run and dance with the rise and fall of the ocean's waves. A continuous pecking around the water's sandy edges, they dine on bits of sea worms, sand fleas, or if lucky, a small crab to grab before the saltwater rushes back, covering the shore line once more with water.

Sitting on a blanket, breathing the cleansing salt air deeply, she watches and listens to squawking sea gulls flying overhead; brown pelicans diving for fish dinners; a slow and steady loner and hunter, the great blue heron spears a baby mullet, then flies off with his lunch. He soon returns to patiently wait for another treat . . . perhaps a handout from a fisherman nearby.

In the watery distance, a school of dolphin dance and roll ceremoniously, whistling family songs to each other in their own playful way.

What a marvelous and pure heavenly paradise. This is peace. And

I thought the desert was earth's only unique place. How naïve; but, I do believe God has given everything on this earth a personal beauty and if the beholder listens to their heart, opens their eyes, they will see God's natural artistry. She falls asleep on her blanket.

Evening is settling in. A huge orange Florida full moon is beginning to rise. She awakens and a heartfelt poem pervades her mind. She composed it for Frank when they married and he was out of town for Boxwood. She recites it to herself at this moment:

Tangerine Moon

A spectacular western sunset lights up the earth's skyline,
an eastern orange moon slowly begins to float skyward.
I wish you were here to explore pristine sandy beaches
and lie with me among tall dunes.

I picture you casting a fishing line into the Atlantic
as singing Dolphin dance and pompano swim near-by.
I think of you every minute while in this paradise,
the spirit of you rolls in on each wave.

I am enchanted by the peace of being together here,
mesmerized by the music of ocean waves and distant fishing
fleets.
I hear your voice harmonize with a seagull's squawk
calling my name with every splash of the roaring surf.

Perceiving your body is walking in step beside mine,
imagining squeaky bare feet leaving imprints on the sand.
I feel your presence on the rays of this huge tangerine moon,
tonight its glowing light will transform our bedroom.
Yearning to share this exquisite sensation with you,

alone with memories of tenderness, warmth and love.
I pine for you to be here or near or coming
on this Florida beach—I am missing you so much, Frank.

She folds her blanket and returns to her condo. Walking to her apartment, she hears the Arabs talking as usual. Her dreams that night are of Frank. Where is he?

━ 53 ━
Deja'vu

The next morning she returns to this beautiful special beach. Walking in the sunshine, she breathes deeply . . . Pure salt air . . . no sand storms here. Relaxing on her blanket, she concentrates on her surroundings: people walking, some jogging along the water's edge, birds cruising overhead, pompano rolling off in the ocean's distance, fishing boats motoring by, the same man fishing along the ocean's edge.

Later, falling asleep, she suddenly senses the sand is shaking beside her. Looking left, reveals a white-socked sneaker, all is in control, calm! *Maybe it's . . . hoping it might be?* One second later, she feels a tap on her shoulder. She hears, "Lillita, mi amour."

The bright sun blinds her vision. Her squinting eyes look up. *Ma Sha'allah, my praise to God.* Now seeing clearly, "It is you!" She screams, "Frank, my wonderful Frank."

He helps her to rise up, "Oh, Frank, thank God, you are alive," a big sigh of thankfulness. Tears flooding both their eyes, run down their cheeks like a water fall.

"Where on earth have you been? They said your plane went down in the Gulf of Aqaba. No survivors. You died. What happened? Why didn't you contact me? Why did you do this to me? You broke my heart when our world collapsed—when your love disappeared. It took me a long time, I tried, but I never really got over losing you."

"I had to return to you, gently and slowly, because I loved you, my Lilli. I love you! I missed you. My dreams were only of you, your smile your goodness." Frank hugged her tightly, close to his heart, not letting her go for some time, tears streaming.

"I had to disappear for your safety, my Lillita. You had to be protected from knowing anything about a very secret mission I was on . . . to eliminate terrorists that want to harm America. Your innocence was essential. The time away from you was unbearable for me. So many times did I want to quit this assignment."

He kissed and kissed her with hugs and couldn't stop. Not releasing her, he whispered, "Mi amour, te amo por siempre jamas. *My love, I love you forevermore*. It broke my heart in two to be away from you. There were times, I felt discouraged and depressed. My thoughts of you lifted my spirits. Kissing your photo, gave me the courage to continue."

They silently sat as one on the blanket, until the sun set and the moon rose, lifting the heavy weight off their souls. He contritely told her the whole story.

"Since my last promotion at Boxwood in Saudi, I began working undercover for a government agency. My new job is searching for and following radical Islamic terrorists. I had orders to get off that Saudia flight to Cairo before it took off and take a flight to London that was immediately leaving. My ticket had already been paid for. With our situation in Saudi, the powers-that-be thought it best to make me dead and allow you to become involved with the ringleader, Saudi Capt. Tariq Rashudi, who had big eyes for you. Luck was with me that I wasn't on the flight to Cairo."

"But why didn't you call me?"

"I am so sorry, but they didn't want your life to be in jeopardy. That was so hard for me to do, my love. Every week, I was sent a report about you, your health and every day's whereabouts. Lilli, I have been working under another name. The Government has been trying to get pilot Rashudi and his group for several years. After your call, we finally got them all red-handed. They were arrested in the hotel room shortly after you called. That's why no explosion occurred in Chicago, thanks to you. Lilli, you saved so many American lives, thank goodness. I was elated when they told me you were the woman who called."

He continues, "The bombs were found in place at the top of the Sears Tower. They also caught the other Cyber terrorists in the cities you mentioned. So thanks to you, many more lives were saved. Hopefully, this will help discover and stop future attacks. Terrorists are here, Lilli! America is in deep trouble."

"I would have never, ever dreamed all of this could happen." Lilli was seriously concentrating on Frank's every word.

Then, she shared her story about how she accidently got stuck on that hotel's 37th floor. "To me, it was scarier than being in the Saudi house prison, because I thought I was alone up there with no phone connection, no way out, never imagining I would overhear familiar voices with plans for exploding our Sears Tower or promulgating a Cyber Attack on many large American cities. I almost had a heart attack. I will never forget that day. In a state of shock, I called the police, as you know. I made a difference, didn't I, Socks?"

"My darling, you are a hero. I want you to know, you were followed on every departure from Saudi, including to Chicago, my dearest. We knew about what happened in the Saudi jail. I told them about Faisal, Nancy's husband. He helped get you free."

"I hope you will forgive me for my deception, but now that you are back in the states, I can expose my past, but only to you.

We can do whatever you wish. I pray you'll have me back, my sweetheart."

She loved hearing the word sweetheart again, "I would have you back in a heartbeat, Frank. God has looked out for us always and now He gave me back my first love. I didn't know I was secretly helping the best democratically free country in the world . . . my home, America!"

"My Lilli, you made a big difference and I am positive you are going to make many more. Oh, how I've missed you."

Laying back on the blanket, their arms tightly encircle their bodies. Lilli's ordeal was over and another new life opened its doors to her . . . to them. *This is a night to remember forever.*

Planet Venus, along with thousands of stars, dazzle the galaxy's heavens delivering their brilliance earthward. In the distance, salt water meets a dark blue sky at earth's visible edge. Endless white-tipped curling ocean waves dance along the shore. A strikingly huge, gorgeous orange moon has begun its ascent to the firma-ment, illuminating earth–scintillating these lovers lying romanti-cally on this sandy beach. The two are reflecting on their past and future with love overflowing in their hearts, absorbing all God's glory.

As they lie there, they hear a slight shuffling. They see several little baby turtles running to the ocean's edge hoping to gain their freedom and live for forty to sixty years.

"We are like baby turtles, beginning a new life to protect the continuation of our freedom and liberty. Pray the best is yet to come, my dearest. I love you my sweets, so much. Words cannot express how I missed you. We will swim in untraversed waters, but together. Our future is made of gold, Lilli."

On the moonlit walk to the condo, "I love you, too, Frank. Not everyone gets the chance to start over. We are beginning again. A new and wonderful life awaits us, doesn't it? But, my heart is heavy for my relationship with Tariq Rashudi. I am so sorry, Socks."

"And, my dear, it is I who is responsible for your relationship with Tariq. You were left alone without my love to rely on. I am sure your life became empty. It was planned to be that way. It saddened me. I am sorry, too. Let's forget the past. The best of happiness and living free is at our fingertips, Lilli, my love. I feel my heart will never beat one more time without you. Hurry, let's go home to bed."

The huge Florida golden moon romantically lights the lover's path. They walk up the stairs to Lilli's apartment instead of taking the elevator. Passing by the Arab's apartment again, Arabic voices are heard as usual. The conversation resonates down the hall.

Lilli and Frank's night is one of love and serenity flooding their dream world with positive anticipation.

~ 54 ~

One Life Adventure Ends—
Another to Begin?

Frank, stationed in Washington, works only for government agencies as an undercover agent. He returns to Florida most weekends. Lilli stays close to her parents and also has a two day a week, substitute teaching position at a local school. She teaches Spanish when needed. She has heard nothing about Tariq.

Their life returns to an almost normal one. Lilli occasionally flies to Chicago on long weekends when Frank is there on business. Sometimes she brings her parents along.

Months later, September 2001, Frank has a three week vacation and Lilli asks for one as well. They spend their days walking the beach, fishing the surf, catching up on the latest movies, shopping and just relaxing. Time flies by too quickly.

Every day they walk past the Arab's condo. The chatter never ceases.

On this day, Sunday, September 9th, no voices are heard. They notice the door is wide open revealing a deserted room. A cleaning lady is vacuuming. The manager walking down the hall toward them, "These eight guys lived here for nine months. Three days ago, they told me they were leaving. They left in one big hurry. Their lease of a year was paid for. It isn't up yet. They spoke English when they had to . . . but speaking to each other, they used some foreign language. Very polite guys, though."

"That sounds peculiar," Frank suspiciously whispers to Lilli.

"I certainly hope not."

~ 55 ~

September 11, 2001

The next morning, Lilli and Frank sit on the sofa, cuddling and drinking coffee, watching the T.V. news. Suddenly they see the unbelievable! A plane actually crashes into a New York skyscraper. The announcer, in a state of shock, excitedly describes the explosion seen happening at this moment on the screen . . . 'A plane has just flown into one of Manhattan's two Twin Towers of the World Trade Center—here in our New York City. Mountains of smoke are bellowing from the building sides. There are people inside. Oh my God!'

In a state of shock, Frank stands up yelling, "What the heck! These are terrorists. Gotta be more terrorists! Unbelievable! How did we miss discovering these guys before they did this? I am sure they have been planning this attack for some time. Our government agencies have been working diligently for several years to locate where, in America, terrorists might be. We suspected some were here, like Rashudi, but maybe terrorism wasn't taken seriously enough."

"Frank, I can't believe this."

Two minutes later they are still glued to their couch. They see and hear, 'Another plane, another plane! It has circled around and flown into the side of our second tower. Fire and smoke is encompassing this whole area. Workers from the first explosion are running down the street. Thick clouds of smoke follow them. What a disaster!'

The announcer continues, 'No! Oh, my God! This is horrible. It can't be happening! People are jumping out of windows now. It's either that or be slowly burned to death . . . either way it's death. So sad. I can't believe this is happening to us, in America—our country, on our soil.'

Their eyes do not depart from the TV set for most of the day. They watch both towers melt and finally collapse to the ground. People scrambling everywhere.

Frank exclaims, "This day in Lower Manhattan will visually stay with us forever. Men and women running for their lives through rubble . . . coughing, faces and clothes blackened with soot, noses and mouths covered so as not to inhale the dirty putrid, thick smoke. Pieces of steel buildings flying everywhere. This is all unreal. Am I dreaming? Is it really happening?"

"An actual horror movie is currently playing in front of us. Frank. You must continue trying to keep our America safe from terrorists." Later another announcement, 'Two more planes have crashed. One, Flight 93 into a field in Pennsylvania and the other, Flight 77, has crashed into the Pentagon in Washington, D.C. This day will live forever in our memory, never to be forgotten.'

The next morning, "Lilli, come quick, listen to this T.V reporting."

'We can now announce that three thousand plus, innocent Americans, were killed yesterday, September 11, 2001, by Al-Qaeda radical Islamist extremists. Most of the terrorists that hijacked those four planes were radical Muslims from Saudi Arabia.'

"This action is going to develop into a third world religious war because of these religious zealots. They want to murder those who won't convert to Islam—non-believers or infidels, as they call them. It's one thing to chop off a head in punishment for a criminal act. Another, to decapitate a person because of their religion, sect, nationality, or their country has different religious beliefs," Frank disgustedly argues.

"Frank, it's crazy because we all believe in the same God, just different ways of reaching Him. Thank God, the majority of Muslims are peace-loving. True Islam rejects religious extremism and terrorism. It preaches tolerance and moderation. We know that for a fact, having lived among them so long. Our Muslim friends are wonderful . . . giving, caring and loving people. Islam, is being perverted by a minority of radicals whose interpretation of God is wrong—murderers, who think God's way to paradise is their way . . . killing and domination . . . not peace, forgiveness and love, as Christianity teaches. This situation is very disconcerting."

Frank confides in Lilli that he feels, "We are at war with a hate movement . . . religious locos. All nations world-wide have to join together with our Muslim friends to defeat these killers."

"Lilli, consider working together with me. And Lilli, Frank Martinez is dead. I have another name now. I am Mister Richard Dupree." Lilli, in a confused shock from all the recent happenings, is not sure what she wants to do, other than teach and be close to her parents.

"I will have to think and pray about it, my love. Whatever God wants me to do, He will signal me. Time will tell. I am positive my life has been in His hands all these years.

"Yes, my dear, I believe so, too."

Frank reminds her that she would be playing an integral part in keeping America free and its people safe.

Lilli loves teaching and of course, the beach. She wants to live here in her ocean front condo. She plans to sell the Chicago condo.

Tariq is out of her life forever. After personally experiencing the plans of terrorists, and the suffering of what happened to thousands of innocent Americans, she feels work is needed to make a difference so America can remain free.

Frank reminds Lilli, "Someone once said, 'when religions ruled the world, they called it the Dark Ages because religious zealots were blinded by light and truth.' Do you remember America's symbol is an Eagle, meaning strong and free? We must protect our liberty, freedom and laws because bad happenings are possible in any society."

"Frank, I do believe God is love—Love is God, Allah is love—Love is Allah. Love never, ever kills."

That evening, the lovers cuddle together on their porch swing enjoying the sounds of the ocean's gentle ripples washing the sandy shores. They sight Venus again, the most brilliant planet in the solar system as it ascends to its usual position in the heavens.

Their whole being is absorbed by light from millions of twinkling stars and the glimmering radiant waves of luminescence bursting from a full moon. Both souls are at peace.

Silently meditating, they wonder what new adventures their future might reveal.

"We must protect our country's freedom before the doors are closed, Frank. *Assalamu Aleikum*, peace be upon us and the world."

"Amen," Frank adds.

CPSIA information can be obtained at www.ICGtesting.com
Printed in the USA
BVOW08s2303090316

439676BV00001B/3/P